THE KOKOSCHKA CAPERS

THE KOKOSCHKA CAPERS

A Megan Crespi Mystery Novel

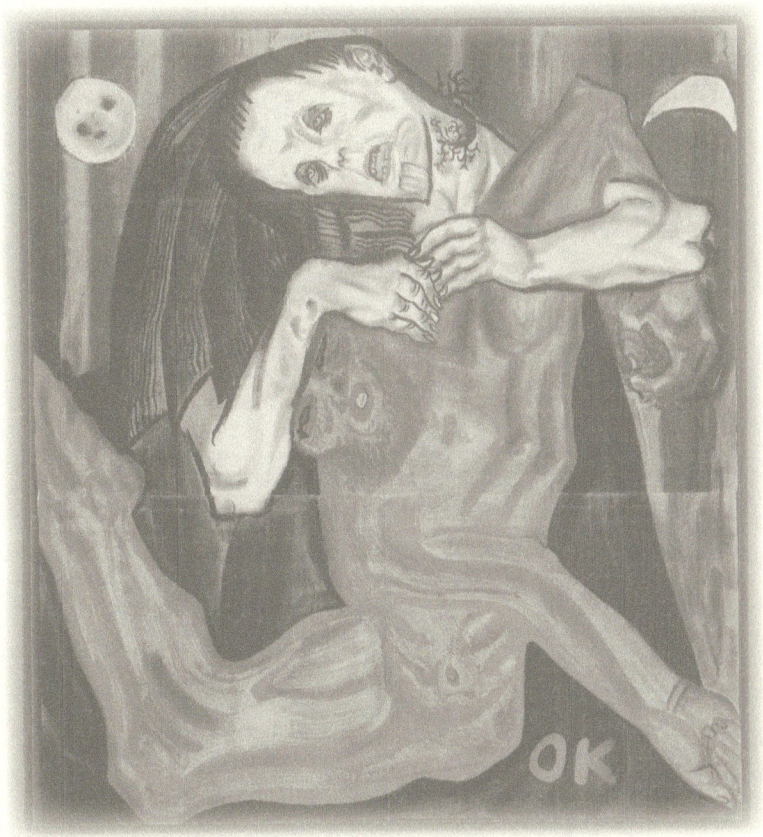

Alessandra Comini

SUNSTONE PRESS

SANTA FE

This is a work of fiction. Names, characters, businesses, places, events, and incidents are either the products of the author's imagination or used in a fictitious manner. Any resemblance to actual persons, living or dead, or actual events is purely coincidental.

Sunstone books may be purchased for educational, business, or sales promotional use. For information please write: Special Markets Department, Sunstone Press, P.O. Box 2321, Santa Fe, New Mexico 87504-2321.

Book and cover design › Vicki Ahl
Body typeface › Bernnhard Modern Std
Printed on acid-free paper
∞
eBook 978-1-61139-397-2

Library of Congress Cataloging-in-Publication Data

Comini, Alessandra.
  The Kokoschka capers : a Megan Crespi mystery novel / by Alessandra Comini.
    pages ; cm
  ISBN 978-1-63293-077-4 (softcover : alk. paper)
  1. Murder--Investigation--Fiction. 2. Art thefts--Investigation--Fiction. I. Title.
  PS3603.O477K65 2015
  813'.6--dc23

                    2015024139

WWW.SUNSTONEPRESS.COM
SUNSTONE PRESS / POST OFFICE BOX 2321 / SANTA FE, NM 87504-2321 /USA
(505) 988-4418 / ORDERS ONLY (800) 243-5644 / FAX (505) 988-1025

To Renée Price
valued colleague, cherished friend

1

"He shot me once in the head, stomped on me with his heavy boots, and left me for dead." Oskar Kokoschka turned in his chair to see the effect of his statement on his forty-three-year-old interlocutor Megan Crespi.

Entranced, she had been listening to the famous if idiosyncratic painter who was nearing his ninety-fourth birthday that year of 1980. It was early February and they were sitting on the glassed-in terrace of his atelier-home at Villeneuve, where the artist had lived for many decades with his adoring wife Olda, twenty-nine years his junior. Before them was icy blue Lake Geneva; behind them towered the snow-covered Alps.

Megan, who lived in Dallas, had been urgently petitioned to come "with all haste" to the small marina town on the Swiss Riviera by the man who in his youth had competed with the artist of her expertise, Egon Schiele. Both had striven to see which one could more outlandishly shock their native city of Vienna. Which could be the greater *Bürgerschreck*—shocker of the bourgeois. During his short lifetime, Schiele, who died at twenty-eight just as World War I was ending, had won the unspoken contest with the riveting images he had created of sexual arousal and suffering psyches.

A short, lively woman who still dyed her hair brown, Megan had been a Schiele scholar since coming upon his explicit drawings in a small 1963 exhibition at the University of California in Berkeley. Acknowledged now, at the grand age of eighty, as one of the leading authorities on the artist, her early books on Schiele had set the bar for further work and she had recently curated a hugely successful exhibition of his portraits for Montreal's Art Austria Museum.

And now, thirty-five years after her dramatic onetime encounter with Kokoschka, she found herself thinking intensely about him again as she read the front page article above the fold in *The New York Times*. The headline read: "Fourteen Kokoschka Works Disappear from Austrian Art Storage Vault."

Megan vividly recalled the artist's tumultuous life story as told to her in his own words. How he had survived the wounds of World War I—not only a shot in the head, but, in another encounter, a bayonetted lung. Due to the head wound his hearing and balance had been compromised for the rest of his life. And now there was an urgency in his voice.

"Do not take me for an old fool, Frau Doktor Crespi," he had said to her, gripping her arm. "I have always had intuitions that proved right. And now I have the overwhelming feeling that someone wishes me ill. I cannot prove it but I *know* it."

"Have you any idea *who* might be wishing you ill?" Megan had asked concernedly.

"No, but I know someone wants to hurt either me or my Fourteen Stations."

"Fourteen Stations? And what are they?"

"I cannot tell you. Works from my youth. Juvenilia. Not even my wife knows. They are in a storage vault in Vienna, have been for decades. But I feel harm is going to come either to them or to me."

Well, Megan now speculated, Kokoschka had been wrong about harm coming to him—he died a peaceful death from "natural causes" just a few weeks after their meeting. But he was preternaturally correct about harm coming to his Fourteen Stations, as he mysteriously referred to them. It was not known what the works were. It had only been established that fourteen crates had mysteriously disappeared from the Austrian art storage company where they had long been kept and, according to the newspaper, were to continue to be held "in perpetuity" under the terms and payments of Kokoschka's will after his death in March of 1980.

Megan was intrigued. Her "trio" of Austrian turn-of-the-nineteenth-century artists—Gustav Klimt, Egon Schiele, and Oskar Kokoschka—had now all emerged from the fog of forgetfulness during World War II to vast public interest and Internet scrutiny in recent decades. Yes, risen to new popularity *and* to criminal acts regarding works by the first two, she thought grimly. She had recently been involved in ferreting out the whereabouts of some newly discovered Klimt masterpieces—works thought to have been destroyed by fire during the war. After a round of dangerous adventures, including attempts on her own life, Megan had found them secreted in a remote Alaskan hideaway. The subject matter of the artworks had been a huge surprise and changed conceptions of Klimt permanently.

As for Schiele, Megan had found herself battling against a secret clan in Austria, whose object was the destruction of all "pornographic" works by the master. Several murders and a number of robberies and vicious vandalism accompanied her trepidatious probing of events and in the end a surprise trove of unknown Schieles had been discovered, much to the joy of Viennese museums.

But while substantial, Megan's engagement with Kokoschka, who continued painting all his long life, had never filled her with the same enthrallment as had Klimt and Schiele. These two artists had far shorter careers than the nonagenarian. Both men died in 1918, Klimt from the after effects of a stroke at the age of fifty-six, the twenty-eight-year-old Schiele from the influenza ravaging Europe at the end of World War I.

On the other hand, Megan told herself now, she had a unique connection with Kokoschka, one she had, of course, not been able to have with either Klimt or Schiele who had both died long before she was born. But Kokoschka she had actually met face to face, and at his urgent bidding. "I chose you because of your work on my Vienna rival," the painter told her engagingly at the beginning of their prolonged and informative interview in Villeneuve, in a home Kokoschka had built in 1951. During their lengthy talk she was permitted to take photographs and record the artist's rambling account of his life, work, and loves.

Kokoschka's most famous liaison was not with his devoted wife of many years, but with a woman quite famous in Vienna during the early years before the Great War. She was Alma Mahler, widow of the composer Gustav Mahler, who died in 1911. Seven years older than Oskar, Alma continued to enchant men of note, entering into a brief marriage with the architect and founder of the Bauhaus, Walter Gropius, and then a longer wedlock to the author of *Song of Bernadette*, Franz Werfel.

But Alma's link with Kokoschka endured all her life. Megan thought of the fervent descriptions of their affair given by them both in their respective memoirs. When Alma, widowed for a second time, became a septuagenarian in 1949, Oskar wrote her a birthday reminder of what their love had been. "There has been nothing like it since the Middle Ages, for no couple has ever breathed into each other so passionately." And in 1958, Alma in turn reminisced: "Years have passed, but the sensations of that time will be equally strong in me as long as I live. On one stormy, agonized day when he loved me passionately, but selfishly, torturing us both, the world around me suddenly melted away."

Megan reasoned that what Kokoschka had dismissingly referred to as "juvenilia" to her, could be the fourteen unknown works stolen from the Vienna vault—presumably the Fourteen Stations. Could they refer to those passionate three years through the outbreak of World War I in 1914?

2

Megan had broken off her train of thought for a moment. She needed to go upstairs and pull out a few of her various volumes on Kokoschka and Alma Mahler-Gropius-Werfel. She was thinking about the notorious life-size doll in Alma's likeness Oskar had commissioned a seamstress in Stuttgart to hand-sew after their breakup. He had provided meticulous drawings and written instructions. His wishes included the doll's mouth—"Can the mouth be opened? And has it got teeth and a tongue?"—and the genitals—"the *parties honteuses* must be made perfect and luxuriant and covered with hair." Settled in Dresden after the war, far away from the then unobtainable Alma Gropius, Oskar kept the doll with Alma's unmistakable facial features on his studio couch, where startled visitors thought at first that they were seeing her in the flesh. Upon hearing about the life-size doll in her image Alma wrote bitterly: "At last, he had me where he wanted me: helpless in his hands, a docile, mechanical tool."

In 1922 Oskar immortalized his fetish in a bizarre *Self-Portrait with Life-Size Doll Made in the Likeness of Alma Mahler*. The "mad" painter pointed possessively to his naked cloth companion, his left hand on her raised left knee as she faced outward. Alma was nothing but a limp, staring partner, a mindless manikin. Megan did the mental arithmetic: let's see, Oskar was born in 1886; he would have been thirty-six years old in 1922. Could this still be considered as juvenilia?

No, she concluded. Far more apposite would be the painter's large 1914 oil *The Bride of the Wind— Die Windsbraut*—also called *The Tempest*. She had photographed and studied it several times in Basel's venerable Kunstmuseum. Suspended in tempestuous space, Alma, naked to the waist, is shown lying against her lover's flank and left shoulder in peaceful sleep while a recumbent Oskar, also naked to the waist, grips his fingers together and stares resolutely into the whirl storm of agitated brushstrokes swirling around them—a true storm of blue and purple strokes that create tremendous depth without the use of geometrical perspective.

This could be the concluding marker of Oskar's juvenilia, of his passionate youth, of his three-year affair with Vienna's most gossiped-about femme fatale, Megan thought. She remembered Alma and Oskar's early descriptions of each other. The newly widowed Alma recorded:

> "There's a poor, starving genius around," my step-father told me one day in the winter of 1912. "If I were you, I'd let him paint me." And Oskar Kokoschka came. But his shoes were torn, his suit was frayed. A handsome figure, but disturbingly coarse, I thought. His eyes were somewhat aslant, which gave them a wary expression; but the eyes as such were beautiful. The mouth was large, with the lower lip and chin protruding. We hardly spoke—and yet he seemed unable to draw. We got up. Suddenly, tempestuously, he swept me into his arms. To me it was a strange, almost shocking kind of embrace; I did not respond at all. He stormed out. In a matter of hours I held the most beautiful love letter and proposal in my hands: "If you can respect me—if you want me to be as pure as you were yesterday then make a real sacrifice and become my wife; in secret, while I am poor." The three years that followed were one fierce battle of love. He was jealous of all things in my life.

Oskar's reminiscence ran in a similar, if more profuse manner:

My face was thin and drawn and the eyes were too big in it, eyes full of the insolence of an alert will, in contrast with the sleepy people around me. I was beginning to realize what I amounted to. I knew this society lady, a young widow. She wore a purple dress of goffered Venetian silk that was so fine that one could have pulled the whole dress through a wedding-ring. Her hair gleamed like that of the penitent Magdalenes painted by Venetian masters. We went for drives in a carriage with rubber-tired wheels, we sat in her box at the opera, she gave me the key of her house so that I could come and go without being noticed. On summer nights I preferred to climb up the rose-espalier to the balcony leading to her bedroom. There was the awe of the first human sacrifices, from reluctant yielding, all the way to complete abandonment, tumult, quarreling, bliss of self-mutilation until one found oneself again. I would have thought it impossible that at my beck and call the beloved would come, atremble with shameless pleasure. I shut my beloved off from all society, because I sensed a rival in every man.

The possessive Oskar did indeed have many rivals to be jealous of, ranging from Gustav Klimt to Alexander Zemlinsky, teacher of Arnold Schönberg. But the strangest competitor of all, Megan thought, was the death mask of Gustav Mahler which, at Alma's insistence, traveled with them. Alma had alluded to it specifically and Megan looked up her account again in the woman's voluble autobiography:

We thought and talked often and earnestly about our future, and Mahler's death mask, which had come by then, made a powerful canto fermo for the grave choral chant of these discussions. Wherever I lived after Mahler's death I would put on his desk his music and his pictures from childhood through the last years. One day Kokoschka suddenly got up, picked up Mahler's pictures, one by one, and kissed Mahler's face. It was an act of "white magic"—he wanted to combat the dark, jealous urges within him. But I cannot say it helped.

Megan laughed to herself as she opened Kokoschka's memoir to refresh her recollection of how he remembered this "white magic" moment:

When one opens a door there's something on the far side that was not there before. I had a premonition that it would be irrevocable when, from a crate filled with wood-shavings, or curly paper, she unpacked the death mask of her late husband. When the crate with the undesirable contents, the mask, destroyed my love that March day, I clenched my fists and screamed into the dead man's face, that's to say, at this yellowish wax mask with the closed eyes: No I won't have it, you can't be there between us.

Megan put away her Alma and Oskar books with a vivid image in her mind of Kokoschka's emotional contretemps with the Mahler death mask. Then she went downstairs and entered the music room of her Dallas home and stared at her own not very good copy of Maher's death mask—a second or even third cast which she had picked up at an antique show in Honolulu of all places. Even so his distinctive features were entirely recognizable.

She was reminded of Beethoven's death mask of 1827, of which she had a third or fourth generation copy. Next to it she also had a late plaster copy of the composer's life mask taken by the sculptor Franz Klein in 1812. She thought happily of the essay she had once written about the grimacing life mask, a short piece entitled "The Visual Beethoven: Whence, Why, and Wither the Scowl?" Her argument was that for generations and in all countries Beethoven's "frowning" life mask had been mistaken for his death mask. Such prominent cultural figures as playwrights August Strindberg and Gabriele d'Annunzio, and the painter Rosa Bonheur had proudly displayed the life mask in the erroneous belief that, because of the prominent scowl, it was the composer's death mask.

On the contrary, Megan had pointed out, it was the *life* mask, and the scowl reflected the fact that, his face covered with fresh plaster, cotton balls over his eyes, and breathing through two straws in his nostrils, Beethoven had suddenly felt suffocated. He ripped the still-setting mask off his face and threw it on the floor where it broke into several pieces. The composer fled the premises never to return, but Klein was able to put the pieces together and this had been his model for the famous bust he created of the master that year.

Decades of Beethoven imagery, cascading right into the twenty-first century, had borrowed the scowl of Klein's bust, contributing to the popular notion of the composer as grumpy at the least, irate at the most. Megan had followed the story of Beethovenian imagery from contemporaneous depictions to modern times in her 1986 book *The Changing Image of Beethoven. A Study in Mythmaking.* She had not realized it at the time, but she was engaging in what musicologists called reception history--*Rezeptionsgeschichte.*

And now she was thinking of Oskar Kokoschka's *Rezeptionsgeschichte.* How he reveled in being the bad boy of Vienna when he was in his twenties—both in his art and in his conduct. Only Egon Schiele, four years younger, provided any competition. But Kokoschka was under the sponsorship of the city's famous minimalist architect in an age of over-decoration, Adolf Loos, and so moved in more elite circles than did Schiele. The satirist Karl Kraus, feuilletonist Peter Altenberg, composer Arnold Schönberg, and philosopher Ludwig Wittgenstein numbered among his "Young Vienna" circle of friends. They were friends of Loos and therefore, by default, friends of Kokoschka, who painted agonized "pathological" portraits of some of them in a roiling style that would soon be called Expressionist. Kokoschka placed his oddly gesticulating subjects in voids that were animated by a torrent of brushwork. Physical likeness was not the object. Tunneling into the individual's psyche and putting it on agonized display was the objective. This was the artist's early, and, for many scholars and collectors, best period—the beginning decades of the twentieth century.

As Megan recalled Kokoschka's extraordinary images she began to wonder why she had never authored a book on the artist. After all, she had written extensively on his compatriot, Schiele, and even on Klimt, but never more than paragraphs on Kokoschka. Was it because over the decades his later portraits were far less frenetic? Or because he had turned to cityscapes and landscapes that, while animated, did not truly invoke the genre of Expressionism? When she had visited the artist in Villeneuve that fateful year of 1980 he had shown her his latest works. They were the opposite of angst, placid and pleasant, certainly not riveting. Most of them were views of Lake Geneva seen from on high.

Just then Megan's phone rang. Irritated that her Kokoschka reverie had been interrupted, she let her answering machine take over. A man's voice with a pronounced Swiss-German accent announced that he was calling from Basel's Kunstmuseum and needed to speak with Frau Doktor Crespi—*dringend*—urgently.

With that Megan picked up the receiver and identified herself.

3

"Ach, wonderful that you are there," said the voice jubilantly. "This is Doktor Hans Tietze, director of the Kunstmuseum Basel."

Megan knew immediately who this Tietze had to be. He was the great-grandson of the man painted in Kokoschka's 1909 double portrait of the two art historians, Hans Tietze and Erica Tietze-Conrat. Both known for advancing the cause of contemporary art, they had asked the twenty-three-year-old artist to paint a marriage portrait for the mantelpiece over their fireplace. The impoverished Kokoschka eagerly accepted the commission from the couple, who were socially prominent. He asked, however, that he be allowed to paint them individually—absorbing their unique astral glow—before combining them onto a single canvas. The Tietzes had readily agreed and soon they and their gesticulating, nervous hands were registered in oil on a large canvas with Hans in profile on the left, facing his wife, with raised fingers traveling toward her. Erica, facing front, had her hands crossed against her chest, the outspread fingers of her left hand almost touching the tips of her husband's outstretched left hand.

The resultant electricity was enhanced by traces of the artist's own fingernails pulling colors across the canvas. A canvas which was free of any environmental surround such as chairs or sofa. The Tietzes existed in existential space and the artist signed the canvas on the lower right with the large initials "O K." He himself described his two sitters as "closed personalities so full of tension." The world at large did not see this early Kokoschka double portrait until the couple moved to New York in the year of the Anschluss and the Museum of Modern Art acquired it the following year, 1939.

So, yes, Megan knew of the man who was calling, and said so.

"Are you calling in regard to the Kokoschkas stolen yesterday from a Viennese storage company?" she asked.

"I *wish* that is why I were calling," Hans Tietze said ruefully. "No, I am calling because our Kokoschka *Bride of the Wind*, you know, *The Tempest*, was sliced out of its frame and stolen last night.

"What? Why that's not possible!" Megan exclaimed, knowing how tight the Basel museum's security was.

"But there is more. An outspread canvas weighted down by four brass weights was left on the floor below where the Kokoschka had hung. It is a perfect duplicate of his painting, in size and technique, but instead of Alma Mahler's famous features is the face of another woman!"

"Incredible! What does she look like? Is she recognizable?" Megan was bursting with questions.

"Not identifiable to any of us here at the museum. She is presented as young, younger than Alma Mahler, and as a blonde with long, luxurious hair. Her eyes are blue and they are wide open. She has a small, narrow nose and voluptuous red lips. She looks innocent enough but her sensuousness jumps out at you. Whoever painted her was good at his craft."

"Have you been able to determine whether or not this substitute *Tempest* is a *new* creation or could it date back to Kokoschka's original?"

"What an intriguing question, Frau Doktor. This is exactly why we are calling you. You have a unique and creative scholar's outlook. So different from our police here, who care only about how the substitution was made, not what the *meaning* of the substitution is. Well known to us are your successes in solving the mysterious factors surrounding the recent crimes concerning works by Klimt and Schiele. If your schedule permits, we should like you to come to Basel and consult with us. By the time you arrive we should have more leads, at least about how the break-in occurred. Please, oh, please say that you will let us fly you over."

Megan weighed her present situation. She had only just returned from Canada to Dallas where she had taught at Southern Methodist University for thirty-one years, after leaving her ten-year position as assistant professor at Columbia University back in 1974. Her exhibition on Schiele's portraits, curated for Montreal's Art Austria museum, had opened a few weeks ago to rave reviews and blockbuster crowds.

And this past weekend she had lectured at the Dallas Museum of Art concerning its dazzling acquisition of the eight million dollar 1908 silver showcase by Wiener Werkstätte artist Carl Otto Czeschka. The first owner of the vitrine—bought right out of the Kunstschau where it was on display—was the Vienna billionaire Karl Wittgenstein, father of the philosopher Ludwig Wittgenstein.

So all Megan's latest projects had come to fruition. She had, at the moment, no deadlines to meet. And she had been happy to get back into her daily exercise routine of treadmill, recliner bike, mild weight-lifting, and Pilates. The petite "retired" art history professor might be eighty, but she wasn't giving up on keeping fit. And a bit of vanity kept her coloring her hair chestnut brown every few months.

The only thing that could arguably keep Megan in Texas was her darling fifteen-year-old, blind little Maltese dog Button. She had spent so little time with him lately and he had developed a congestive heart condition that caused him to emit a continuous honking cough. Oh, it was pitiful to hear him cough. But she knew that, if asked, her good friend Claire Chandler would happily keep Button for her.

Megan heard herself saying to Hans Tietze: "If you can give me two days here in Dallas and if you fly me over and back business class, I shall come." Now that she had turned eighty, business class had become increasingly attractive to her. In addition to terrestrial and cyber mail, she had a number of small tasks on the home front to wind up. She truly needed two days to herself.

"Excellent! Frau Doktor, excellent. We shall make the Swissair reservations for you with an open date for your return, and of course it will be business class. But of course!"

4

It had not been difficult for Megan to put her affairs in order during those two hot June days in Dallas. And Button was thrilled to be visiting Claire Chandler's house with its large, always mysterious backyard full of unfamiliar scents and suspicious noises. Yes, he gave his human full permission to leave the country for a short time.

Megan's early afternoon flight took her by way of Chicago's International Airport and Zurich before her one-hour flight at noon the next day from Zurich to Basel. Business class had been delightful and she had drunk her fill of Baileys Irish Cream, the only alcoholic beverage she liked other than red wine sweetened with Dasani drops. In an email exchange with Hans Tietze during her layover in Zurich, Megan learned that reservations had been made for her at the Rochat, a charming hotel where she had twice stayed during her pursuit of Schiele works in private Swiss collections. It was right in the center of the medieval town and very near the university. Megan knew from past experience that if she walked from the Rochat over to the elegant Grand Hotel Les Trois Rois, she could slip out onto its terrace and enjoy a splendid view of the Rhine. She had done this on New Year's Eve once and enjoyed the firecrackers as they burst into colorful bouquets and then sank majestically into the river. She still remembered the enthusiastic comments of the Baselers around her, with their distinct Alemannic dialect known as Baseldytsch and its many borrowed French words, due to its proximity to France's border.

After checking in at the Rochat, unpacking, and downing a light lunch, Megan meandered through the old town toward the Basel museum where she had a four-o'clock appointment with Hans Tietze.

She took a slight detour toward the red sandstone, tile-roofed Münster with its twin gothic towers. But this, her body told her, was as far as she could comfortably walk. Her fallen arches—too much ballet training as a youngster—were beginning to complain. Gratefully switching to a taxi, she arrived at the museum with five minutes to spare. She was surprised to see that an extension to the old museum building was being built. Wooden fences partially blocked both buildings, and construction crews and machinery were everywhere. No wonder Tietze had told her he would meet her outside the museum on the Sankt Alban-Graben. And sure enough, in front of the museum's ground-floor exterior arches, there stood the spitting image of the director's great-grandfather Hans Tietze, as portrayed by Kokoschka. Right down to the trim moustache.

"Frau Doktor Crespi?" he asked as Megan approached him.

Megan smiled at him as they shook hands. She remarked on his resemblance to the original Hans Tietze, something of which, she learned, the present-day Tietze was very proud. Dr. Tietze sized up his diminutive American visitor, noting how agile and animated she seemed, despite her, what must be—from the early dates of her scholarly publications—advanced age. She probably dyed her hair, as it was brown with a trace of white showing along the roots. Well, never mind: he also dyed *his* hair and moustache and he was only in his sixties. The two exchanged pleasantries as they avoided noisy workmen on their circuitous way to the director's office.

As they walked through the museum's older galleries Megan caught intriguing glimpses of works by Hans Holbein, Lucas Cranach, and Konrad Witz. Hans led her through the courtyard with its life-size group of Rodin's *The Burgers of Calais* and they entered another gallery on the far side. It contained a large trove of works by one of Megan's favorite nineteenth-century artists, Arnold Böcklin of Basel, including his haunting *Isle of the Dead*— one of six celebrated versions.

Some forty years ago she had once rented a rowboat to take her out to the rocky islet of Pontikonisi, a half-mile off the coast of the island of Corfu in the Adriatic, just to see and photograph what was believed to be the site for Böcklin's mysterious painting. In the painting a lone oarsman ferries a coffin draped in white and a standing female figure wrapped completely in white across dark water to the rocky islet with its white tombs, chapel, and giant stand of dark green cypress trees. And white tombs cut into the rock face, a small chapel, and tall cypress trees were exactly what Megan saw as she landed on the tiny island.

The strange scene had inspired an eponymous symphonic poem by

Sergei Rachmaninoff as well as appearing in several Hollywood films, including one of Megan's favorites, *King Kong*.

Salvador Dalí with his ironic wit had created his own version of it as a deserted beach in his painting titled *The Real Picture of the Isle of the Dead by Arnold Böcklin at the Hour of the Angelus*.

And soon after Mahler's death, Alma herself visited Corfu in the company of Joseph Fraenkel, the physician who had tended to her husband in his final illness and who was then—unsuccessfully—courting the glamorous widow. It had not been Alma's first time in Corfu. She had been taken there as a child of eight by her painter father on a commission from Crown Prince Rudolf.

All this Megan quietly discussed with Dr. Tietze, as though putting off encountering the ersatz Kokoschka that had been left behind in place of the stolen original. But they could delay no longer. Tietze opened the door to his office and there on a large, square table lay the rolled-out canvas. Except for the Alma substitute it was an exact replica of the Kokoschka original. Magnificently executed, they had to agree. The weight and wielding of brush strokes were the same as those of Kokoschka's. The museum's two conservators would be joining them in a few minutes with their analysis of the canvas's probable date of origin.

"If I didn't know the circumstances of this painting's having been left in place of the original, I would be darned if I didn't think this too was by Kokoschka," Megan said half reluctantly.

"I am astounded to hear you say that," Hans Tietze almost whispered. "I have had the same gut feeling."

"Is there anything on the back of the canvas?"

"No. We had wondered the same thing but there is no trace of anything on the verso. After determining that, we put the canvas—which had a few wrinkles from having been rolled—into these stretcher bars here."

There was a knock on the office door. Two young people entered.

"Frau Doktor Crespi, may I introduce our two conservators, Fraülein Rebecca Paratur and Herr Reno Sachs."

"Shall we proceed to first names?" Megan smiled. There was comfortable assent and the conversation moved to the quick.

"We have *lived* with this fascinating painting for three days now," Rebecca began enthusiastically.

Reno picked up the thread: "And we have subjected the front and back of the canvas to all sorts of tests. It is medium brown in color and is of closed weave, signifying an early twentieth-century origin."

"Infrared reflectography revealed no under drawing, no pentimenti of any sort nor grid, so the paint was applied without any underlying guide. We conducted microscopic analysis of the paint layers and their superficial craquelure, as well as the crystallinity of the pigments," said Rebecca, "and based on our results we can date this painting back to the opening decades of the twentieth century, say the first twenty-five years."

Hans and Megan drank in this information. It was data that seemed to confirm their instincts that the painting could actually be the work of Kokoschka.

"Judged solely on style, the painting is a dead ringer for Kokoschka's self-portrait with Alma in *The Tempest*, only with a different female," declared Megan, looking at Hans.

"And your tests point to the very period that Kokoschka painted *The Tempest*," Hans said, turning to the two conservators.

Silence ensued as they all stared at the picture.

Megan took the leap. "I think we are looking at an actual work by Kokoschka, one painted at or near the same time as your stolen Kokoschka."

Hans spoke up. "I have to agree," the excitement in his voice audible to all. He added: "I don't know whether I'm happy about this or furious!"

They circled round the canvas, looking appreciatively at the two semi-nude figures lying against each other in a storm of agitated brushstrokes.

"It looks as though your burglar did not want the museum to lose a Kokoschka and so he substituted what seems to be a genuine Kokoschka for the one he took," Megan offered.

"But how could he have gotten by security, loaded down with four weights and a huge canvas roll?" Reno asked indignantly. "And when he sliced out the Kokoschka from its frame did he roll that up as well? Did he think of the *damage* doing something like that could cause?"

"What have your surveillance cameras shown, Hans?" asked Megan.

The museum director stared at his feet for what seemed like a full minute. "I am chagrined to tell you, to tell all of you, that because of the construction taking place connecting our building to the new extension, some of the security cameras have been on the blink this past week. Sometimes they work and other times they don't. We've had countless repairmen come out but so far they haven't been able to stabilize the camera feed. What we do have on tape is a tall workman carrying a large roll across the courtyard at two-ten in the morning the day of the robbery. When nobody else was at work. Our foreman swears he does not recognize the person. That he is not a member of his crew. But that's all we have to go on. The police have no likely suspects so far."

Still embarrassed at having to divulge such a security gap, Hans stared at his shoes in silence.

After some moments had passed Megan said encouragingly: "If we can figure out *why* the paintings were exchanged, then perhaps we can discover *who* is responsible for the theft. It can't be a coincidence that during this same week in two different countries and at two different facilities, works by Kokoschka were stolen—one from your museum, Hans, and fourteen crates of art, all presumably by Kokoschka, from a Vienna storage vault."

Hans looked mildly comforted. "So you are saying that the same person, or persons must have been involved with the two thefts?"

"It is possible. I think, first and foremost, we should attempt to identify *who* the blonde woman is in this substitute Kokoschka painting. Although she is the same size and assumes the same pose as Alma Mahler, she is not Alma Mahler. Like Alma, however, she commands an identical storm-tossed environment. On another tack, it is possible that if we check the provenances of works by the artist done in this same period, we may come across a useful list of previous owners, some of whom may have had direct contact with the artist. Who knows, they might be related to this mystery woman. After all, Kokoschka had a number of commissions for portraiture, especially during his early years, and we know about them all. Or at least think we do!"

"Those are good ideas, Megan. At least it gives us something to hope for, something positive to do!" exclaimed an encouraged Hans.

"We can both work on that. But what I think I should be doing now is visit the art storage company in Vienna where the fourteen Kokoschka crates were stolen. I could at the very least obtain their exact measurements.

And those measurements might give us some idea of what the artworks might be—whether small cityscape or larger portrait or allegory."

"Don't you think this is something that could be done by phone or e-mail? After all you only just arrived here in Switzerland. I should tell you that I have, of course, contacted the Kokoschka Foundation in Vevey in case they could shed any light on our drastic situation."

"Oh, that's the collection founded by Kokoschka's wife Olda after he died, isn't it?"

"Quite right. All the paintings and works on paper that Olda had access to are now in Vevey's Musée Jenisch."

"Is Olda is still alive?"

"No, no, she died ten years ago. But she did live to the age of eighty-nine. Almost as long as her beloved Oskar."

"So that means she was sixty-five or so when I met her in Villeneuve back in nineteen-eighty. Did you know that she never addressed Oskar in the intimate form? She always said 'Sie' to him, never 'Du,' and when she referred to him in conversation she never called him 'Oskar' or 'Herr Kokoschka' but simply 'OK.'"

"I suppose, since she was so much younger than he, she just couldn't bring herself to say the 'Du' to him. She must have been in continuous awe of him. How lucky he was to have such a caregiver, such a respectful wife!" Hans said appreciatively.

Megan exchanged an amused smile with Rebecca who had been listening intently to their conversation.

"But wasn't she responsible for getting him out of Czechoslovakia just before the Germans invaded?" asked Reno.

"Indeed she was!" Megan affirmed. "In nineteen-thirty-eight her father was a high-ranking official in Prague's legal system, and he learned that Kokoschka was on the Wehrmacht list of people first to be arrested when the country was invaded. Kokoschka had already been denounced as a 'degenerate artist' by Hitler's regime—hence his defiant self-portrait with arms crossed which he titled *Self-Portrait of a Degenerate Artist*.

"But this list indicated that he would be executed without trial. Olda immediately arranged to flee with him to London and they got out just in time! Theirs was the last flight out of Prague before the Nazis took over.

That was the impetus for the saying people used to quote: 'Without Olda, Oskar would be nothing.' There is some truth to that."

If they knew each other that early, in the nineteen-thirties, could it be Olda who is portrayed in our 'substitute' painting here?" asked Rebecca.

"Ah, if only it were that simple," Megan said, raising her outspread hands. "The trouble is that Olda was a brunette, and the woman in our painting here on the table is definitely a blonde. Plus your laboratory dating of the canvas to sometime within the first two-and-a-half decades of the twentieth century doesn't jibe with the dates of Olda and Oskar's first meeting, which was in Prague, probably in nineteen-thirty-four or five."

"Well that nixes my theory then," Rebecca murmured, making a wry face.

"Don't feel too bad. As far as relationships are concerned your hypothesis makes sense since it is obvious that, whatever the identity of the woman in this painting, Kokoschka was making an intimate and positive statement about her. *Her* eyes are open. Quite the contrary of the dependent, sleeping Alma in the painting that has been stolen. And this blonde girl is definitely much younger than Alma."

"Don't you have any idea, Megan, as to who this mystery woman might be?" Hans asked.

"Well, I am churning over some possibilities in my mind right now. For instance, since it is not Alma, she could be one of a number of tumultuous love affairs Kokoschka had during his postwar years in Dresden. He taught briefly at the Art Academy there, so it might have been a student. Or daughter of a colleague.

"After Dresden he traveled extensively—Europe and North Africa, then back to Vienna temporarily before moving to Prague in nineteen-thirty-four after his mother died. The trouble is, no names jump out at me. I—we—would have to go through the legions of rhapsodic letters, poems, plays, memoirs, short stories, manifestos, and polemics Kokoschka produced during this still early period of his life when he was known as the 'mad' Kokoschka."

"Where could we find all this material?" Reno asked.

"The major part of his literary legacy is in Vienna at the University of Applied Arts' Oskar Kokoschka Center ," Hans answered for Megan.

"Another reason I should go there," said Megan eagerly, always happy to return to the font of her research on Schiele and Klimt.

"It was an honor to meet you," said Rebecca to Megan as she and Hans made their farewells.

"And what do you think we should do now with our new Kokoschka?" Hans asked after the two restorers had gone.

"Well, of course, call in some other Kokoschka experts to examine the work and give their opinion. Janette Killar of the Galerie St. Sebastian in New York, for instance. But in the meantime I think you should mount the canvas in its predecessor's leftover frame and display it along with a full didactic explaining the theft "exchange" and that there is an ongoing effort to affirm its authenticity and to locate the kidnapped Kokoschka canvas. Holding a press conference wouldn't hurt either. In fact it might increase museum attendance."

"You are right about that, Megan. Indeed, there has been a noticeable increase in museum visitors since the story broke three days ago. Yes, a press release about the substituted Kokoschka is an excellent idea. I'll set it up tomorrow morning. But now it's getting late and if you don't have any plans for this evening I should be honored to take you to dinner."

"I would love that, Hans."

"How well do you know Basel? Do you have a favorite restaurant?"

"I've only been here twice, years ago, in regard to Schiele oils held in private collections, but during those times I had some of the best restaurant meals I've ever experienced in my life."

Hans grinned. "And do you remember the names of any of those restaurants?"

"I don't, unfortunately. But I can describe where my favorite Italian restaurant is. It's not on street level, it's up a floor and their zabaglione is unforgettable."

"Italian? And upstairs? You must be thinking of the Trattoria Aroma on the Sattelgasse. I'll call and make reservations right away."

* * *

Hans was lucky to get the last table available and an hour later the two art historians were seated next to one of the restaurant windows overlooking the Sattelgasse, talking animatedly over red wine. To Hans' horror Megan had sweetened hers with the Dasani strawberry-kiwi sweetener she always carried with her.

They continued to speculate about who the blonde woman in Kokoschka's painting could be.

"Two notions keep recurring to me, but both seem too fanciful to be realistic," Megan mused.

"Tell me regardless," encouraged Hans.

"All right, but please don't laugh."

"Of course not. *Any* theory at this point should be thought through and considered seriously."

"Well, I keep wondering whether it might be a case of righting what may have been perceived as a great wrong. We know that Alma truly disliked the way Oskar depicted her in *The Bride of the Wind*—making her seem so passive and blissfully unaware as they are tossed about in a small boat during a tempest at sea. She had written about it in no uncertain terms: 'he painted me relying utterly on him for help, while he, tyrannical in his expression and radiating energy, calms the waves.'

"The first title Kokoschka gave to the painting struck a Wagnerian note—*Tristan and Isolde*, as you doubtless know. The two lovers who would be united in death. And decades later, on Alma's seventieth birthday, Oskar wrote her that they were 'united for eternity' in his painting of them. Given that she had since had two husbands, she may not have felt the same way. After all, Mahler remained the center of her life, in her thoughts and in her memoirs."

Hans nodded his head in agreement.

"To say nothing of the fact that, after their three-year affair was over, terminated by war and by Alma herself, the next thing she heard about the 'mad,' super-intense Kokoschka was that he had had a life-size doll made in her likeness."

"Oh, yes, I am acquainted with that bizarre story. A figure complete with orifices. *All* of them. Right?"

"Right. It was a doll he not only displayed in his Dresden studio and introduced to people, but a doll that he included in a large double portrait with himself—he dressed, she nude. You don't have to imagine what Alma thought of all this. She expressed her revulsion in letters and in her two published autobiographies."

"So" asked Hans, "are you saying that Kokoschka painted a second version of *The Tempest* starring another woman in order to right the wrong perceived by Alma?"

"No, I don't think so. If Kokoschka had done such a thing you can be sure we would have heard about it in the chatty, overwrought "autobiography" he titled *A Sea Ringed with Visions*. And it makes sense that the art world would know about such a large painting. That Janette Killar, who recently put together the revised oeuvre catalogue of his works, would be acquainted with the painting."

"Yes, I suppose it would have been difficult to keep secret such a large work," agreed Hans. "Unless Kokoschka put it into storage somewhere, as he did with those fourteen art crates stolen in Vienna. Hold on, Megan! Is it possible that this second *Tempest* was in one of those crates?"

"Hm. If so, the transfer from Vienna to Basel would have to have been accomplished with lightning speed."

"Yes, I give you that, but then why the theft of those crates just four days ago? Surely the two acts are related and not coincidental."

"Yes, indeed they do seem to be connected. As to *who* might have initiated the two crimes, I am wondering whether, if it is the same person in both cases, it could possibly be some *direct descendant* of Alma, someone living right now. So in that person's mind, Alma's 'shame' has been righted, avenged with the *Tempest* substitution of another woman, one clearly not Alma."

"Ach! I like your thinking, Megan. All I know about Alma's descendants is that she was survived by a daughter, Anna Justine, who sculpted."

Megan laughed. "There's a great deal *more* to know about that daughter. Her mother's string of affairs and marriages obviously damaged her. Although Anna Justine was able to become a successful sculptor—she made bronze busts of composers like Schönberg and Alban Berg—psychologically she was a wreck. She married various musicians, the first one when she was only sixteen. She left her fifth and last husband at the age of seventy-five."

"That is some history. I have seen a few of her composer heads: Bruno Walter, Otto Klemperer, Artur Schnabel, and Rudolf Serkin. Certainly a distinguished list. But tell me, did Anna Justine have children?"

"She had two girls from two different marriages. They were named Alma Otilla and Marina, and the first one, Alma Otilla, provided three great-granddaughters for Alma. She also gave birth to a son out of wedlock, one Bruno Fichte—Alma Mahler's unacknowledged great-grandson—still unacknowledged when she died in New York in nineteen sixty-four. Bruno, if he is still alive and kicking, most probably lives in New York."

"So it's Bruno, the great-grandson of Alma Mahler-Gropius-Werfel, you're thinking could conceivably have had a hand in our museum theft?"

"I think he might be a bit too old to have figured personally. If he were born in the early forties, let's say, he would be seventy-five or so now. But, if he is carrying a torch for righting the 'wrong' committed against his great-grandmother Alma by Kokoschka, he might have transmitted this ambition to a son or daughter. Or even hired someone to substitute paintings. Of course, one would have to know how *he* came to be in possession of the painting that was switched for your painting."

Hans looked thoughtful. "Some might say the connection is too far-fetched, but, knowing the history and passions stirred up by both Alma and Oskar over the decades, I think it is an idea worth exploring. The thing to do now is to find out whether or not there is still a Bruno and if he has or had children."

"Let's give the Internet a try, just for fun," said Megan, pulling her iPhone out of her purse and typing in the name Bruno Fichte-Mahler. Some irrelevant images and a few possibly pertinent entries immediately appeared, but only one of them seemed related to her search person's decade of birth. Under the name Bruno Fichte, not followed by Mahler, she came across a Hunter College retired professor of art history, "son of the industrialist Hugo Fichte." Never heard of his father or of him. Probably some esoteric field. Something to explore next time she was in New York, Megan thought.

As they finished dinner and were preparing to leave the restaurant, Hans' cell phone rang. He listened intently to the message, then turned to Megan.

"There has been a murder at Vevey's Kokoschka Foundation!"

5

Retired Hunter College professor of art history Bruno Fichte, unacknowledged great-grandson of Alma Mahler, waited impatiently in his luxurious New York apartment across from the Metropolitan Museum for the call he expected from his son in Switzerland. A limber man of medium height with abundant curly hair that was still mostly black, he carried his seventy-four years well, appearing much younger to his acquaintances. Acquaintances, because he entertained no real friends. No one who could have an insight into the overriding passion that ruled his life: assembling the largest collection of Alma Mahler material in private hands. Bruno's wife had died young, but not before giving birth to a son, who had been taught by his father to keep the Mahler connection in their lives secret. Secret because so much of Bruno's collection had been assembled by devious means. Felix, black-haired, tall and limber like his father, was an intense recluse with a gift for languages. He had never married and now, at the age of thirty-six, he shared in his father's obsession concerning all things having to do with their famous relative, despite the fact that in her lifetime she had never accepted Bruno as a blood descendant. Felix had been in and out of jail on various charges having to do with attempted thefts of artworks from New York galleries and homes. He now occasionally taught German at a Berlitz school near his father's midtown Manhattan apartment.

Both father and son realized how important it was to sidestep their familial lineage publically. They could not afford to have prying eyes viewing their complicated affairs, their shady contacts, their customs-dodging maneuvers, their actual thefts. The collection of Almariana they had assembled in New York was impressive and represented all major periods of Alma's long life. Through an Austrian gallery, the two men had been able to acquire previously unknown diaries from Alma's early Kokoschka years, hidden in the attic of her former home in Breitenstein on Semmering, the Haus Mahler.

And thanks to a discreet connection in Basel they were hot on the trail of a tremendous memento of Alma's three-year affair with the artist. Between 1912 and 1915 Kokoschka had painted seven goatskin fans for his inamorata. Decorated with fanciful depictions relating to their passionate but turbulent relationship, all except one, apparently, had been preserved.

The seventh fan, according to Alma, had been burnt in a fit of jealousy by her second husband, architect Walter Gropius. But, as so often in her writing, Alma had fudged the facts. In this case she was purposefully misleading. She had in fact saved the fan and it was found hidden among her effects at the time of her death in 1964. Her namesake granddaughter sold it, along with the six other fans to Hamburg's Museum für Kunst und Gewerbe where all seven fans were on permanent display.

But in early 2015, what appeared to be an eighth fan from the series turned up in the estate of a fanatical Austrian collector, Julius Messerschmidt. His estate was put up for auction at Vienna's renowned Dorotheum and the Vevey Kokoschka Foundation had made the winning bid for the artist's painted fan. The treasured item, its imagery a definitive prototype for *The Tempest*, was about to be put on display for the public by the Foundation.

This was the bit of news Bruno's discreet contact in Basel had conveyed. And just in time. The exhibit was due to open on the following Wednesday. Felix had managed to arrive in Zurich from New York on the Sunday before, and by Tuesday afternoon he had sized up the Vevey building's layout. No security cameras were in evidence, nor were there more than two guards on duty when he entered the Foundation on the pretext of looking at Kokoschka's correspondence of the 1970s with his Swiss gallery director. Wearing a blond wig that covered his black, curly hair, he had an animated discussion with the curator of the Kokoschka collection and learned that the restoration room was just down the corridor beyond the library and café.

Shortly after midnight, Felix reentered the Kokoschka Foundation premises by way of its ground-level garbage storage bin. It had one opening facing the alley for after-hours pickup, while a second opening gave directly onto the ground floor corridor, closed off by a sliding, unlocked metal door. Making his way directly to the restoration room, Felix quickly located the Kokoschka fan, its untanned goatskin leaves splayed out in a frame and its astonishing imagery articulated with India ink and watercolor. Two naked figures, male and female, their recumbent bodies intertwined as they lay within a small boat, raised their Liebestod goblets and toasted each other in a Tristan and Isolde farewell that would unite them in a love death. Their features were unmistakably those of Oskar and Alma.

The fan was virtually priceless, Felix declared to himself as he carefully lifted off the glass cover and slowly disengaged the fan from its mountings. Success. But just as he turned to leave the room he heard steps coming down the corridor. Damn! The Foundation paid for a night watchman. That had not been in Felix's calculations. He picked up a hammer from the restorer's table and placed himself behind the door. Perhaps he wouldn't need to use it. Perhaps the man would not enter this room. But he was wrong. As the night watchman got closer another sort of sound attracted Felix's attention. It was the excited whining of a guard dog. A large one. Suddenly the dog began to bark and it was clear that the man on the other end of the leash was being pulled along the corridor past the library and café to the restoration room. As soon as they entered Felix sprang into action, leaping out from behind the door. His first hammer blow was for the straining dog, who fell to the ground with a single whimper. The second blow caught the night watchman full face, knocking him down on his back. Felix delivered two more hammer blows to the man's head, then stepped back. His work was done. Too bad about the killings, but they had been necessary. It was the Basel contact who had been remiss in his assessment of the Kokoschka Foundation's security system.

Within minutes Felix was out of the museum by way of the helpful two-way garbage disposal unit and on his way back to Basel for his return flight to the States via Zurich and Frankfurt. After breezing through the Basel airport security—he had added a few children's dolls to the satchel carrying the fan, now in cotton wrap—Felix finally called his father. Success. And yes, the fan was in excellent condition. Unfortunately a life had to be taken, but the man was quite old, more a pensioner than a regular guard. And, oh yes, a dog had to be put out of commission. What kind of dog? A Swiss mountain dog, what else?

Megan, at Hans Tietze's urging, had agreed to stay in Basel another day before continuing on to Vienna to try to examine the storehouse vault from which the Kokoschka crates had been stolen. She would drive up to Vevey with Hans tomorrow to discuss what else, if anything, had been taken. She was eager to make the visit, as she had never been to the Kokoschka Foundation. She was familiar with the collection of his papers in Vienna, but had never had the scholarly need to study what Vevey held regarding the artist.

In the meantime, after a restful night at the Rochat hotel, she decided to start an examination of the numerous women in Kokoschka's passionate early life, with an eye as to who the blonde woman in the substitute *Tempest* might be. The first one about whom anything was known was a seventeen-year-old girl by the name of Lilith Lang, a fellow student at the Vienna School of Decorative Arts. She was the sister of the artist Erwin Lang—colleague of Kokoschka and Schiele—and the daughter of the Viennese feminist and theosophist, Marie Lang. Blonde, blue-eyed and slight of frame, Lilith had been the inspiration and subject matter for much of Kokoschka's early work, ranging from stark drawings of her in the nude to a "children's book," *The Dreaming Youths—Die Träumenden Knaben*, commissioned by the Wiener Werkstätte.

It was a book that precipitated a public scandal when exhibited at Vienna's 1908 Kunstschau. Eight color lithographs were accompanied by a staccato-versed poem by the twenty-two-year-old artist. A rich gestural repertoire animated the nude, pubescent figures. Accompanied by loosely associated illustrations, one boldly titled *Eros*, Kokoschka's text evoked the image of a voyage of awkward adolescent sexuality in search of self-expression. The passionate desire to communicate and experience release was built up though the use of abruptly shifting images, a constellation of sexually suggestive symbols—fish, knife, flower, lake.

The opening color lithograph presented a sleeping young girl with long blonde hair—Lilith—seated on a tiny island no larger than herself and observed by two predatory red fish. The accompanying text began:

Red little fish,
little fish red,
stab yourself
with the triple knife dead,
slit yourself with my fingers in two,
that the silent circles may be through.

It was fascinating, new, and definitely *not* a book for children.

The concluding illustration, titled *The Girl Li and I*, showed two dreaming youths—the artist and Lilith—standing frontally and naked, each isolated from the other in their own spherical white surround and individual reverie. They were separated by a bulbous red area over which two golden birds flew.

Megan wondered whatever happened to the girl who so dominated Kokoschka's thoughts when he was in his early twenties. She had starred in the poster he had made for the 1908 Kunstschau. It presented a lyrical yet simultaneously agitated image of a girl smelling white flower blooms that, with their black cavities, looked like tumbling skulls. Was this a hint of things to come?

In retrospect, this was not a bad question, considering that Kokoschka's color lithograph poster for the following year's Kunstschau had lost all its lyricism. Instead it showed a blood-red man—the artist himself—being flayed alive by a deranged, pale woman in black behind him, both figures posited between sun and moon. What was this blasphemous, modern *Pietà* all about?

The answer, Megan knew, was that, five years before the outbreak of World War I, visible gaps were appearing in the beauteous façade of the Viennese Waltz Capital. And what lay behind was dark and disturbing. It was the individual suffering *psyche* with its consuming angst that demanded to be seen. Kokoschka was asking: Who am I? Who are you? Why do you wish to murder me? Key to these questions was the drama the artist had written that year of 1909 and which the riveting poster advertised, *Murderer, Hope of Women*—a harrowing play, performed only once, about a literally bloody battle of the sexes.

Had Lilith jilted Oskar that year of 1909, Megan wondered as she called the bizarre poster to mind? If so, was this Oskar's extreme reaction? Could the question ever be answered? She would have to reread the artist's meandering autobiographies, that was clear. But her books were in Dallas. She called Hans at the museum to see if their library contained any of the pertinent volumes.

"Yes indeed. You're welcome to come over, or shall I have them brought to your hotel?"

"Oh, no, I'll come over there, now that I know you have them."

"Let's meet half-way. I'll bring the books with me if you come to Les Trois Rois hotel for lunch," said Hans.

"What a lovely idea! Shall we say one o'clock?"

"See you then," Hans promised.

Megan thought she would get a cat nap in before lunch, but when she lay down all she could think of was the two Kokoschka posters, so vastly different from each other. Was Lilith Long at fault? What could explain the drastic change? Does art follow life, or does life follow art? She fell asleep pondering these imponderables.

⌐

Leo Lang knew his obsession was dangerous. But now he was committed and the lure of what was to come was irresistible. A thin, nervous man in his late fifties with receding gray hairline, long-boned face, and gray stubble on his chin, he looked down appreciatively from the center balcony of his sprawling house in Vienna's fourteenth district Penzing, with its partial view of Otto Wagner's Church am Steinhof. The Art nouveau villa had been inherited by him from his wealthy father Oskar Lang, who had made a fortune in the manufacture of artificial rubber and had served on many school and hospital boards. Although rising to social prominence, Oskar's origins were humble enough. He had been born out of wedlock to a young Vienna artist, Lilith Lang. Lilith would never reveal the identity of the man who impregnated her. Her domineering mother Marie took over care of the child and Lilith had distanced herself from them both. A taciturn, single woman who worked as a librarian at Austria's National Library, Lilith died in 1952 at the age of sixty-one.

It was then that the object she kept hidden all her life was brought to light. When her estranged son Oskar cleared out his mother's modest but book-filled apartment he found, hidden under her bed, a large roll of canvas. One more thing to throw away, he had thought with irritation. Unrolling it impatiently, he found himself nonplussed. He was staring at his mother's features as she must have looked when she young. As he knew her from an early photograph. Her half-naked, recumbent body was alongside the bare torso of a protective male companion. Both were pressed together in what looked like a small boat that was being tossed about by turbulent waves. The man looked steadily ahead; his mother was staring at her companion with wide open, cerulean eyes.

What could this mean? Oskar remembered his mother had attended art school for a few years when she was a teenager, but he didn't remember his grandmother talking about Lilith's having had her portrait painted there. Especially not a half-naked, embarrassing one such as this! It was a very compromising picture and Oskar thought his uncommunicative mother certainly did the right thing in hiding it away. It was a wonder she hadn't thrown it away, except that her features were too recognizable. He decided to take the picture over to his own home and store it in the cellar until he had time to find out more about it. The portrait was far too embarrassing to show to his wife.

A few years later Oskar chanced to see a poster decorating the entrance of Vienna's Albertina Museum advertising an Oskar Kokoschka retrospective. The image on the poster was titled *Bride of the Wind. The Tempest.* Except for the brunette woman with closed eyes in the picture, the image was exactly the same as the canvas roll in his basement!

Although Oskar had little knowledge of art, he did have an uncle who was an artist, Erwin Lang, his mother's brother and husband of the famous Viennese dancer Grete Wiesenthal. In October of 1956, Oskar had invited his painter uncle to come over to see his newborn son, Leo, and added mysteriously that he would also show him a "bizarre" portrait of his sister as a young girl. Erwin could not resist the double offer and, after admiring the baby, followed Oskar down into the cellar to view the painting.

"Why, that's Kokoschka!" he exclaimed. "It's his *Tempest* portrait with Alma Mahler, except that the woman in this painting is my *sister*, not that wretched femme fatale."

Oskar nodded in assent.

"Is it dated or signed?" Erwin asked out loud as he looked the canvas up and down. There, on the lower right, in orange against the swirling blue and violet background was the characteristic "O K" along with the date, 1914.

"You realize, Oskar, don't you, the *value* of this picture?"

"I suppose so. But I would not want it to go public, not with my mother being half-naked in it. I could never stain our family with something like this."

"Forget the 'stain'! Don't you realize that this picture is worth at least two hundred million Euros? This is no time to be prudish."

Oskar was staring fixedly at the date on the canvas. "Do you realize, Uncle, that the year Kokoschka inscribed this picture is the year of my birth?"

The two men looked at each other in astonishment. Neither wanted to be the first to express their common thought.

Erwin broke the silence. "This is a picture of patrimony. By including your mother and signing and inscribing it with the year of your birth, Kokoschka is admitting that he is…your father!"

A stunned silence followed.

"If this is really true—and perhaps a DNA test could prove it—then at last I know who my *father* is!" Oskar cried. "And to think, he was a famous man!"

"*Is* a famous man. He is still alive and lives in Switzerland," Erwin informed his nephew.

"Do you think I should contact him?"

"I would think about that very carefully," said Erwin slowly. "He is quite mad, you know. Still writing manifestos, railing against governments and nations, joining unpopular causes, a complete madman. Yes, he might acknowledge you as his son, but you can bet he would emphasize his *bastard* son. And who knows how many other sons and daughters he might have fathered? Would you really want that kind of *publicity*?"

"No," answered Oskar meekly. "But I would like the world to know some day of my Kokoschka portrait and its connection to my mother."

"Then wait till Leo grows up and let *him* take care of it. By then enough time will have passed and the family name will not seem so tarnished. And by then Kokoschka will have passed away."

"All right," Oskar responded sadly, bowing to his uncle's wisdom.

"And by then, should he want to, Leo could sell the portrait to a museum or through a gallery to a private collector."

This thought cheered Oskar and he agreed to keep the canvas a secret until his son was old enough to cope with the fallout.

Leo grew up to take over the family business and for a number of decades the painting in the villa's basement was forgotten, in spite of the fact that Oskar had finally shown it to him. When Kokoschka died in February of 1980, Leo, whose son had just been killed in a car accident, barely took notice. But when his father Oskar passed away in 2000 at the age of eighty-six, he began to think about the Kokoschka in the cellar.

Over the next decade and a half Leo began to form a plan. Selling the canvas held no interest for him. He wanted the world to know that his father had been Kokoschka's son. During the next fifteen years he acquainted himself with every detail of the artist's life and work—both literary and imagerial. Working alone, and visiting countless museums, he had become a Kokoschka connoisseur and could spot a forgery within minutes. The Kokoschka *Tempest* in his father's basement—now *his* basement—was genuine.

Slowly an idea had taken shape. Money was no object. A recluse widower who lived alone, he was a wealthy man, having more than doubled his father's rubber business income. There would be no point in selling the work to a private collector where it would be hidden away from the world. What he wanted was a large audience. A museum audience. And a European museum, where Kokoschka had long been known and represented. His appraisal of Austrian museums left him unimpressed. Not even Vienna's Belvedere, which did own a few of his grandfather's paintings, seemed worthy of the canvas. His research turned to Switzerland—Geneva and Zurich museums. Nothing in either institution gave him the incentive to expand their collections. In fact, he also realized, there was no guarantee that any museum would be willing to pay the price his Kokoschka would have to command. That could be embarrassing. He did not want simply to bestow the thing. He wanted a venue that would make the portrait go viral.

By the time he was about to turn sixty, Leo's pondering had produced a novel idea. Museum *thefts* always triggered publicity. A major museum robbery always attracted world attention. What if he were to initiate a "trade"? But a trade on *his* conditions. The Basel Kunstmuseum was the obvious target as it owned the Alma Mahler version of *The Tempest*. It was doubtful whether the museum would display both *Tempest* paintings side by side: not enough funds and not enough space most likely. And he did not want simply to give away the artwork. No, it would be up to him to engineer things in what could only be characterized as a forced trade. Leo had found the answer.

He would employ a professional thief, a known master, to switch the two paintings. The Lilith version for Basel, the Alma version for himself. A simple switch. And certainly a fair trade. Even if both paintings would have to be fit to new stretchers and frames. It was a brilliant idea! The journalistic and television publicity would be worldwide, the crowds would come by the thousands and YouTube, Facebook, and Instagram would do the rest.

Finding the right person to do the job had not been as easy as he thought, but finally, through contacts he would be embarrassed to acknowledge, the right agent was located. She was a private restorer, Swiss, from Basel, and six feet tall. Her code name was Agnes Sauer and she had a long and successful history of small painting, jewel, and manuscript "acquisitions," as she called them. After a lengthy phone conversation—an interview of sorts—Leo gave her the measurements of the canvas that would have to be rolled up for transport. Soon afterward, they met face to face at his villa and once Leo felt confident about her credentials and professional attitude, he took her to the basement to collect the cargo. Sauer had brought with her a cardboard container tube measuring some two feet in width and six-feet-ten-inches in length. The tight transfer was made without any glitches.

And now—after the switch event—their most recent phone conversation had provided Leo with all the details he craved to know about the successful switch. How convenient it had been that work on the Basel museum's new addition had frazzled the security cameras. Agnes Sauer, dressed as a laborer, her long brown hair swept up under a workman's cap, had entered from the extension under construction with the Lilith *Tempest* roll and crossed the inner courtyard at ten minutes after three in the morning. In the main entrance foyer two night watchmen were chatting before going on their hourly rounds. Agnes had a full fifty minutes in the gallery room that housed the Alma *Tempest*. She leaned the Lilith *Tempest* roll, enveloped in bubble wrap, against the wall and slid the four heavy weights off her belt. She carefully sliced the Alma canvas from its black frame, rolling it up gingerly on the floor, then standing it on end next to the substitute *Tempest*. She fit a width of thin bubble wrap around the Alma roll, securing it gently with plastic ties. Then she unrolled the Lilith *Tempest* onto the floor directly beneath the empty frame and pinned down its corners with the four brass weights. No note of explanation or demand. Simply a substitution—with no loss to either party.

Agnes Sauer had finished her task with twenty minutes to spare. Picking up the Alma roll she retraced her steps through and out the main building, crossed the courtyard, and entered the half-completed extension. Emerging from a back door, she walked up the street to where she had parked her blue Volvo station wagon. Quickly, she loaded the roll in the back, placing it in the container tube that would be sent through as baggage. Two minutes later Agnes Sauer was on her way to Zurich and the early morning flight that was to take her to Vienna. There she would deliver the Alma *Tempest* to Leo Lang and collect her fee. Mission accomplished. Or so she had every reason to think.

8

Megan had arrived at the Grand Hotel Les Trois Rois a few minutes late, much to her chagrin, as she had always been a stickler for promptness, usually arriving far too early for appointments. Hans was waiting for her in the reception lounge and greeted her with a wide smile. He thrust an elegant Kunstmuseum sack in her hand; it was heavy with Kokoschka books. Megan beamed her gratitude and they went out onto the hotel terrace for lunch. There, with an ideal view of the Rhine before them, Hans ordered a bottle of pinot noir while they studied the attractive lunch menu. They decided to share a fondue that came with thin slices of potato for dipping along with a small green salad each. Megan then eagerly peeked into the museum sack, exclaiming at the finds Hans had brought along from the museum library. Both of the artist's autobiographies were there, although Megan knew that it was challenging to extract fact from philosophical reflections and character judgments.

She opened the one titled simply *Mein Leben* to a description of the genesis of *The Dreaming Youths* book and came to Kokoschka's description of "the young girl Li," who wore "a red hand-woven peasant skirt, something unknown in Vienna. I was in love with the girl," the text continued, "the book was my first love letter, but she had already disappeared from my circle of acquaintances when the book appeared."

She read the passage aloud to Hans.

"Well, that seems definite enough," he commented. "It would seem that Lilith was in and out of his life very briefly."

"I wonder about that," said Megan broodingly, thinking again of the youthful girl with blonde hair Kokoschka had portrayed in the substituted *Tempest*. Hans had already put it on display in his museum with an appropriate and lengthy label. In fact the didactic ended with the promise of a reward of 25,000 Swiss francs to anyone giving a lead that resulted in the return of the stolen *Tempest* to the museum. This had brought more press and television coverage.

"What if they met again?" Megan queried. "And during the year when Oskar broke up with Alma for the last time? Perhaps he took Lilith back into his life, even if only briefly."

She thought about how, after Alma broke off their tumultuous relationship for good in 1914, Oskar had, with the help of his loyal patron Adolf Loos, joined a regiment of dragoons after World War I broke out. His mother paid for the horse; Loos for the elegant dragoon uniform in which Oskar had himself photographed. All this, and riding off to war in an effort to forget Alma. But could Lilith have reappeared in his life at this time? Might they have become lovers? Could this second *Tempest*—Megan presumed it was the later work—be a testament to that love? It was absolutely intriguing that Kokoschka had duplicated his painting down to the last detail, that the only difference was the face of the woman. Megan would have loved to compare the two canvases brush stroke by brush stroke.

Megan turned to Hans after they had finished their delicious fondue. "I'm hatching a fantasy scenario and would like to pass it by you, just for fun."

"Of course! Go ahead, Megan. I'd love to hear it."

"Well, presuming that Lilith reappeared in Kokoschka's life, what if he got her pregnant? What if his second *Tempest* was a declaration of his love renewed?"

"Hm. Well, it would have been a very short period of love, considering all the female company he kept in Dresden right after the war. And we hear no more of Lilith in his life."

"Oh, I'm not saying it lasted. I'm just wondering if perhaps he fathered an unacknowledged child by Lilith. One who grew up not knowing who his or her father was."

"Let's say your fantasy theory is correct. The child would have been born in nineteen fourteen, the date of *Tempest* number two, or nineteen fifteen at the latest. That would make her or him one hundred years old now, or a hundred and one. Not much to go on there, even if your hypothesis is correct."

"Yes, but say the child had offspring, and they inherited the strange painting, not realizing that it was by a famous painter. Perhaps they gave or sold it to someone who *did* know who Kokoschka was."

"But that doesn't explain why the painting's owner, whoever that might be, would want to replace the Alma version with the Lilith version. The break-in was bold and it was professional, that much is clear. The substitution was carried off without our night guard's knowledge." Hans looked doubtful.

"So, again, the big question. *Why* would someone want their version of the Kokoschka to be 'gifted' to your museum? And why would they take the Alma version? Certainly it could not be sold. The art world would learn soon enough if it were put up for sale. But an unscrupulous gallery or private collector could sell it to another party without the world market being any the wiser."

"Is it your conjecture then that whoever the owner of the Lilith painting might have been, that person for some reason or another craved owning the Alma version? And out of some weird sense of obligation, exchanged the Lilith one for it?"

"I guess it is. But my supposition seems to raise more questions than answers."

"Don't abandon it completely, Megan. You may indeed have something here. We just don't have all the pieces of information we need at the moment." He turned to the waiter who had laid a dessert menu on the table. "Would either of you care for a *Nusstorte*?" the young man inquired. Hans looked at Megan and she nodded an enthusiastic yes. "Make that two," said Hans.

"Well," Megan persevered after the waiter had left, "I have one practical idea. Let's look up the surname Lang in the Basel cyber telephone book. There are doubtless hundreds, but, what if the child were male and named in honor of his father—Oskar?"

"Probably farfetched but why not give it a try?" said Hans gamely.

From a light shoulder bag Megan whipped out her iPhone and conducted a search. After a few minutes she made her report. "There are three Oskar Langs listed in Basel. Shall we check them out?"

Hans was bemused. "And how will you go about doing that?"

"Just watch me," said Megan as she dialed the first number she came across. "Hallo," she said when a female voice answered. "My name is Dorothea Lang and I'm trying to locate the man who may have been my grandfather. Might I ask if the Oskar Lang in your family had an ancestor of the same first name?"

Megan's question was answered with pithy alacrity.

"Nein."

Hans smiled ruefully as he heard the barking answer come through the phone.

Undeterred, Megan dialed the second number. Same routine, same answer.

But the third call produced an unexpected result. The man who answered said he had a great-uncle named Oskar and that he had died in America, owing taxes to the Swiss government. This did not seem like a good candidate.

Megan was tireless however.

"Let's try Zurich and Geneva," she said, typing in an entry. After multiple calls, all with negative results, Hans suggested that she try the city in which Kokoschka had met Lilith—Vienna.

"Oh, of course! I should have thought of that at once. You're a genius, Hans."

"That will only be determined if we get results," Hans smiled.

Oddly enough, there was only one Oskar Lang in Vienna, Megan's research showed. An answering machine affirmed that an Oskar Lang lived there but was "away until July on another gig." Hardly a likely candidate.

Undeterred, Megan then began a search for any Lilith Langs that might be listed in Basel, Zurich, Geneva, or Vienna. No luck. The mythic name that for centuries had signified seductress or murderer was obviously not popular. Megan could see how it might be the real-life Lilith who was the man-flaying woman in Kokoschka's poster advertising *Murderer, Hope of Women*. His battle-of-the-sexes play ended with the man murdering the woman, thus explaining the quixotic title. Perhaps in real life Oskar may have turned on Lilith. After all, he had written laconically that she was "out of his circle of acquaintances."

However, there was another way into the haystack, Megan thought. What about looking at death records for an Oskar Lang? Her perusals of information for Basel, Zurich, and Geneva produced nothing, but when she scanned the Vienna files, a search of the main cemetery came up with life dates on one Oskar Lang, born 1914, died 2000. The right birth year! He would have been eighty-six when he died. The question was: if he was the lovechild did he *know* about the painting of his mother? She must have owned it, considering neither of the two oeuvre catalogues—that by Wingler, and the newer one by Killar—made mention of such a work. She must have kept all knowledge of the portrait quiet. The great question was did Oskar know about the portrait and did he inherit it when Lilith died? One fact that was known was the date of Lilith's death. She died in 1952 at the age of sixty-one.

Yet another reason to travel on to Vienna after their outing to Vevey tomorrow, Megan told Hans. She would seek out any living relatives of Lilith's locally famous brother, the painter Erwin Lang, and see what she could come up with.

Lunch over, they returned to the hotel, Hans carrying the heavy museum book sack. "I'll pick you up at ten o'clock tomorrow morning," he said in farewell.

"*Wo ist Alma?*"—"Where is Alma?" the headline on the front page of the *Basler Zeitung* ran as news of the daring art heist spread. A heist that pertained to the legendary femme fatal Alma Mahler. Other cities picked up the story. In Berlin, at his penthouse apartment overlooking the famous zoo, Helmut Haesslich read the account in his *Berliner Morgenpost* with growing interest. Owner of one of the city's most prestigious if secretive— some might say unscrupulous—galleries, he had two painter passions: the nineteenth-century Swiss artist, Arnold Böcklin, and the twentieth-century Austrian artist, Oskar Kokoschka.

At present the walls of his gallery were hung with Böcklin drawings showing figure studies for some of the artist's famous mythological paintings. Public response had been gratifying and the show was already very nearly sold out. Haesslich's best sellers, however, were hand-embellished giclee color reproductions printed on archival canvas of the Swiss artist's 1872 *Self-Portrait with Death Playing the Fiddle*. The original was in Basel but it was one of the artist's best-known works. Haesslich's educated clientele knew and appreciated the painting's link with Mahler's Fourth Symphony. In her memoirs Alma Mahler explained that the second movement's *danse macabre*, featuring a solo violin with strings tuned a tone higher—a scordatura, was inspired by Böcklin's haunting painting in which a grinning skeleton plays its violin next to the painter's head.

Five days earlier a young art restorer identifying himself as Niki Deschner, had visited his gallery *Am schwarzen Schwan—At the Black Swan*—with a canvas roll under his arm and an unusual proposal. In his free time he liked to copy old masters at Berlin's Alte Nationalgalerie. Recently he had switched his attention to the Swiss artist and painted a near-perfect copy of Berlin's version of Böcklin's *Isle of the Dead*. Of course, he had complied with museum rules and worked on a canvas of different proportions from the original. But, as Haesslich rolled out the canvas, it was obvious that the copy was extraordinarily well done and, were it the correct size, could have easily passed for the original.

It occurred to him, young Niki Deschner explained eagerly, that since one of Böcklin's six versions of his popular *Isle of the Dead* was known to be lost, he would be willing to provide, at the right price, a fine portrayal in the right size of what he was absolutely sure the missing image looked like. Just the slightest variation on the five known versions in Berlin, Basel, Geneva, Leipzig, and New York.

Helmut Haesslich feigned shock. "Do you realize what you are proposing, young man?" Actually he was intrigued by the idea as something not to sell, but for himself, for the inner sanctum of his penthouse. After all, he already had his own color reproduction on canvas of Böcklin's *Self-Portrait with Death Playing the Fiddle* hanging in his den.

Niki Deschner looked unrepentant. "I just thought you might like to display it in your gallery, signed by *me* of course."

"Of course."

A silence ensued.

"I was only thinking that one of your clients might like to be *reminded* of the real thing. Kind of like a theme with variations, you know. They know the theme, so they buy the variation."

Haesslich marveled at the boy's audacity. "Young man, I have no interest in your proposal of resuscitating a lost Böcklin by creating a new one, no matter how close it might come to what we all expect the original looked like."

Niki Deschner's face was a study of surprise and disappointment.

"I tell you what I will do, however," continued Haesslich. "I appreciate the work that went into the copy you made at the museum. It is quite good and I will purchase it from you for one thousand Euros."

Niki smiled broadly. He was off the hook. "I accept your offer, sir, and just want you to know that I am available, should you ever desire a copy of any work."

"Give me your e-mail address and I will keep it on file," answered Haesslich, opening his wallet and taking out two five-hundred Euro notes.

Niki Deschner walked out of the *Am schwarzen Schwan* a happy man. His career as creative "copyist" was just beginning.

10

Standing five-foot-eleven, with a long, aristocratic nose and slender body, Desdemona Dumba absent-mindedly touched her rich black hair which was pulled back away from her face in an abundant bun. She was staring out the window of her spacious Vienna apartment that encompassed the top floor of the building that, in the days of Emperor Franz Josef, used to be her great-grandfather's private home. Of Greek descent, multi-millionaire Nikolaus Dumba had been a renowned industrialist and patron of the arts in

Vienna. It was he who commissioned Gustav Klimt to paint two sopraportas in the music room of the palatial residence he had built in Vienna's inner city on the Ringstrasse. A lover of Schubert, he had collected some two hundred of the composer's musical manuscripts by the time of his death in 1900. He left them to the City of Vienna and even now Schubert's *German Mass* was performed in his honor.

Dumba's great-granddaughter Desdemona had carried on the tradition of patronizing the arts and was a collector as well. She had assembled an impressive array of Kokoschka's cityscapes of different European cities. Born in Vienna in the mid-1970s, Desdemona was a throwback to the nineteenth century in her absolute worship of Elisabeth—Sisi—Austria's beautiful but tragic Empress. After the double murder-suicide of her only son Crown Prince Rudolf and his mistress at Mayerling, she fled Austria and wandered aimlessly around Europe virtually alone. A student of all things Greek, thanks to her court reader Constantine Christomanos, Sisi built herself a palace on the Greek island of Corfu in 1890, and called it Achilleion in honor of the mythical hero Achilles.

Like Sisi, Desdemona was fluent in Greek, obsessed with beauty, and, also like the Empress, she was anorexic. Having no wish to marry, she had used her exquisiteness and the millions she had inherited to great effect, charming a Greek government official into granting her permission to buy the small, unimportant rock of an island that to her looked so like a painting she had seen once as a child and never forgotten. It was on this small island, which she christened Xenia—stranger—that she had her villa erected, built out from the rocky rise with an imposing stand of cypress trees. Yes, stranger. Like Sisi, a worshipful stranger, but for Desdemona, a stranger in the land of her ancestors.

And it was at Xenia that the contents of fourteen crates her man Theo in Vienna had recently taken charge of would ultimately be displayed. Displayed for an awed audience of one.

11

Walter Fortier, curator of the Kokoschka Foundation, warmly greeted Megan and Hans when they arrived at Vevey from Basel. Despite all his goodwill, Fortier was not able to shed more light on the theft of the Kokoschka fan. The local police had identified the means of entry and exit as the garbage disposal area with its two doors, one opening to the outside, the other accessing the building's interior. Fortier had immediately checked with the city's Musée Jenisch, which owned a number of important Kokoschka late works, but no signs of an attempted break-in had been discovered there. What could not be determined, however, was whether or not the robbery was a local job. Common sense suggested that it was not, Fortier concluded, nodding his head sagely.

Megan asked if he had heard about the theft of fourteen crates of Kokoschka works in Vienna. Fortier had not and was immediately interested, almost comforted that his was not the only institution robbed. That there was an international market for the artist was a given, but that his works were now being *stolen* was quite new.

After Megan assured the concerned curator she would let him know what, if anything, she learned about the Vienna theft, she and Hans left for a brief tour of the pretty little town with its palm trees and plethora of bright flowers lining the lakeside promenade. They slowed down to admire a life-size bronze effigy of Charlie Chaplin, who had spent the last twenty years of his life at Vevey. On his head was the famous bowler hat.

"Did you know that Vevey is the home headquarters for Nestlé?" asked Hans as they passed an ad for Nestlé chocolate bars.

"No, I didn't realize that. But my favorite Swiss chocolate bar is Lindt. Their dark chocolate with 'a touch of sea salt' is so incredibly good that I no longer eat any other sort of chocolate. I have one square of Lindt every morning after breakfast and I break that square up into ten pieces, slowly sucking each one and waiting for a single grain of sea salt to land beneath my front teeth so I can deliberately crunch it. Divine!"

"Well, you may make me an instant convert. Shall we stop and buy some here?"

"Not on my account. I brought a supply with me, although it's back at the hotel."

"But now I'm really eager to try your sea-salt Lindt, so let me pull up at this pharmacy and see if they carry it. You can stay in the car."

A few minutes later Hans emerged from the pharmacy triumphantly holding up a sea-salt Lindt chocolate bar. He was in the company of an elegant young woman with brown hair, dressed in white slacks with a tailored white jacket over a rose-colored blouse.

"Guess who I met in the pharmacy?" Hans exclaimed happily. "Beatrice Beauchamp, the director of the Jenisch Museum!" He introduced the two women and within seconds Beauchamp was urging them to stop in at the two-story neoclassical villa that was the Musée Jenisch. There was a special *Kokoschka et la Musique* exhibition that had just opened, one they really must see.

Megan readily agreed. She knew about the artist's early and close ties to music, as evidenced during the Alma breakup in a series of eleven lithographs responding to his favorite Bach cantata, *O Ewigkeit Du Donnerwort—O Eternity Thou Word of Thunder*. Relying more on the words than the music, the artist had responded to the libretto's dialogue between Hope and Fear, casting himself as Hope and Alma as Fear. In the next-to-last print he had shown himself standing in a grave, "slain by my own jealousy," he later admitted.

"Part of our accompanying program to the show," Beauchamp was saying, "is a performance of Paul Hindemith's operatic setting of *Mörder, Hoffnug der Frauen*." Megan did not care for the one-act opera with its dissonant portrayals of the archetypal Man and Woman and she secretly wondered how the residents of serene Vevey might respond. But she smiled encouragingly at Beauchamp.

"And we have hung our new Kokoschka hall walls with color photographs of his stage-settings for *The Magic Flute*," continued Beauchamp.

"So, from the profane to the sublime," proffered Hans.

Beauchamp climbed into the car with them and they drove the three short blocks to the Musée Jenisch. Megan had not been there for a number of years and, as she studied the eleven lithographs inspired by the Bach cantata, she was glad they had accepted the director's invitation. The artworks were images of pain, anxiety, and the eternity of hell. Yes, Kokoschka was certainly hard on himself in this series. Once again Megan marveled at the enduring impact Alma had had upon the men in her life. No wonder people were still writing books about her!

"Shall we stop for lunch before we drive back to Basel?" asked Hans after taking in the exhibition and bidding farewell to a gracious Beauchamp, who had loaded them down with catalogues to Kokoschka shows past and present.

"Good idea. I'm starving. How about eating at a café on the beach?"

"I know a very good one. It's a trattoria with a marvelous view of the lake on the Corseaux Plage. I think you'll like it, considering your Italian background. *And*, it's practically next door to Le Corbusier's villa *Le Lac*, which he built for his parents and which shares the same view as the trattoria."

"Killing two birds with one *lac*," Megan agreed happily.

Over lunch they discussed how, of all the countries and capital cities to which Kokoschka either made pilgrimages or in which he lived, Switzerland offered him the peace and security for which he had always searched.

"Yes, his agitated cityscapes sum up his residencies in Berlin and Prague and Dresden and London and Paris—the list goes on and on," Megan mused.

"To say nothing of his dips down into North Africa and Asia Minor," added Hans, spreading his hands wide.

"I think Greece must have been his favorite country. He was there in sixty-one, I think, and went the rounds to Athens and Delphi and Olympia, drawing everything that pleased his eye from temples and sculptures to tomb reliefs. I've studied the chalk lithographs that resulted from that trip and can almost *feel* his awe."

"Do you think his interest in Greece could have originated with the portrait he painted in Vienna of Constantine Christomanos? When was that? Early, I think," said Hans.

"Oh, yes. It was done in nineteen-nine; one of his earliest 'psychological' renderings. He dispensed with a mimetic mirroring in order to probe the psyche. In Christomanos's case, the anguish Kokoschka perceived and presented via his device of having the man's arms wrap around his twisting body was real. Did you know that he was a hunchback?"

"Ach! Well, that explains a lot," said Hans. "About how old was Christomanos when Kokoschka painted him?"

"In his early forties. He died just two years later. Actually he was an amazing man. His father was a professor at Athens University and he reaped the benefits of growing up in an academic atmosphere. He wrote poetry and was in love with the theater, even wrote plays."

"Why did he leave Greece and go to Vienna?"

"Ostensibly to further his education. And he had an introduction to one of the city's great art patrons, a fellow Greek, Nikolas Dumba."

"Oh, Dumba! Yes, still a famous name in Vienna."

"Christomanos was twenty-one when he arrived there. He must have made splashes because three years later Kaiser Franz Josef hired him to teach modern Greek, read to, and accompany his peripatetic wife Sisi on her travels. It was he who showed her Greece, introduced her to the island of Corfu, consulted with the locals when she decided, under his guidance, to build her villa and temple to Achilles there. She was thirty-three years his senior and he was, in his own way, in love with her, although it is doubtful whether, in her continued mourning for the Crown Prince, Sisi was even aware of his infatuation."

"Didn't Christomanos publish his memoirs of Sisi after she was assassinated?"

"Yes, he certainly did, all based on his meticulous diaries. The public learned, for example, that it took over an hour for Sisi just to be laced into her corset. And how her heavy, ankle-length hair took as many as three hours to dress. Publication of such an intimate view of the Empress caused a huge scandal in the press and ultimately Christomanos fled Vienna and returned to Greece."

"What about Kokoschka's portrait of him? Where is it now? I don't recall ever having seen it in the flesh," Hans asked.

"You haven't seen it because supposedly it was destroyed by fire at the end of the World War One. But when I interviewed Kokoschka in nineteen-eighty, he thought he remembered painting a religious scene over it in nineteen-eleven. On the other hand, the portrait must still have been in existence between nineteen-twelve and nineteen-sixteen, because the Berlin publisher Herwarth Walden, with whom Kokoschka worked, had it reproduced for a photo album of his magazine's picture collection."

"And where is the photo album now?"

"No idea. Both oeuvre catalogues of Kokoschka's work—which reproduce the painting in black and white—list it simply as 'private collection.'"

"Well, you'd think some enterprising art dealer would have tried to track down that album. In fact to track down the portrait itself."

"I agree. I think there is every likelihood that the portrait does still exist and is in private hands. Christomanos could have taken it with him when he returned to Greece, for example. There is no record of his having married or of any offspring. He died relatively young, at forty-four. I believe there was a younger brother, so the portrait might have gone to him. But this is only a hypothesis. It could just as easily be in Vienna or, more likely, Berlin, since Walden was based there. Perhaps Kokoschka brought it to Berlin from Vienna on one of his many trips there in the years before the first world war broke out. There is a history, after all, of the artist's sitters refusing to buy the angst-ridden portraits he painted of them during those years."

"So it could be that Christomanos disliked the painted result of his sittings for the artist and that he left the portrait behind when he returned to Greece."

"I can certainly imagine his not liking the portrait: he seems to be shivering in it and ridden with anxiety."

"Speaking of angst, my museum staff are probably wondering where their director is," joked Hans. After downing espressos *con una scorza di limone*, the two friends—and by now they were friends, united by Kokoschka—returned to Hans' car and headed back to Basel. Megan's flight to Vienna left early the next morning.

12

Agnes Sauer, the Alma *Tempest* roll safely in the plane's cargo hold, was flipping through the magazines supplied by Austrian Airlines when a man's authoritative voice crackled through the loud speaker.

"Attention, please, ladies and gentlemen. An incident concerning this plane has been reported. We are changing routes and heading for the nearest airport, which is Innsbruck. Please remain calm. Further information will be given as we receive it."

Alarmed voices sounded all around Agnes and she felt her heart sink. What was the "incident"? Was it a bomb? Would they all be blown up in the air? How could something like a bomb escape airport security? Was it a device worn by one of the passengers or something that was in the hold? She found herself staring around, studying her fellow passengers apprehensively. Her glances were returned with equal suspicion. The minutes seemed to pass with excruciating slowness.

"Please be sure your seat belts are fastened. We will be landing at Innsbruck Airport in a few minutes."

Agnes was among those who uttered sighs of relief. The landing was a bit rough and when the plane pulled up to its gate she could see that it was being surrounded by uniformed police.

"Leave all carryon luggage onboard and prepare to disembark immediately. Take nothing with you as you exit the plane. Speed is of the essence."

Agnes was not about to leave her ID or cellphone on board. Quickly she slipped them out of her leather backpack and into her jacket pockets, then stepped briskly into the crowded aisle. In another few minutes she and her fellow passengers were standing in an area of the airport terminal that had been sectioned off with yellow police tapes. Thorough body pat-downs were under way and after that the passengers were asked to pass through two different screening points. There had obviously been a bomb scare. What about my checked luggage, Agnes wondered. Are they going to open up the tube?

An announcement over the airport's loudspeaker advised passengers that all cargo baggage was being screened. Owners of suspicious items would be questioned. After that, luggage would be reloaded and passengers could board the plane for the continuation of its flight to Vienna. Impatient groans were heard from some of the passengers. They had left their laptops and cellphones on board. No entertainment to pass the time.

Will I be one of those questioned, Agnes worried. She tried to remain calm by arguing to herself that a cardboard tube with an old canvas inside could hardly be considered dangerous.

Some forty-five minutes had passed when the announcement came over the loudspeaker. "Agnes Sauer please report to the security desk." Trying to control her anxiety Agnes strode with false confidence up to the agent at the desk. The man looked up at her, no hint of his thoughts on his expressionless face.

"We must ask you to open the cardboard tube you are sending through as baggage."

"Of course," Agnes answered, following a security officer who led her outside to a group of bags that had been set aside on the tarmac. Her cardboard tube was among them. Under the watchful eyes of the officer she pried off the metal cap at one end of the tube.

"And what is inside?" The officer pushed a finger tentatively at the bubble wrap.

"An old painting of my father's I just inherited from my mother's estate."

"And that is all?"

"Yes, that's all."

"All right. It was the metal caps that attracted our attention. Sorry to inconvenience you, Fräulein. You are free to return to the waiting area. The plane should be boarding in another half-hour or so."

Back inside the terminal, Agnes' relief soon gave way to new apprehension: could the canvas have been damaged? And what about Leo Lang, who had planned to meet her plane? In her worry over the painting she had forgotten to advise him of the arrival delay. He must be anxious. She slipped her cellphone out of her jacket pocket and called him. His voice was strained. He had indeed been worried about the plane's not having landed in Vienna yet.

"We've had a bomb scare," Agnes explained. "It's delayed us by a couple of hours, but we're going to be allowed back on as soon as security has finished its search."

"What a relief! I was worried sick. I will track your arrival time and meet you at the airport."

Reassured, Agnes could only hope that the painting had not suffered any damage and that she could still collect her fee. Her underworld reputation for success must not be stained. If Herr Leo Lang did not judge her work a triumph—which it was—she had her own means to silence him.

13

Felix Fichte was sitting in his father's spacious New York apartment looking thoughtfully out the window across the street at the Metropolitan Museum's front steps and the milling throngs climbing up and down them. Little did any of those museum-goers know that a precious, unique work of art was within walking distance if they only looked up. Playfully he picked up the Kokoschka fan, spread it open and waved it at the people below.

"What the *hell* are you doing?" growled his father Bruno. "Get away from that window at once and put down the fan. It's not a plaything, you know."

"Aw, Dad, I was just having fun. You're gonna lock that fan up under glass soon enough."

In truth, Bruno was deeply disappointed by the fan. He had expected a new scene by Kokoschka of himself with Alma, not simply a miniature of the famous *Bride of the Wind—The Tempest*. Of course it was still a work by the artist, and in an unusual medium, and about his great-grandmother, but the disappointment was still there. Palpable.

Bruno, however, was contemplating something that took his mind off the fan. Something daringly ambitious. He had been reading in the newspapers about the theft at Basel and the replacement of the *Tempest* with a duplicate in all details except for the face of the woman. It was not Alma's face. Someone else's. He didn't care about who the replacement was—she had not been identified in the press—but he did care about a stolen *Tempest* that pictured Alma. Yes, he and the international police as well.

But who could have been so interested in his great-grandmother that he would steal her portrait with Oskar from a *museum*? Whoever it was, he certainly operated on a scale far grander than he, Bruno, had thought of doing. For decades he had collected his Alma material through European galleries and dealers, most of them unsavory, true, but all of them reliable in that they turned to him first when something related to her came through their hands. But now it would appear he had a rival. A rival on a grand scale.

Emboldened by the Basel art theft, Bruno told himself that he too must think big. There was a famous Kokoschka depiction of Alma in the States, in Boston, Massachusetts, as a matter of fact, that deserved his attention, now that he was thinking big. He began to formulate a daring plan.

14

Unlike Agnes Sauer's interrupted plane trip, Megan's flight from Basel to Vienna was uneventful and on time, landing at exactly ten-thirty in the morning. She encountered a curious taxi driver who, when he learned she was American, querulously quizzed her on the Bush dynasty of presidents. She arrived at her beloved Hotel Römischer Kaiser half an hour later. The front desk clerk cheerfully assured her that she had reserved Frau Doktor Crespi's favorite room overlooking the quiet courtyard rather than facing the noisy Annagasse. Not having brought anything except her leather *Prima Classe* roller bag and lightweight sling purse, Megan unpacked in record time. Sitting at the room's attractive foldout desk, she checked her e-mail hoping to find an answer from the Vienna storage company she had queried concerning the theft of fourteen crates of Kokoschka art. They had not answered her e-mail. And probably they won't, she thought. I'll just have to go out there in person.

But first she would contact her friend Johannes Ohm, director of Vienna's renowned Leopold Museum. They had worked together on the recent spate of Schiele crimes and he might have an insight on the Kokoschka robbery.

"Megan!" he exclaimed immediately when he saw her ID on his phone. "What are you doing in Wien?" Then, before Megan could answer, he added conspiratorially: "As if I didn't know."

"You've got it right, Hannes. I'm in Europe at the request of the Basel Museum concerning the Kokoschka heist. You know the director Hans Tietze, don't you?"

"The great-grandson of *the* Hans Tietze? Only by e-mail, but he seems an excellent man. He must be at his wit's end about the robbery. The press is having a field day."

"Oh, yes, although museum attendance has really improved, he tells me."

"Well, that's some consolation, I suppose. Now, Megan, what can I do for you, my dear?"

"You could have lunch with me if you're free and advise me how to handle the storage company where the Kokoschka robbery took place. I want to know as much as possible about the sizes and, if known, the contents of those fourteen crates."

"Don't you think the police have found out as much as can be learned from them?"

"I wouldn't expect anything else, Hannes. But there may be some detail, some angle that could be brought to light if I could only talk to them. They haven't answered my e-mail."

"They probably don't feel any need to respond to an art historian from America, given the attention they've received in the press and from the police."

"What if *you* were to go with me?"

"Sure. I'm willing to give it a try but I can't do it today, dear. My calendar is full. But at least we can have lunch today and put our heads together then. How about one o'clock?"

"Perfect! See you in the museum café then."

After hanging up, Megan decided to study the storage company's website she had found on the Internet. She pulled the page up and scoffingly read the proud claims of total security and anonymity if so desired. The site's second page gave a plan of the large, one-story structure with its massive "temperature controlled" basement vaults. Megan was looking for entrances and exits and found that there were four altogether. The main entrance faced the front of the building; the other three faced the rear and seemed to be connected to loading docks. Very convenient, Megan thought, if you were bringing a truck up in the middle of the night. Which must have been exactly what happened, considering the weight of the crates. She was not so interested in how the burglars got in and out as she was in the content of those crates. Knowing their sizes could possibly help.

Lunch with Hannes was lively but there was no more information they could share. He had made an appointment with the firm, however, on the pretext of wanting to inspect their storage facilities in regard to the museum's keeping some artworks there. The ruse had certainly worked. They had an appointment for tomorrow morning at ten.

Megan spent the rest of the day contacting old friends she knew from her student days in Vienna back in the nineteen-fifties. Two of them were able to meet her for dinner at the Wienerwald restaurant across from her hotel on the Annagasse. At the age of eighty, limber as she was thanks to her daily treadmill routine at home, she did not fancy a long walk to a remote restaurant, no matter how delicious the food. Nor did her two friends, Paul Cernak and Karin Schwind. They had come together in a taxi and found Megan awaiting them at a cozy corner table near the back of the popular establishment. Back there they could actually hear one another talk, something rather rare in restaurants nowadays.

After fondly recalling the days of yore in the Wien they knew of some sixty years ago, where being out till dawn at cabarets was not unusual, they settled down to addressing the present. Megan was surprised to find the conversation dominated by an enumeration of the aches and pains her friends now suffered. She couldn't think of any matching disabilities except for the fact that it was getting harder to hear what people were saying—they just didn't speak distinctly nowadays was her indignant verdict.

Ah, but then she did think of something to add to the physical disabilities discussion. For years she had suffered from what was called a "trigger finger"—the middle finger of her right hand tended to freeze in a curl if she tried to peel a pear, for example. And it was most painful to try and dislodge it. Running hot water over it helped. Oddly enough, it had not interfered with the fingering on her musical instruments—piano, flute, guitar—but still she had to be careful. Her doctor had recommended that she wear a finger splint at night, and she had done so for some twenty years.

The disabilities dinner lasted some three hours and they promised to do it again the next time business brought Megan to Wien. Megan had discussed the Kokoschka robberies with them only briefly. She felt superstitious about telling them her plan of visiting the art storage facility the next morning. She didn't want to jinx it.

15

Theo Papadakis, agent-at-large for Desdemona Dumba, was the definition of patience. A short, pudgy man with heavy dark eyebrows and glistening bald head, he had been instrumental through the years in obtaining works once owned by the Greek tycoon Nikolaus Dumba. His success was based on dogged perseverance and the conviction that a surprising number of artworks considered lost were not necessarily so.

His greatest coup so far, acknowledged as such by art historians across Europe and America, was to ferret out the whereabouts of a sopraporta panel by Klimt painted in 1899 for the music room of Nikolaus Dumba. Long considered destroyed by fire in World War I, it showed Schubert in profile at the piano, flanked by a trio of young girls, two of them singing. The whole scene was candlelit and the image had become a symbol of Austria's gentle, *gemütlich* music as opposed to Germany's heavier music epitomized in Wagner.

The canvas turned out to have been hidden in the cellar of a farm house near Schloss Immendorf in Lower Austria and was turned up by Papadakis after paying adjacent farmers enormous fees to let him search their grounds, houses, attics, and cellars. Desdemona had joyously installed the precious Schubert painting as the centerpiece of her small music room on the top floor of her great-grandfather's former residence on the Parkring.

Papadakis, who had presented himself to Desdemona Dumba as an art authority who could be instrumental in locating lost family works, had, of course, scored highly with his discovery of the whereabouts of Klimt's iconic work. Since then Desdemona had retained him on a yearly basis with the hope of turning up more items missing from the Palais Dumba after World War I. She was especially interested in rescuing the immense and famous library of books. Papadakis had held out hope since every volume carried the specially-designed Dumba bookplate. His knowledge of major European antiquaries and bookstores was immense and he was in frequent contact with proprietors who utilized both legitimate and criminal contacts. He had already located the Bösendorfer concert grand piano that used to be in Dumba's music room. It too had been returned to the rightful heir, albeit for the price of 70,000 Euros plus a twenty percent finder's fee to Papadakis.

Desdemona was particularly pleased that her *Schubert at the Piano* was a work enthusiastically judged by a contemporary viewer when it was first exhibited at Vienna's house of modern art, the Secession. The witness was Alma Schindler, soon to become Alma Mahler. At the time of the Schubert exhibition she was being pursued by Klimt and he escorted her to see the work several times. Desdemona had jotted down in her own journal Alma's diary's enthusiastic words of March 17, 1899:

> Party and private viewing at the Secession. Klimt took me personally to look at his "Schubert." It is indisputably the best picture at the exhibition. Schubert sits at the piano, surrounded by ultra-modern young ladies singing. The whole thing bathed in dim candlelight.

Fascination with Alma for Desdemona was second only to her worship of Sisi. And to think! Alma's lifespan interlocked for a period with that of Sisi's: the Empress was assassinated in 1898 at the age of sixty and Alma was born in 1879. That meant their lives had shared almost twenty terrestrial years on this planet.

Desdemona was thrilled by the thought. She felt she had learned so much about life from reading Alma's several memoirs. Her three-year seismic affair with Kokoschka, described so vividly in her autobiographies, had convinced Desdemona not to enter that sphere of human relationships. Nevertheless, she was intrigued by Kokoschka, the creative *artist* if not the hotheaded, narcissistic madman.

And, yes, there was one painting by Kokoschka she yearned to own, would give anything to possess. She would take it with her to Corfu, to her Xenia, if only Papadakis could locate it. Ownership of the work—thought to be lost by many—would connect Desdemona with Sisi in a way nothing else could. Her heart beat more quickly at the mere thought: let providence bring to me the portrait of Constantine Christomanos!

16

The drive from Vienna's Schwechat airport—nowadays grandly called Vienna International Airport—to Leo Lang's villa in Penzing took about twenty minutes. Both Lang and Agnes Sauer were in high spirits. The precious canvas roll was safely in the back of Lang's black Mercedes-Benz station wagon. He carried the cardboard tube up to his private study where a copy of Kokoschka's life-size doll made in the image of Alma Mahler sat stiffly on a chair in a corner of the room. She was clothed in a blue dress and her hands were bound together in front of her by wire. She had inhabited the room for years, ever since Leo had commissioned a copy be made of the original.

Leo eyed the cardboard roll. Now the woman who had lured Kokoschka away from his grandmother would pay the price. She, Alma, would be imprisoned in his house, away from public scrutiny, just as his doll replica was. And Oskar's first love, Lilith, would be the object of the public's admiring eyes. Admired. For centuries to come.

In a few years, Leo had decided, he would destroy the Alma *Tempest*, but for now he intended to enjoy observing her in the prison of his home. That dangerous femme fatale of times past would soon fade from public memory, at least in this Kokokoscha rendition. There were other portraits of her in various mediums ranging from lithograph to oil, but Leo would tend to them later. He had given to the world the true *Bride of the Wind*, his greatly wronged grandmother Lilith.

Leo brought out a bottle of Johnny Walker Platinum Scotch with two glasses which he placed on the coffee table by the couch where Agnes had seated herself.

"Shall we drink to the success of our endeavor?" he asked, pouring them both drinks.

"Perhaps we should wait until we see how much damage the canvas has suffered from being rolled up."

"I'm not overly concerned about that," said Leo brusquely. "The painting's very existence is something I have longed to obliterate for a long time."

"What? But it must be worth a fortune!"

"That does not concern me. Having removed it from the public domain is what matters to me."

Agnes was beginning to wonder whether she was in the presence of a lunatic. "But would you not be interested in selling it to a discreet collector?"

"Absolutely not. This painting is never leaving my house. However, let's give it a look."

Leo downed his drink in one swallow. They both got up and Agnes worked on the tube at one end and then the other, removing the metal caps and setting them down on the floor. Then the two of them slowly pulled out the bubble-wrapped, tightly rolled canvas inch by inch until it was free of the container. Gingerly they rolled out the canvas on the floor. It measured just six-feet, ten inches in length and two feet wide.

Leo had to gasp. Although he had studied the painting in reproduction in books and online, he was still stunned to see how very painterly the work was, how the brush strokes rose in palpable ridges like waves. He had of course seen Kokoschka's handling of paint up close before in the Lilith *Tempest* version that had for so long been part of his family household. But to observe how the blue and green layers of paint joined to support and surround the windswept couple was impressive, Leo reluctantly admitted. Nevertheless, the painting would eventually be destroyed. There would no longer exist an Alma *Tempest*. He would die knowing his grandmother had been avenged.

He looked at Agnes thoughtfully. A full minute went by as she studied the painting on the floor and he studied her.

"Fräulein Sauer. I may have another job or two for you."

Agnes looked up in surprise. She had considered this heist a one-time commitment. And she had never handled anything as large as the painting on the floor before. No, her preferred métier was jewelry and manuscripts. Still, she was curious. Especially considering the handsome fee Leo Lang now handed her in cash.

"What do you mean, Herr Lang?"

"It is my aim to erase as many effigies of this dreadful woman as possible. To rid the world of her painted presence wherever and whenever I can. You could help me in this. Greatly. I am almost sixty and do not like to travel. But you, you are young and strong and not adverse to travel at all, from what I've learned of you. Is this not so?"

"If you mean am I willing to take on jobs that require travel, you're quite right. Not a problem."

"I thought not."

"But if you want me to make any more museum 'exchanges' I'm afraid that really isn't my line. This one was harrowing enough and if it hadn't been for the lucky fact that the museum security cameras and alarms were thrown off by construction, I would not have succeeded."

"What I have in mind, my dear, does mean entering museums, this is true. But it does not entail carrying paintings in and out of buildings."

"Well, that's a relief. What is your proposition, Herr Lang?"

"Simply this. In certain museums and private collections around the world there are images of this shameless woman by her onetime lover Kokoschka. During the three years of his steamy affair with Vienna's merry widow, he made well over four hundred images of her, most of them drawings and lithographs. But several of them are in the form of oil paintings. What I should like to entrust to you is the erasure—call it vandalism if you like—but the obliteration of the woman's features from paintings around the world. What do you say?"

Silence prevailed as Agnes considered his words and their meaning. Finally she spoke.

"And at the same fee as before?"

"Yes, same fee as before. For each assignment. And of course air fare and lodging as well."

"In that case, agreed. You will give me the precise information on the locations of these images and I shall do my own reconnaissance and set my own schedule."

"Agreed! And if I may, I'd like to give you your first assignment now."

11

Megan had gotten up especially early the next morning before her ten o'clock appointment with Hannes at the art storage company. She had not been able to get her Pilates exercises in at Basel and was determined to do so here in Vienna. Still on her bed, she did a few extra "planks" just for good measure and then ten deep knee bends as she faced the bathroom sink. She ended her abbreviated routine by standing on one leg with the other tucked in at knee level for the duration of three circular arm movements, and then the same with the other leg. She knew that good balance could be compromised as one aged and she was determined not to lose hers.

Downstairs in the cheerful breakfast room she sat down at her favorite corner table overlooking the Annagasse. After she gave her order for green tea she went to the buffet and dished out a selection of cereal, yogurt, strawberries, blueberries, and a banana, then went back to her table and mixed everything in a deep bowl, adding a little milk. This is the breakfast that keeps me healthy, she said to herself with approval. And beside that, it's yummy.

At a quarter to ten, dressed in brown slacks with a red blouse and comfortable brown shoes, her sling bag over her shoulder and her tinted Google glasses on, Megan was standing outside the back entrance of her hotel when a smiling Hannes pulled up in his car. He was wearing a dark blue business suit as befitted a museum director making a business call. Fifteen minutes later they entered the front door of *Kunst Sicherheit und Lagerung Firma Moser*—Moser's Art Security and Storage Company. Herr Moser himself greeted them. He was a small, nervous man who kept clasping and unclasping his fingers against his stomach.

Hannes identified himself and introduced Megan as a visiting curator, Frau Doktor Schmidt.

"We are honored that the Leopold Museum is contemplating putting some of its overflow artworks in storage with us," said Moser.

"What we are most interested in is high quality vault storage with temperature and humidity control, of course, but also with self-managing access."

"Yes, yes, that can be done. We have such an arrangement with the Belvedere Museum, for example. The rates are a bit higher for this than for unit control by our own staff members, but we do recognize the need of some museums and individuals to have instant access to stored artworks."

"Can you give us a walk-through of your basement vaults?" Megan asked.

"But of course. Here, please to enter our freight elevator. You can see how the walls are padded and that it has foldout partitions for keeping artworks upright."

"Yes, good idea," Hans said.

The elevator opened onto a veritable labyrinth of ceiling-high units, each with its own combination padlock and deadbolt lock. The units were identified by numbers only, no names.

"Goodness!" exclaimed Megan. "Makes you wonder how on earth those burglars who stole the Kokoschka crates ever managed to do so."

"We're making sure such a thing never happens again," Herr Moser hastened to assure his two potential clients, his cheeks turning bright red.

"How so?" inquired Hans abruptly.

"Well, in the Kokoschka case, the unit's dead bolt and padlock were simply melted down by a blow torch, providing almost instant access."

"But how did the thieves know *which* unit to go to?" Megan asked.

Herr Moser's cheeks burned even brighter. "Um, unfortunately, we think our computer system was hacked and some of our files were accessed. That's how the thieves got the unit number. But now we have a double fire wall, so that is not likely to happen again."

"But didn't the live feed of your security cameras alert the night watchman?" asked Hannes.

"We had two on duty, one making the rounds continuously, the other doing nothing but monitoring the video feed every second. The trouble is that around four in the morning on the day of the robbery, someone rang urgently for admission—not an unusual occurrence for us with self-managing clients. Over the intercom a woman's voice was heard screaming for help, and *both* guards answered the door, each unaware that the other was also doing so until they met at the door. The peek hole showed a lone, hysterical woman. Her face appeared to be bruised and battered black and blue. But the moment the door was opened to her she stepped aside and two burly men wearing gloves and face masks burst their way inside, bludgeoning the two guards unconscious. They turned off the security camera and then commenced to remove all fourteen Kokoschka crates. We have no idea what sort of vehicle they loaded the crates into —a van most likely. The break-in wasn't discovered until six in the morning, when the guards on day shift arrived. They called the police immediately but it was too late of course. Tire tracks indicated a large vehicle. There were no fingerprints anywhere inside although the place was dusted up and down."

"So the crime is unsolved as of yet," Hannes said.

"Yes, unfortunately that is so for now. No leads for the police. And no appearance of any new Kokoschka works for sale either here in Austria or abroad."

"Do you have any idea as to the contents of the fourteen crates?" said Megan, slipping in her key question with a worried smile.

"None whatsoever."

"Wouldn't the *size* of the crates give you some idea?" Megan pressed.

"Well, that's the funny thing. The crates, when originally delivered back in the late nineteen-seventies, are identified in our logbook as being no larger than three-by-three-feet wide and two-feet high. All of them."

Megan was thrilled to have pulled out this precious information from Herr Moser. Now she knew that major canvases had not been stolen. In that case what were they? Not portraits, unless only head renditions. And not allegories, which, with Kokoschka, were always writ large. More likely they were landscapes, or still lifes, both subjects Kokoschka had painted all his long life, often relatively large, but equally often in smaller format. *But why had Kokoschka told her during her interview with him in 1980 that the works were "juvenilia?"*

Hannes, pleased by Megan's success, brought the visit to a close.

"Well, Herr Moser, this has certainly been an interesting and worthwhile experience. We shall probably be getting back to you later, depending on the needs of our registrar."

Back in the car Hannes exploded: "A front-door robbery! How bold. And using a lone, 'assaulted' woman as a foil. Clever, clever."

"Ah huh, I bet she was reveling in having duped the guards with that bit of battered-woman drama. The Moser 'secure' art storage certainly hasn't lived up to its name."

18

Bruno Fichte had hatched a grand plan. Inspired by the daring Basel theft of *The Tempest*, he realized that there was in existence an even more scandalous image of Alma and Kokoschka together. It was the *Two Nudes: The Lovers*—owned by the Boston Museum of Fine Arts. One of his former students, now curator at Buffalo's Albright-Knox Art Gallery, had recently advised him that the museum was about to mount an exhibition called "Famous Artists and Their Lovers." One of the museum's picks for the show was Kokoschka's rendition of himself in lock step with Alma, the *Two Nudes: The Lovers*. Bruno's former student was ecstatic because the Boston museum had just agreed to lend the work to Albright-Knox. Bruno realized that he might very well be able, with the proper tangential questioning, to elicit the transport company's name and date the painting was scheduled to be transferred from Boston to Buffalo. Then, with the help of his son, anything could happen.

19

Theo Papadakis was facing Desdemona Dumba across the table at Café Schwarzenberg, the oldest café on the Ringstrasse and once favorite stopping place of the architect Josef Hoffmann, one of the founders of the Wiener Werkstätte. Papadakis's chubby face was wreathed in smiles and he was speaking in hushed tones to his illustrious patron who was staring at him, an expression of disbelief on her long, beautiful face.

"Yes, it is true. I have come in contact with a distinguished Berlin gallery owner who tells me he may have discovered Kokoschka's long-lost portrait of Constantine Christomanos. He has told no one else, he assures me, but knowing that I represent *you* and what your collecting interests are, he has promised to give us first option if indeed he does acquire it."

"So he does not have it in his possession as of now?"

"Not at the moment. As you know, most art experts, including the authors of the two oeuvre catalogues on Kokoschka's art, consider the portrait destroyed. The fact that—Helmut Haesslich is his name—the fact that Haesslich believes the work to be extant is already a plus. But that he thinks he knows where he might find it is truly exciting, don't you see? Colossal!

"Let's not put the cart before the horse, Theo. If he does obtain the artwork I would have to see it in person, preferably with a restorer at my elbow."

"Oh, yes, of course, of course. But that might entail a trip to Berlin, gnädige Frau, that might entail a trip to Berlin."

"Not an obstacle, Theo. Just keep me informed and I will clear my schedule accordingly."

"On another matter, gnädige Frau. The fourteen crates."

Desdemona's body tensed. "Yes?"

"What would you like me to do with them? Shall I have them opened and unpacked?"

"No, no. They are at your storeroom now, correct?"

"Yes."

"I would like you to ship them unopened, to my warehouse at Corfu."

"How soon would you like me to send the shipment?"

"Oh, right away."

"As you wish, gnädige Frau."

Theo Papadakis was pleased with himself. It was he who, a week ago, had informed this intense, sad woman who never smiled about the Kokoschka trove. His brother's married daughter Sibyl Speros was the registrar at *Kunst Sicherheit und Lagerung Firma Moser* and privy to all sorts of customer information that had been useful to him in the past. Of course he had never managed a break-in before. But when Sibyl had e-mailed him the full roster of customer names and he came across "Kokoschka, Oskar" he knew he had lucked into something highly unusual. Kokoschka was long since dead, so why would possessions of his be in storage, and under his name?

Knowing the keen interest his patron Desdemona Dumba had in all things relating to Kokoschka, he had passed on his insider information to her.

"There are fourteen crates of Kokoschka possessions—possibly artworks—in storage at a facility here in Vienna."

"So many years after his death? In whose name are they stored?" Desdemona had inquired.

"That's the puzzling thing. They are under the artist's name and listed thusly: 'in perpetuity.'"

"Say again?" Desdemona, who was slightly deaf, had asked.

"I said they are stored under the artist's own name and 'in perpetuity'—rather puzzling, don't you think?"

"Ah yes, very puzzling, because as far as I know Kokoschka had no direct heirs."

"True, gnädige Frau, true."

"Does your contact show any visitors to the crates?"

"I have not brought up that subject with my contact, but I can."

"Do so, Theo, do so. If it is true that the items are there 'in perpetuity' as you say, but left unattended to, unvisited, then—how shall I phrase it—it would be a terrible shame not to release the contents of those fourteen crates to someone who would really appreciate them. Do you follow what I am saying, Theo?"

"Indeed I do, gnädige Frau, indeed I do."

"Let me know then if and when you have the crates in hand. Leave them unopened. I do not need to know any more."

Theo Papadakis had been thrilled beyond measure at the turn the conversation had taken. He immediately contacted Sibyl asking for a layout of the Moser building and specifics on the security there, including the number of night watchmen. After studying the data in detail he decided he would need three accomplices: two able-bodied men to effect the break-in and a woman as cover. He would drive the van.

The caper had gone without a hitch.

20

Leo Lang had an immediate assignment for Agnes Sauer. They had been sitting in the den of his Vienna villa looking at the canvas roll spread out on the floor—Kokoschka's *Tempest* version with that slut Alma as his storm-tossed companion.

"What is your assignment, Herr Lang?"

"I have in mind a nineteen-twelve oil portrait by Kokoschka of Alma done at *her* request at the very beginning of their relationship. She's pictured from just above the waist up, with only the upper arms showing, and with long, golden-brown hair falling loosely to her shoulders. She is blue-eyed and her thin lips are pressed together. She has a determined, to my mind, controlling expression. Not at all enigmatic, as with Leonardo's Mona Lisa, which is what Kokoschka's portrait obviously alluded to. Very flattering for *her* of course.

"You might be amused to know, Fräulein Sauer, that the conceited woman thought his portrait suggested she was a modern-day Lucrezia Borgia, attracting great men to her court. Typical of her."

"So she *liked* the portrait, that's obvious. But where is the portrait, Herr Lang?"

"Before I tell you, will you confirm for me that you are willing to travel in regard to our agreement?"

"Yes, I've said that I like to travel."

"Well, Alma, in her vanity, kept the portrait right through her marriages to Walter Gropius and Franz Werfel. It was prominently displayed in her New York apartment when she died."

"When was that?"

"Back in nineteen-sixty-four. She was eighty-five, I think."

"So is the painting still in New York?"

"Um, no. Her descendants finally parted with the thing. It is now at the National Museum of Modern Art in Tokyo."

"Tokyo!"

"Yes, they made the highest bid when it went up for sale."

"And all you want me to do is simply deface it?"

"That's all. But the damage must be permanent. Restoration impossible."

"Give it an acid bath, in other words. All right, I'm game."

"When can you be ready?"

"I have to return to Basel first but I could leave at the beginning of next week."

"I very much like your expression 'acid bath'—let us hope that is exactly what you achieve."

"I am sure I will be successful. This is child's play when compared to the Basel Museum switch-out. And if the situation permits, I shall photograph the results and e-mail them to you on the spot."

21

Megan was back in her cozy hotel room at the Römischer Kaiser and making phone calls. She had told Hans Tietze that she would like to brainstorm with him concerning Kokoschka paintings in private collections around Europe and beyond. After all, it was entirely possible, if not even probable, that the Alma *Tempest* was stolen at the behest of a greedy private collector. One who would, of course, hide the work from the eyes of the world. Killar's oeuvre catalogue of Kokoschka's works was the most up-to-date one, having been published in 2006, but even so, paintings changed hands and recent auction sales and private sales were often difficult if not impossible to track.

The same could hold true for some of the major galleries. They might be able to shed information on contemporary sales that could be helpful. But there were also those galleries, the dealings of which were often cloaked in mystery, that needed to be checked out.

So perhaps if they made separate lists of "possibles" and then shared them, something, some detail, some location, some particularly active collector might register. It was a long shot.

Meanwhile she would visit likely Vienna galleries—both legitimate and shady—while Hans did the same in Basel, Zurich, and Geneva. Megan suggested they confer at the end of the week. Making the rounds in Vienna both online and on foot would certainly take a few days. And then there were the gossip mills—certain art historians and gallery owners who had insider knowledge and reveled in it. She would renew her contacts with them. Obviously several days' work, to say the least.

Realizing the time that would have to be committed to her task, Megan then made a call to the ever-patient Claire, who was keeping her little Button.

"I don't know who misses you more, Button or I," Claire said, glad to hear Megan's bouncing voice.

Megan caught Claire up on recent happenings and then asked tremulously, "So would you mind keeping my Button-boy for another week or so?"

"Now, why am I not surprised by that question?" laughed Claire.

After they had chuckled and talked for a few more minutes, Megan concluded the call after greeting Button, who had been brought to the phone. He had enthusiastically barked his answers to her questions. All was well in Dallas.

Her energy renewed, Megan decided to confront a certain lion in its den by visiting the Galerie Hummel, a firm well known in the international art world for suspiciously lucky finds and extremely profitable transactions. On the Kärntner Ring and right next to the historic Café Schwarzenberg, it wasn't far from her hotel and she felt like walking.

When she entered the gallery she was surprised to see hanging on the walls of the spacious front room nothing but graphics by Kokoschka. About fifty of them. Oh boy, cashing in on the robbery notoriety, she thought to herself sarcastically. She went up close to the wall on her right. And they weren't lithographs, they were chalk drawings! All of them! How could this be? So many original graphics for sale? Glancing from one drawing to the next, some of them showing Christ staggering under a heavy cross, Megan realized she was looking at a series related to the St. Matthew Passion dating from the mid-1920s. The series had never been commercially reproduced. *How did the Hummel Gallery get hold of these?* And at such a propitious time? Kokoschka's name had been bandied about in the newspapers and online ever since the storage vault robbery on Sunday.

Megan looked around at the gallery visitors. There were some dozen of them, mostly foreigners, all murmuring excitedly and pointing to various works. Each drawing had a small label with an explanatory title and a hefty sales price. *A sales price?* How totally gauche, Megan thought. She was beginning to see for herself why the gallery had such an unsavory name in the art world.

She went up to the overly pleasant, elderly receptionist who was seated behind a blond art deco desk.

"Is Herr Doktor Hummel in?"

"Unfortunately not today."

"Oh, that's too bad. I wanted to bring him greetings from Dallas,

Texas. I'll leave my business card for him. My goodness, how did he have the good luck to come across all these wonderful Kokoschka works."

"That I can tell you. He inherited them from a distant cousin."

"A distant cousin?"

"Yes, a distant cousin."

"Well, thank you very much. It's certainly an interesting exhibition you have here."

"Thank you. We just put it up. Please do feel free to take one of our checklists, won't you?"

Megan took the checklist extended to her by the receptionist and made the rounds of the exhibition, writing down the sales price for each drawing on the checklist. Some of the labels had a red dot affixed, indicating that the artwork had been sold. Megan did the mental arithmetic and realized that if all fifty drawings were sold, the profit would be well over one million Euros. She found herself wondering if, somehow, it was the Galerie Hummel that was behind the storage vault robbery. No, too bold, too obvious. And the drawings wouldn't have taken up fourteen crates for storage.

She paused to take Google glass shots of the three walls, then stopped to examine the contents of a glass-topped table in the middle of the room. Again she was stunned at the hutzpah of the Galerie Hummel. On display was Kokoschka's famous exploration of adolescent sexuality in the book done for the 1908 art show, *The Dreaming Youths*. But in this presentation the eight color lithographs had been carefully excised *from* the book and were exhibited as eight separate works of art, each one marked with an individual price tag. The most expensive page was the final one, *The Girl Li and I*—a specific reference to the artist's first love, Lilith Lang. Megan shook her head. She simply could not get over the bad taste and naked greed of the gallery. Unobserved, she took a photograph of the vandalized display and then exited out onto the Ringstrasse with the intention of crossing over to the Hotel Bristol from the Café Schwarzenberg.

She stepped back as a tram was coming toward her in the direction of the Opera House. But a woman about to cross the tracks next to her apparently had not heard the streetcar coming and was stepping directly into its way. Megan yelled a warning, then hurled herself upon the woman, landing them both on the far side of the track without a second to spare.

"Oh! You have saved my life!" cried Desdemona Dumba.

22

Berlin is beautiful in June, thought Helmut Haesslich, as he sat in the front office of his gallery *Am schwarzen Schwan*, with its view of the entrance to the Charlottenburg Palace. Everywhere was green and above his head hung an impressive image of Böcklin's *Isle of the Dead* as concocted by that impudent art restorer student Niki Deschner. The boy has talent, Helmut had to give him that. He had been thinking a lot about young Deschner the past twenty-four hours. Helmut's reliable forger of many decades—he preferred to think of him as restorer—had died recently and so far he had been unable to find a suitable replacement. Should he give the youngster a trial assignment? Would the boy be discreet, able to keep a confidence? Not convinced of this, Helmut decided to camouflage his assignment. The situation was just too ripe not to take advantage of it.

Yesterday morning he had received a most interesting phone call from Vienna. The caller identified himself as Theo Papadakis, agent-at-large for a "very esteemed Viennese patron of the arts." She was most interested in learning what she could about a reputably lost painting by Oskar Kokoschka. His portrait of Constantine Christomanos. Helmut knew the history of the portrait well: how it had been considered lost, and how the painter himself remembered having painted a religious scene over it. If it did exist, it was more likely in Greece, if Christomanos had taken it with him when he returned there, or languishing in Berlin, where it had been photographed for Herwarth Walden's *Der Sturm* magazine's picture collection.

Since the painting had not shown up in the past twelve decades, it was highly likely that it was indeed irrevocably lost. But Helmut Haesslich was in the business of reversing irrevocable losses. And a black-and-white photograph of the shuddering figure was known. It had been reproduced in both Kokoschka oeuvre catalogues.

Helmut made his decision. He would advise Niki Deschner that he had decided to give him a test. See what he could do in colorizing the black-and-white image of a lost Kokoschka portrait. He should study color reproductions of other early portrait paintings by the artist in order to acquaint himself with the manner in which he yielded the brush and which hues he favored. The copy should be done on antique canvas, which he would provide, and the size should match exactly the size given in the oeuvre catalogues. The test was about two things: how well the color copy came out and how totally confidential Deschner could keep his assignment. The reason for this particular image? Haesslich wanted to hang it in his home.

Niki Deschner was at the *Am schwarzen Schwan* within fifteen minutes of receiving the e-mail from Haesslich. The provisions of the test were gone over and Niki was asked to sign a contract, which he did without question, barely glancing at it. Who would, when the payment was going to be five thousand Euros?

"How soon do you want it?" Niki asked, his face flushed with excitement.

"As soon as you can do it while exercising caution and total privacy. And remember, *varnish* it. Kokoschka always used varnish on his paintings."

"You've got it!" Niki fairly leaped out of the gallery, holding the precious Kokoschka oeuvre catalogue Haesslich had lent him close to his chest. A roll of one-hundred-year-old canvas was loaded in his backpack. Haesslich watched as he disappeared down the street. If the painting turned out well, he would have good news for Papadakis and his anonymous Vienna client.

23

Bruno Fichte was filled with excitement and frustration. According to his former student, now curator at the Albright Knox, the date for transfer of the Boston Museum of Fine Arts' Kokoschka *Two Lovers*, showing himself and Alma Mahler in the nude, was coming up in five days. For Bruno, it was not enough merely to own one of the Alma fans anymore. Now he wanted to own a major Kokoschka work in which his great-grandmother figured. This would involve a daring intervention. He had the invaluable transit information, but he needed professional thieves to do the physical work. His son Felix would be in charge, but two more men were needed. Where might he find such personnel?

He decided to surf the Internet, in particular websites dealing with recent museum thefts around the world. He was surprised by the spate of robberies that had occurred in the last decade. Various methods had been utilized, including the waylaying of vans conveying art—exactly what he planned to have done.

He decided to look under the categories "transport" and "removal." After some forty minutes of checking various unpromising sites, he came across an unusual one with the logo *Remove Nudity in Museums*. He pulled up the explanatory text.

"Help us rid museums of art that shows women and men unclothed. Public nakedness is condemned by God." The text went on to explain that many offensive works now in public museums were restituted works from after World War II and that their owners had "shamelessly" sold them to museums for immense financial gain. Clicking on the "contact us now" button, Fichte was soon in live cyber conversation with a professional-sounding correspondent who explained the purpose of the organization, allowing that it was theoretically possible to engage help for the removal of offensive works from their respective museums. Fichte was asked if he would be willing to enter into a Skype exchange for the purpose of a personal interview. No sooner said than done, as Bruno was an avid Skype conversationalist.

"We are interested in your being a supporter of our cause but, as you can understand, we need to know more about you."

"I can supply you with a short curriculum vitae, if that would help. Or even with my credit rating, if that is what you are interested in."

"No, no. We will e-mail you a questionnaire and depending upon your answers we will Skype you again."

"But what sort of answers are you looking for?"

"We need to *know* you, that's all. What your aims are. And we expect your answers to be truthful."

"I also need to know what I can expect from *you*," Fichte said with some irritation.

"The next step is a personal meeting with one of our representatives. You have to realize that we must be sure you are not connected with the police."

"I can assure you I am not," laughed Fichte. "So go ahead and send me the questionnaire."

A few minutes later he was filling out a very long list of questions, most of them asking how far and in what way he was prepared to go to help rid museums of nakedness. Thinking of his son Felix's daring feat at the Kokoschka Foundation in Vevey which resulted in a necessary murder but also in success as far as securing the Alma fan, Fichte answered truthfully that he was prepared to go the limit if a specific work of art, chosen by him, were the target. He then hit Send on the completed questionnaire.

24

The vast metropolis of Tokyo spread out like an endless patch quilt before her as Agnes Sauer stared out the window of her Lufthansa flight from Basel's EuroAirport. It was a direct flight and her business-class status had given her a luxurious seat that lowered into full recliner position for sleeping. She had slept long and soundly. She had arranged for limousine service to pick her up on the morning of her arrival and sure enough, as she cleared customs and entered Haneda airport's arrival hall, there was a widely smiling young Japanese man holding up a chalk board with her name on it. Agnes congratulated herself on getting the metal-tipped glass syringe with its dangerous ingredients stored in her checked bag past security and through customs. She had not been asked to open either the bag or her backpack.

Some twenty-five minutes later the limousine pulled up at the small and conveniently located Sakura Hotel Jimbocho where she checked in. The

National Museum of Modern Art was a short walk away, just across from the Imperial Palace grounds. Agnes had one final purchase to make before paying the museum a visit that afternoon. With the hotel concierge's help she was directed to a nearby camera shop. There she bypassed the cameras for sale and bought a capacious cloth camera container that could be worn as a fanny pack on a belt. In the empty pouch would be her glass syringe with two ounces of concentrated sulfuric acid—sufficient for her purpose. She then went up to her room to unpack and relax a bit.

Aware that her unusual height might attract unwanted attention at the museum, warranting perhaps a thorough purse check, she decided to place the syringe and its contents in one of her tall boots before she entered the premises. Then she would transfer it to the camera pouch in the privacy of a restroom. The glass syringe had a metal stopper that made it safe to carry the acid, and the opening was wide enough to enable a powerful jet of liquid when the syringe plunger was pushed down abruptly. Agnes knew that her two-ounce dose of sulfuric acid would cause extreme damage to the face in the painting. The muriatic acid would react violently with the humidity naturally present in the varnish, the paint, and layers of different materials in the painting and it would permanently modify the nature of those materials. The damage could not be undone.

Although she wasn't hungry, Agnes knew she should eat something before embarking on her first mission. The little hotel buffet advertised sandwiches as well as Japanese dishes and she settled for a turkey and Swiss cheese along with a pot of delicious white tea. She would be making two trips to the MOMAT, as the museum was called. One exploratory visit this afternoon and tomorrow at noon—the busiest hour—the real thing.

25

Desdemona Dumba repeated her grateful words to the kind stranger who at the last minute had knocked her out of the way of the oncoming streetcar. "You have saved my life!"

She was lying on her side on the pavement where both women's bodies had jettisoned under the weight of Megan's sudden throwing of her body over Desdemona's. Both were panting heavily and a group of inquisitive bystanders was beginning to gather. Megan rolled off the younger woman and sat up, looking around blankly. All she remembered was the frightening sound of the approaching tram and hurtling herself at the woman crossing the tracks in front of it. How they both avoided it was miraculous, she thought.

Desdemona tried to pull herself up from the ground and yowled in pain. "I think my wrists are broken," she sobbed, frightened by the out-of-whack appearance of her hands, which were splayed back unnaturally.

"Don't move anymore. I'm calling an ambulance," commanded Megan, her wits returning to her.

"We just called one," a helpful bystander said reassuringly.

Megan stood up and checked her limbs. Other than a stinging sensation all over her body, everything seemed all right. She looked with compassion down at the woman she had saved. She noticed what had to be her purse on the ground a few feet away and went over to pick it up. *Limped* over would have been a more apt description, she thought, still feeling pain in her joints. She wanted to hand Desdemona the heavy purse but realized that she wouldn't be able to hold it, so she simply murmured to the woman that she would take care of her purse and stay with her. Another minute passed and then, its siren blasting, an ambulance pulled up onto the sidewalk. Two attendants jumped out and Desdemona's transferral to the back of the van was quickly accomplished.

"I'm going with her," Megan said, climbing into the back with Desdemona and showing her that her purse was safe.

"Oh, bless you, bless you!"

"Not to worry. I'm going to the hospital with you."

"Your accent sounds slightly Italian. Are you?"

"Well," said Megan with the first smile to cross her face since the streetcar incident, "my surname is Italian but I'm American. My name is Megan Crespi."

"And I am Desdemona, Desdemona Dumba and terribly indebted to you."

"Dumba? Any relation to *the* Dumba of Franz Josef days?"

"Indeed I am. Niklaus Dumba was my great-grandfather."

"Oh, how marvelous! I am such an admirer of how he decorated his palais and his passion for collecting Schubert manuscripts."

"How do you know about all this?"

"That's because I am an art historian and my special field is art and music in Vienna at the turn of the last century."

"Megan Crespi. Megan Crespi. Your name sounds familiar to me now. Could I have read a book by you perhaps?"

"Yes, that's possible. I have written on Klimt and on Schiele. And Beethoven—a study of his changing image over the centuries, ending up with Klimt's *Beethoven Frieze*."

"But yes, that's it!" Desdemona said happily. I believe I have one of your Klimt books at home."

"Well, I'm flattered," Megan smiled at the brave woman who must have been in excruciating pain but was making an effort to be conversational with a total stranger.

Just then the ambulance pulled up at the emergency entrance to the city's *Allgemeines Krankenhaus*–the General Hospital. Desdemona was helped into a wheelchair and Megan followed her inside. During the wait for medical attention, after Megan filled out the forms at a disabled Desdemona's instructions, the two women discussed Nikolaus Dumba at greater length and Desdemona explained how her family line extended from her great-grandfather down through his son and his son's son to her.

"And I suppose you've visited Greece where it all began?"

Desdemona, despite her pain, smiled happily. "Oh, yes, Greece is my spiritual homeland. In fact…how long are you in Europe? You must come with me to see *my* Greece!"

Desdemona had surprised herself by the impetuosity of her invitation to a perfect stranger. She had never had a guest at Xenia. But this woman had saved her life. And, she was an art historian of her great-grandfather's period

Megan could see that her aristocratic interlocutor was serious. She marveled at the generous spontaneity of a woman waiting in a hospital emergency room to be examined for possible broken bones and sprained wrists.

She began to speak again but just then a nurse came up and led Desdemona into a small examination room. She was unable to get up on the examining table so the nurse placed her gently in a chair alongside it. Megan stood by her side.

Some minutes later a physician entered the room. She took a look at the completed forms and the chart a nurse had filled out, then turned to Desdemona and smiled.

"Let us hope that two sprained wrists are the only damage your fall has done to you." She examined her patient carefully up and down, tapping her rib cage gingerly, had her slowly stretch her arms and legs, twist and turn sideways, lean forward and backward, and finally turn her head from side to side. When asked if she experienced any pain other than in her wrists, Desdemona shook her head no.

"I don't think we need to take any X-rays. Aside from some black and blue spots that will soon get larger before they get smaller, and aside from your sprained wrists, you are in quite good shape. It is lucky you didn't fall on your head. That would have been an altogether different story. But your hands braced your fall and that, of course, is why your wrists are now sprained."

Desdemona looked slightly comforted. She was not prepared for the doctor's next question.

"Now, do you have someone who can help you at home? You will have to have your wrists in a cast at first, but all your fingers will be free so at least you can go to the bathroom by yourself.

Desdemona and Megan exchanged worried glances.

"Will I be able to take a shower by myself?"

"That would be difficult. You would have to keep the casts absolutely dry."

"Oh, dear. I have a butler who takes care of my place here in Wien, and I have a daytime maid and cook. But none of them would be suitable for helping me into the shower."

Megan intervened. "But couldn't she put plastic bags over her hands and throw a bath towel over the shower bar to provide balance as she enters? By keeping her casts dry with the plastic covers, she could use her fingers to wash, even though they are inside the plastic bags." Megan was speaking from vicarious experience. Her friend Claire had been disabled in the same way Desdemona was now and had devised this way of coping.

The physician looked dubious but allowed that it could possibly be done that way, as long as the casts were kept absolutely dry.

"Well, there you have it," Megan beamed at Desdemona who returned her confident smile with a grateful one.

After being released from the hospital, Megan hailed a taxi and within a few minutes they pulled up to the corner of the Parkring and Schwarzenbergplatz. It took a monumental effort for Desdemona to steer her fingers inside her purse for her wallet. "I insist upon paying for this," she was saying.

"Absolutely not! I'm taking care of it," said Megan, appreciating her friend's effort to deal with the awkward situation.

After paying the driver Megan went around to the other side of the taxi to help Desdemona out. She was quite shaky on her feet and it was good that she had someone to aid her in walking to the side entrydoor of the palatial building that was once the Dumba palace.

"Won't you please come upstairs with me and let me give you—us—something to drink?"

Megan realized that Desdemona was still in a state of shock and that what she needed was rest, not company.

"I really don't think you are up to entertaining anyone right now. It's best that you lie down and give yourself a lot of rest."

"Well, yes, I suppose you are right. Thank you. But how about coming to lunch tomorrow?"

"Excellent! I should love to do that. What time?"

"Would one o'clock in the afternoon be convenient?"

"That would be fine. I shall look forward to it. But to be on the safe side, why don't I telephone you in the morning just to be sure you are feeling well enough to have company."

"Yes, that makes sense. Here," Desdemona said, trying to dig down into her purse, encumbered by the cast. "Let me give you my card, if I can reach my card holder."

"Here, wait, let me get it for you." Megan pulled the thin silver holder out and opened it up. She took one of the beautifully printed cards, noticing that it was in three languages, German, English, and Greek. Helping Desdemona grapple with the elevator, she pushed the penthouse button for her at her direction, watched the elevator door close on her, then left by the side door she had come in, as the front of the Dumba building was given over completely to shops.

But now she was feeling regrets. Regrets that she had not accepted Desdemona's invitation right away. Patience, she counseled herself, patience. Looking up at the Dumba palais with the knowledge that now she knew the distinguished inhabitant of the penthouse was enough for one day.

26

Megan glanced at her watch. She realized she did need some nourishment before continuing her gallery snooping so she stopped in at a fruit smoothie bar a few blocks away and in the direction of the next gallery she wanted to visit. This time it was not a shady establishment but one of Vienna's most venerable galleries, the Christian M. Nebehay Antiquariat right on the Annagasse, just steps from her hotel.

She entered and found the proprietor, Dr. Hanskarl Klug, seated at the front desk examining a folder of color prints.

"Megan! How lovely! What brings you to Wien?"

"I'm here in pursuit of Kokoschka this time."

"Oh, yes! The series of robberies, here and in Basel and Vevey. Absolutely intriguing. And it's funny that with the painter's name spread all across the newspapers, people have been dropping in, even here, to inquire whether we might have Kokoschka works for sale, although all we have are some of his early Wienerwerkstätte postcards. I should say *had*, because I sold the last one just yesterday."

"Sold to anyone special?"

"No. Just a regular, professional comber of antiquariats. His name is Theo Papadakis. A pleasant enough fellow. I know he has clients all over Europe and America."

Megan took note of the fact that the man's name was Greek. "Do you think he has Desdemona Dumba for a client?"

"Oh, I know for a fact. He has been able to find books and even a piano that belonged once in the Palais Dumba."

"And all on the up and up?"

"As far as I know, yes."

"Well, what are the gossip mills saying about the robbery of those fourteen crates from Moser's?"

"Not much. There simply haven't been any clues as to who was involved, whether a local or someone outside Vienna. The police know *how* it was done—you've seen the accounts in the paper—but not *who* did it."

"And do you have any private ideas or theories?"

"I do. I think it had to be an inside job of some sort—computer hacking probably. The storage units are not identified by owner name, I've been told. So someone must have been tipped off as to which, of all those units, contained the Kokoschka works."

"That makes sense. But who do you think was the recipient of the crates?"

"Possibly someone who lives in Austria, I'm thinking. There is that famous collector of all things Kokoschka who lives in Graz, for example. He's a real recluse, however. Lives in a country house full of Kokoschka graphic works."

"Any oils?"

"Yes. A number of cityscapes from Kokoschka's later periods and several still lifes."

"What's his name, just so I have it in my mental files?"

"You're going to be surprised. He is Greek. His name is Kallias Andriopoulos."

"Yikes! Let me write that down; I could never remember how to spell correctly such a name."

Megan printed the name into a miniature notebook she always carried with her and then turned to other topics of mutual interest, especially what music events were taking place in Vienna right then. *Das Rheingold* was going to be performed at the end of the month at the Vienna State Opera and there were a few interesting organ concerts coming up.

After a half-hour's chat Megan stood up to leave, hoping to get one more visitation in before the day was over. She and Hanskarl embraced and she reminded him that he was still storing one of her music stands for her, just in case she ever found someone in Wien to play duets with. But she had not brought her flute with her on this business trip; hadn't even thought of doing so.

Now she walked up the Annagasse and over to Vienna's main shopping area, the Kärntner Strasse, a pedestrian-only street. She strode all the way down to the Stephansplatz and an auction house behind the cathedral. Situated right next to Mozart's house, at Domgasse 7, the auction house was named, appropriately, Amadeus Auktionshaus. Megan had noticed the way it was able to hold its own in a city where the greatly esteemed and large Dorotheum auction house held sway with its forty specialization departments and some hundred experts on call. Amadeus was a horse of a different color. It was an online auction platform. Amadeus had an extensive cyber address list and Megan was on it. She had even made a successful bid once for a small interior scene by Denmark's Anna Ancher, one of the many Scandinavian painters who worked in the village of Skagen on the northernmost tip of Denmark. And she had written about her in a book called *World Impressionism*.

Now she had a specific question for the owner whom she recognized chatting with a customer. While awaiting her chance she looked with interest at the reproductions on the wall of early nineteenth-century items that would be offered for sale in the next auction. The actual works could not be maintained in Amadeus's small premises. Instead, they were at a local storehouse and Megan hoped it wasn't Moser's. None of the items scheduled for the next auction were Kokoschka works, but still Megan wanted to ask her question.

Finally Cornelius Weber was free and turned inquiringly to Megan, who he was aware had been waiting to speak to him.

"May I help you?"

"Yes, thank you. I'd like to know whether you have had any recent additions to what you'll be putting up for your next auction. Works other than the ones you have reproduced here on your walls."

"Actually, we received something this morning that will be going into our new cyber catalogue."

"And what was that?" Megan asked with what she hoped was innocent enthusiasm.

Cornelius Weber eyed her appraisingly. "Are you one of our clients?"

"Yes, I am. I made a successful bid for the Anna Ancher interior you put up for sale a few years ago."

"Ah ha, I see. Let me just look that up in our data bank. Anna Ancher, Anna Ancher. Oh, yes. Your name?"

"Megan Crespi."

"Ah, yes, here you are. Well, I can tell you that someone came in this morning offering us the preparatory drawing for Oskar Kokoschka's nineteen-nine poster for the Vienna Kunstschau. The one advertising his play, *Murderer, Hope of Women*. It was in surprisingly excellent condition; had never been rolled up. It's out of our field of expertise, of course, but I thought it would make an interesting addition to our offering, especially with all the hoopla surrounding the artist's name just now."

"Might I see the poster drawing, since I'm here in Wien?" Megan asked, affecting a more pronounced accent in German than she usually had.

"Ach, you are from out of town. May I ask from where?"

"From Dallas, in Texas."

"Oh! The city that killed Kennedy!"

"One deranged man killed Kennedy, not the city."

"But now you have had Ebola outbreak. It is a very unlucky city where you live."

"Yes, one could say that." Megan was having trouble containing her irritation.

"I suppose we could show you the drawing, since you are here from abroad." He signaled to an employee who had just come from the back of the shop.

"Fetch the Kokoschka poster drawing that came in this morning and bring it here," he instructed. The assistant disappeared momentarily and returned with a brightly colored gouache-enhanced drawing suspended in his hands and held high above his head.

Megan saw immediately that it was a forgery. A very good one, but nevertheless a forgery. Should she say anything? She certainly did not feel well-disposed toward the Amadeus owner. Before either man could stop her, she pivoted around to the back of the poster and saw affixed to it a large seal that read: "Collection Kallias Andriopoulos."

Megan stepped back to the front of the drawing again. An interesting coincidence, considering she had just learned about the fanatical Graz collector an hour earlier. It was very clear just why he was letting this "Kokoschka" go. Anyone who was familiar with the artist's early works, as indeed she was, could have seen that the gouache sketch was not authentic. The pressure of the lines was wrong, the wielding of the brush was much too controlled.

Megan's art-historian conscience got the better of her. "This is indeed an interesting sketch, so similar to the famous Kunstschau poster, but independent authentication is always important, don't you think?"

"Authentication! Do you realize this artwork comes from one of the greatest collectors of…" Weber's voice trailed off.

"Just a suggestion from a humble art historian who hails from Dallas, Texas," Megan said over her shoulder as she headed for the door. Whew! Glad to be out of there, she thought to herself. To cheer herself up she made a brief visit to the Mozart House—actually apartment, and up several floors from the arched entryway. When at last she stood next to the bronze bust of Wolfgang facing a wall panorama of Vienna as it looked when he lived there, she began to feel better.

But now a new thought possessed her. What would a known and apparently respected collector of Kokoschka be doing placing a questionable work by the artist on auction? And interesting that he hadn't placed it with the Dorotheum but with the Amadeus online auction house. Was this a one-time incident or were there other questionable works from the Graz collection that were making their way to the market? If she stayed in Europe longer, she might be able to snag an invitation to visit the collection. Graz was the home of the Fogarassy family that had helped her so much when she was first studying Schiele. She had been invited to spend a week with them and to examine their extensive collection of works by Klimt, Schiele, and Kokoschka. And Megan was still in contact with all four daughters of the family. Yes, the prospect of a visit to Graz was certainly inviting.

And a train ride through the Semmering Pass would take her very near Breitenstein am Semmering, where the Haus Mahler had been built. The retreat to which Gustav never had the chance to go while it was being built in 1910. Terminally ill, he died a year later without ever seeing it.

Alma brought her new lover Kokoschka there in 1912 and he painted a gigantic tempera-and-oil mural measuring some thirteen feet long and approximately two feet high. It was placed above the oversized fireplace of the living-cum-music room. The frieze, Oskar had explained to Alma, was a continuation of the dancing flames from the fireplace and showed him standing in a hell of snakes and death, the bright sky above him a ghostly irony. She, by contrast, was shown with arms flung wide, supplicating the heavens.

Alma had thought that wall-painting was lost when the house went into Russian hands during World War II. But in 1987 a couple who bought the villa unexpectedly came upon the mural when they were removing the ugly wallpaper that had covered it for some seventy years. The unusually long frieze was later transported from Austria to a bonded warehouse in Zurich. Megan knew that sales to various museums had failed. But after a rare exhibit of it in 2008 in connection with a Kokoschka exhibition at the Belvedere Museum in Vienna, it was bought right out of the show by a famous nonagenarian private collector in Berlin. Margareta Nussbaum was her name and Megan had visited her once in her remote Babelsberg villa in Potsdam, just outside Berlin.

In the meantime, Megan thought, should she make the trip to Graz, it would be delicious fun to jump off at Semmering and see the Mahler House for herself. Franz Werfel's writing desk was still there, that she knew for sure.

And she also knew for sure that her stomach was rumbling, so she left Mozart and Kokoschka behind and returned to the Annagasse where she had dinner in her favorite Italian restaurant, Sole. She spent the evening making notes and went to bed at midnight, early for her. The Kokoschka poster forgery danced in her mind's eye as she tried to fall asleep. Finally, thinking instead of little Button, she drifted off.

21

Reconnoitering the MOMAT was not quite as productive as Agnes Sauer had hoped it would be, but she was glad she had checked it out the day before her actual maneuver. The three-story, in-your-face modern building by the beautiful Imperial Palace had easy enough entry; the guards checked only purses and briefcases and not cameras or camera cases. And there was a women's restroom nearby. There, in the privacy of a booth, Agnes, wearing a blonde wig, would be slipping her glass-and-metal syringe with its two ounces of concentrated sulfuric acid from her boot into the camera pouch she would be wearing on the back of her Gucci leather belt the next day. Only there would be no camera in the pouch. Just her tools. Exiting the restroom she continued down the long hall leading to the Crafts Gallery and the Exhibits Gallery. She observed that one guard covered three exhibition rooms on average and that one of his main duties appeared to be urging groups of reverent schoolchildren to continue circulating. Certainly there were plenty of visitors, but most of them groups rather than individual. The individuals seemed on the whole to be European or North American rather than Japanese. Photography was allowed, but no flash.

More difficult was locating the Kokoschka. The museum's map indicated European art was on the second floor at the far end of the building.

When she got there she was reminded of Paris's Musée de l' Orangerie, since the Japanese museum seemed to be flooded with Monet at first glance. But a second room had greater variety. There were works by Pissarro, Picasso, Braque, Arp, and Chagall. Only when Agnes entered the third room did she find Kokoschka's "Mona Lisa" portrait of Alma. It was on the far wall and in the fitting company of Max Ernst and Kandinsky on either side. And the room was full of visitors, Japanese as well as Westerners. They simply packed the room. Their respectful, quiet, but overcrowded presence made Agnes decide on a maneuver and tool she had not planned to use but for which she had come prepared.

The next day at exactly noon, wearing her empty camera pouch at the back of her belt under a jacket, a blonde Agnes passed easily through security—only her shoulder bag was examined. She then went directly to the women's bathroom where she transferred the loaded syringe from her boot to her pouch. From the other boot she pulled out a slim, three-inch folding knife with wooden handle. It too went into her waist pouch which she had pulled around her belt to the front. She then took the stairs to the second floor and walked to the third room.

The small room was appreciably more crowded than the day before— just as she had hoped. She positioned herself in front of the thin-lipped Alma portrait and feigned interest while at the same time slipping out her knife. When she felt someone back up against her she turned quickly and expertly stabbed the woman in the back at heart level. The woman fell to the floor with a scream, a scream echoed by Agnes who pointed to the fallen woman, urging people to help. An excited crowd, their backs to the room walls, immediately formed around the woman and its very density pushed Agnes up almost against the Kokoschka. The syringe was in her hand now and, wheeling once again and aiming at the painted face, she pushed the plunger all the way down in one swift motion. Then, turning back around, she too stooped with the noisy crowd around the fallen tourist. No one had noticed.

Within minutes the Kokoschka portrait evinced terrible, irreparable damage. By violently reacting with the humidity naturally present in the varnish, the acid had permanently destroyed the paint. Alma's unsmiling face had been transformed into a dark brown, foul-smelling crust.

Seeing the guards come running and their frantic attempt to get through the crowd to reach the shrieking woman on the floor, Agnes quickly turned back to the painting for a moment and, from her kneeling position, took a photo of the damage with her cellphone. Another second and it was on its cyber way to Leo Lang. Their second collaboration had turned out to be a most successful caper. A Kokoschka caper.

28

"Your suggestion about using plastic bags over my casts was *so* helpful," her hostess said to Megan over lunch in the Dumba palais penthouse. Megan had arrived promptly at one in the afternoon and was greeted at the door by Desdemona herself. A discreet maid was to be seen in the background, but Desdemona had already mastered using only her fingers so well that she did not need the maid's help.

"I only knew about that tip because a dear friend of mine broke both *her* wrists a few years ago and that's what she figured out to do when taking a shower."

"It's such a relief not to have to change my daily routine despite this handicap. Showers feel so good on my back."

"And that handicap is only temporary," Megan assured her smiling hostess.

A delicious lunch of gazpacho followed by a tuna casserole had been served by Desdemona's attentive butler, and Megan was feeling in fine spirits. She had earned this time off, she told herself, because she had made the rounds of two more galleries that morning, although she had elicited nothing that could be useful.

"After dessert I will give you a tour of the flat, should you so desire."

"I would love that."

The butler reappeared with two servings of one of the most delicious zabaglione concoctions Megan had ever tasted. It was perfectly whipped and slid down the throat leaving a lovely aftertaste.

"Might I congratulate your cook on this wonderful meal?"

"You are too kind. I'll ring for her."

A pleasant, slender, black-haired young woman in an apron tentatively opened the swinging door from the kitchen and looked inquisitively toward them. Megan thanked her profusely and the girl grinned from ear to ear.

Following her hostess's lead, Megan stood up from the table and walked after her into the music room. It had two items that made Megan gasp aloud. Klimt's *Schubert at the Piano* sopraporta, displayed on two easels at the far corner of the room, and a Bösendorfer grand piano in the near corner, placed with the same orientation as the piano in the Schubert painting.

"What a privilege to see this in person," Megan breathed. "And what a story of restitution it has had. I've, of course, followed the history of its recent discovery."

Megan went up to the Klimt and caressed it with her eyes. "Ah! Now I clearly see the tall male figure in between the women. He's in three-quarter profile looking at the piano. Do you think it could be Schubert's favorite singer, Johann Vogl?"

"I am certain that is who it is. Once they met they were inseparable musically. Vogl was the first to sing *Der Erlkönig*."

"Yes. It was written with his beautiful baritone voice in mind. And do you know Franz von Schober's caricature of Vogl and Schubert?" Megan asked.

"Oh, yes, indeed I do. The one in which the very tall, majestic Vogl is walking along in profile and behind him, his arms huddled about himself, is a very short Franzerl looking out at us and clutching music scores to his chest."

"Exactly. You have a good visual memory, Desdemona."

"Thank you. Look again at Klimt's picture. Do you notice anything else?"

"Yes. Something I've always wondered about when looking at reproductions of this painting. To the right of the singers and Vogl, but quite small, is the figure of another man."

"Quite right. Do you have any theory as to who the man might be?"

"Your great-grandfather, the patron who commissioned the Schubert painting?"

"Exactly right! It is Nikolaus Dumba himself. A surprise compliment from Klimt, my father told me."

"That's marvelous. A delicious homage. And a great postscript to add to the painting's history," Megan said.

"Did you know that Vogl sang a complete performance of *Winterreise* on an anniversary of Schubert's death?"

"No, I did not, but I can certainly understand why. It is rare in music history that such a partnership between singer and composer has existed." Megan looked back from the Klimt toward the Bösendorfer.

"And is that an inheritance from your great-grandfather?"

"Well, again it a story of discovering where it ended up after the palais's contents were distributed in the nineteen-thirties."

"And are you a pianist?"

"I have been in the past. Not so much now as I am traveling a lot lately. And certainly not *now*," she laughed, holding up her two casts. "And you?"

"My instrument is the flute, but I do like to play songs by ear on the piano."

"Oh, do play me something!"

"Only if you will too."

"What? With these casts?"

Megan laughed and sat down on the piano bench, looked at Desdemona, then began playing the well-known theme from the film *Never on Sunday* for her."

"Thank you for the Greek homage," Desdemona laughed when Megan finished with a flourish.

"But as you see, I only play in the key of C or C minor."

"But that's good enough for many, many tunes. Too bad you don't have your flute with you; we could play something together. Or we could have if I didn't have these," Desdemona said, waving her casts in the air.

"My trip over this time was for business and not for pleasure, unfortunately." Some instinct told Megan not to tell her hostess why she was in Europe.

"Now it's your turn to play something on the piano for me, even if it's only with two fingers."

Gamely, Desdemona went over to the wall switches and turned off the overhead light. An electric candelabra on the piano lit up.

"You see how I have tried to recreate the atmosphere in Klimt's candle-lit painting," she said, slipping onto the piano bench.

"Now I line myself up exactly with Schubert," she said, looking at the painting and pushing the bench in so that her profile was on the same sight line as Klimt's painted Schubert. Then she began awkwardly to play. She was tapping out Massenet's *Méditation* from his opera *Thaïs*. In spite of her casts she played with extraordinary feeling and composure.

After Megan had expressed her appreciation, she said: "You won't believe this, Desdemona, but I love that arcing melody so much that I have it as the ring tone on my iPhone."

"I must hear that!"

Megan obliged and the two women laughed together.

"Mine is only the marimba sound, but you've inspired me. I shall download a more suitable piece, perhaps the same as what you have. But now let me show you my study."

They walked down a picture-hung, carpeted hallway toward another room and entered. It was a large, wood-paneled library with a long table and two chairs in the middle. On the table was a desktop Macintosh computer with a very large screen. On the back wall of the room was an enormous three-part color photograph that extended across the length of the wall. The subject, obviously taken from the air, was a small island with white cliffs and a cluster of green cypress trees.

Desdemona saw Megan looking at it keenly.

"Commanding, isn't it? It's an aerial view of my beloved island off Corfu, my Xenia."

"So! You've found it!"

"How do you mean 'found it?'" Desdemona looked at Megan perplexed.

"You've found Böcklin's *Isle of the Dead* in the flesh."

"I'm afraid I don't know what you mean. *Whose* isle and why of death?"

"Do you not know Arnold Böcklin's famous picture called *The Isle of the Dead*? It was a major motif in his work in the eighteen-eighties. He had visited Corfu and sighted your tiny island. It intrigued and inspired him. He actually painted six different versions of it. In fact I was just admiring the first version at the Basel Museum the other day."

"But I can't believe I don't know about this picture, or, rather, these pictures."

"Yes, there are others: in Berlin, a bit more whitish than the Basel one, another, smaller one at the Metropolitan Museum in New York, another in Geneva, and one in Leipzig, more golden in hue. The sixth one is lost. The color photograph of your island has the same rising cliffs on either side of a group of cypress trees and the same indications of tombs carved into the cliff on the right."

"I absolutely have to see this, Böcklin, you said his name was?"

"No sooner said than done. I'll Google it for you on your Mac if you like."

Megan walked over to the table as Desdemona hastened to turn the computer on. Within seconds Megan had beamed up a URL that showed her a color image of the artist's haunting *The Isle of the Dead*. The one in Basel.

"*But this is the picture I saw in my childhood and never forgot!*" Desdemona gasped. "This is remarkable! *So* like my island. You know, the Greek government allowed me to purchase it. Let me see the other Böcklin images." Megan obliged, bringing up the image at the Metropolitan, the one in Leipzig, then Geneva, and finally the one in Berlin.

"These are all wonderful. But you said there were six versions by Böcklin. Where is the sixth? Why isn't it here?"

"Because it is presumed lost, the one painted in eighteen-eighty-four. Supposedly in Berlin during World War II."

Desdemona stood looking from the images on her screen to the vibrant, elderly woman who had beamed them up. She was silent for a long minute watching Megan expertly pull up details from the Böcklin images to match the photographic spread on the wall.

"How long will you be in Europe?"

"I'm not sure. I had thought it would only be a few days, but now I think I shall be staying longer."

"Then you know what?" Desdemona had made her decision. "You are going to come with me to Greece, to Corfu, to *my* island. I want to show you Xenia. You have earned it with this Böcklin revelation. *Please* say you will come!"

Megan laughed. "It's a lovely idea, but I do have some business to attend to."

"Ah! You said *'some.'*" This means you can do me the honor to come to Xenia. You simply must not say no."

"I'd have to see how things go," Megan said, warming to the idea in spite of her Kokoschka mission.

"Well, how about this? We go to see one of the Böcklins together. Either Berlin, Leipzig, Geneva, or Basel—your choice. Even New York, if you wish. What do you say? *The Isle of the Dead*," Desdemona said, stringing out the words dramatically.

Megan had to laugh at her new friend's spontaneity. But she decided she needed to rain a little on her burst of enthusiasm.

"As a matter of fact, Böcklin did not believe in titling his works. He thought that his paintings ought to evoke a mood in the beholder. He did not want to prejudice this mood by providing an instructive title. Just the way Beethoven's so-called *Moonlight Sonata* was dubbed that by a music critic, not by the composer."

"Oh, yes, of course I know. The Piano Sonata in C Sharp Minor. Just that; no descriptive title."

"Well, so it was with Böcklin. It was his art dealer Fritz Gurlitt who baptized the painting with a descriptive title in the eighteen-eighties."

"Gurlitt? Any relation to the Cornelius Gurlitt in the headlines now for having a cache of some fifteen hundred artworks seized recently from his Munich apartment?"

"Yes, it's the same family. But the other members were honest art dealers. One was even a very successful artist."

"This is all too complicated for me. Come, decide which city we will go to and see the Böcklin death isle."

Megan's defenses were down. She felt sorry about having flung herself on the endangered Desdemona with such force that two sprained wrists were the result. On the other hand, if she hadn't leapt on the woman, the streetcar would have run over her. A choice not allowing for nuanced falls.

"All right. Next week I do have to return to Basel. We can go together if you like."

"And you will let me pick the hotel and be my guest?"

"Yes, yes," said Megan in capitulation to this amazing woman's passion.

What am I doing, she asked herself back at the Römischer Kaiser. But she already knew the answer: surrendering to her unquenchable thirst for adventure and the unexpected.

29

Leo Lang was enormously pleased by the success of Agnes Sauer's Japan mission. The Internet was full of reports about the vandalism, even supplying images of the damaged portrait that no longer had a face. And the police had absolutely no clue as to who the perpetrator was. He really had to congratulate Sauer. Why, she had even managed to send him a photo of the eradicated Mona Lisa Alma just moments after having squirted it with the contents of her syringe. He really must ask her what chemical she used to do such a thorough job.

And he would have a chance to do that in just a few minutes. She was due to arrive at his villa in half an hour. This time he had an assignment for her closer to home: the Museum Folkwang in Germany's bustling city of Essen. The Alma object this time was a double portrait Kokoschka had painted of her with him, clothed this time—she, apparently on his lap, both of them about to clasp hands and looking out at the beholder with serious faces. The portrait dated from soon after their fateful meeting in 1912 at the house of Alma's stepfather, Carl Moll—the one who had recommended that she ask the painter to do her portrait.

Leo filled the half hour he had to wait for Sauer by reading again the two conflicting accounts of their meeting and its hectic aftermath. Oscar's recollection, as told to the Hungarian photographer Gyula Brassaï was:

Mahler had been dead for a year when I met her, which was in 1912, at Carl Moll's, a painter who often invited his friends to dinners in his mansion, dinners followed by chamber-music concerts. It was on one of those occasions that I first came face to face with Alma. She had just returned from abroad. How beautiful she was, and how seductive she looked beneath her mourning veil! She enchanted me! And I had the impression that she was not indifferent to me, either. In fact after dinner, she took me by the arm and drew me into an adjoining room where she sat down and played the Liebestod on the piano for me. I was dazzled by her, she disturbed me.

Alma's version of meeting the peculiar young artist, seven years her junior, was vastly different. Although it did confirm the piano playing:

> He had brought some rough paper with him and wanted to draw. But after a little while I said I couldn't be stared at like that and asked him if I could play the piano meanwhile. He began to draw, coughing intermittently and trying to hide his handkerchief because it had specks of blood on it. We barely spoke, but even then he could not draw. We stood up—and he suddenly embraced me wildly. This kind of embrace was alien to me. I did not respond in the least and it was precisely this that seemed to affect him.

Over the course of the next two and a half years Oskar wrote some four hundred letters to Alma. The first one was a proposal of marriage:

> My dear friend, if you can respect me and wish to be as pure as you were yesterday, when I recognized that you are superior to and better than all other women, who only ever brought out my baser self, then you will be making a true sacrifice for me and will be my wife, in secret while I am still so poor.

All their friends were aghast at Kokoschka's conduct, including his mother, who threatened to shoot Alma. But Oskar was undeterred, recalling "I obeyed nothing but our mutual passion." He spent the next months either in her house with her or pacing below her bedroom window until two or four in the morning, to be sure she did not receive other visitors.

All this Leo Lang recalled as he eagerly awaited his agent's arrival. Finally he heard the sound of her taxi in the drive. He met her at the front door, smiling widely.

"You have achieved a wonderful success, Frau Sauer, simply wonderful."

"You received my photo then?"

"I have printed it out and placed it in my missions album along with shots of the Alma *Tempest* which you so successfully brought to me."

Agnes Sauer again wondered whether she might be dealing with a lunatic. "Where is your *Tempest* now?" she asked.

"Oh, it's rolled up in the cellar. Nicely out of sight where it won't offend my eyes."

"I cannot understand why you don't place it on the, shall I say, black market? It must be worth many thousand Euros."

"It probably is. But money does not interest me. Ridding the world of images of that hideous, grasping woman is what I care about. She was a voracious octopus! Reaching out with her tentacles for famous men. And she stole my grandmother Lilith's lover, Oskar, from her."

"Oh, so the *Tempest* version you had me substitute for the Alma version is of your *grandmother*?"

"Jawohl! But you are never to speak of it, not to a living soul, is that understood?"

"Of course. It is our secret, and since it is I who achieved the switch, I am hardly likely to talk to other people about it, Herr Lang."

Agnes was now utterly convinced she was dealing with a madman. But he was a generous one she thought, as she counted out the banknotes he handed her. And apparently a man with an endless font of missions. He had already brought up the next one.

"Essen's Museum Folkwang is a modern building that admits lots of light from a glassed inner courtyard," he was telling her. "I cannot tell you where in the museum the Kokoschka target is but you will easily recognize it. Here," he said reaching for the Killar oeuvre catalogue, "this is what it looks like. Just look at that witch! And poor smitten Oskar! You understand, do you not, that Kokoschka was my *grandfather*?"

"Indeed yes, Herr Lang. And it is your grandmother Lilith whom you are rightly avenging." Agnes had decided to throw the word "rightly" into her answer to demonstrate her loyalty to her employer.

"How soon do you think you could travel to Essen?"

"Again, Herr Lang, I must first go home to Basel for a day, but after that my schedule is clear, so sometime at the end of the week."

"Excellent!"

"Might I ask one question, Herr Lang?"

"Yes?"

"Is the life-size doll in your study the one Kokoschka had made in the likeness of Alma?"

"Oh, no it is not. Grandfather Oskar finally burned the Alma doll, but not before he painted her twice—once alone, dressed in blue, recumbent with breasts bared, and the other time spread out naked before the viewer's gaze in front of him as he points to her pudendum."

"Pudendum?"

"External genitals."

"Oh. Rather gross."

"Exactly. I simply cannot understand how my grandfather could have been so taken by Alma that he would have had a Doppelgänger doll made of her after they broke up. She totally bewitched him and at the same time she was seeing and sleeping with other men. She went ahead and married Walter Gropius in nineteen-fifteen. That broke grandfather's heart. And then she was already sleeping with Franz Werfel before she divorced Gropius in nineteen-twenty. A total whore."

Half an hour later Agnes Sauer left Leo Lang's house with a new assignment and a new understanding of why he himself was so "bewitched" by a woman who had been dead for over fifty years.

30

Bruno Fichte had begun to think he would never hear back from the *Remove Nudity in Museums* people, but at the end of the week, Friday, he received an e-mail asking him if a visit from one of the organization's representatives could be scheduled. He hastened to offer several dates and nearby public locations—god forbid that they should learn about his Almariana collection—and received confirmation of time and locale almost immediately. The meeting was set up for that afternoon at three at the Bocado Café on Lexington at 87th Street.

He got there a few minutes early and wore a hat—a golf cap—as instructed. A tall, thin man with white hair approached him. "Are you Mr. Fichte?"

"Yes, I am." Bruno decided not to insist upon being addressed as "Professor."

"We are interested in your request for aid and would like to know the details and location of your target object."

"I have a photograph of it here—you see the naked 'dancing' couple—and on this second sheet are the names of the institutions involved and a description of the mission I would like help with." Bruno gave the man, who had not offered his name, time to look over what he had been handed.

"The artwork concerned will not be in either museum then?" he asked at last.

"No, it will be in a moving van, being transported from the Boston Museum to Buffalo's Albright-Knox Art Gallery. I have the exact time, date and route that will be taken. What I need is to have the van stopped en route, preferably where there is the least traffic so that the artwork can be speedily removed and placed in a second van. The trip from Boston to Buffalo takes about six-and-a-half hours via interstate Highway Ninety."

Bruno beamed up a map on his mini iPad.

"Let's see," said the man. "The van will go through Albany and Syracuse, on Highway Ninety the whole time. That's not good. Can't waylay a van on a major highway. The best thing to do would be to catch it after it bypasses Syracuse—see here, Highway Ninety is to the north of town—and halt it on the turnoff for Lake Onondaga to the west. This is how we can handle it."

Bruno listened to the man's bold plan that would involve three men and realized that there was no place for his son Felix.

"I would want my son to go along, just in case there is a hang-up."

"No can do. Mission initiators of removal actions are not allowed. Should our men get stopped, which is highly unlikely considering the ruse we will be undertaking, the trail would not lead back to you but to a non-existent shipping company."

"And after the hijack the painting will be delivered to me as requested?"

"Yes, our main goal is to prohibit the installation of the nude thing in yet another museum. We can either destroy it or, as you have asked, deliver it to you. But I would advise you against this, as it opens the procedure up to the possibility of interception, especially if it's to be delivered to your Manhattan address."

"Ah, but I have an isolated country home in Nyack, New York. That is where I would have you deliver it, free of spying eyes."

"All right. You provide us with that address as well and we shall deliver it. Absconding with the artwork is our business, and it's gratis, but delivering it to a private address is a horse of a different color. We should have to charge you for the inconvenience."

"I understand."

"Then our business is concluded. The transfer date, according to your data, is Monday next. We shall contact you by e-mail upon completion of the transfer."

"Then here is a third sheet of information for you with a map and instructions on how to find my house in Nyack. Do you think that might be accomplished on the same day?"

"It's possible. The pickup in Boston is scheduled for nine in the morning; we will be intercepting the van around two in the afternoon. There is no reason why our men couldn't deliver the artwork to Nyack by early evening."

"Then I shall await you there."

The two men shook hands and walked off in different directions.

Damn lucky about that former student-curator of mine, Bruno thought to himself. He has proven to be an embedded treasure at Albright-Knox. And now Felix and I shall be in possession of one of Kokoschka's most glorious depictions of my grandmother. Who would have thought that a fanatical organization I found on the Internet would be willing to do the legwork! They will have fulfilled their mission of removing nudity from museums and I shall have my greatest Alma yet!

31

Helmut Haesslich was stunned. The unframed portrait on stretchers placed on the easel in front of him by the kid Niki Deschner was dazzling. Constantine Christomanos was breathtakingly *present*. The expression on his contorted face exactly matched the black-and-white photograph in Killar's oeuvre catalogue and yet the pale, sickly yellow of the skin was Kokoschka through and through. So too were the short, abrupt brushstrokes. Urgently applied, jagged, and exuding turmoil, they complemented Christomanos's exposed anxiety as the hunchback wrapped his arms around his quivering torso. The colors agitated the empty surround with typical Kokoschka hues—blues, purples, grays, and blacks. A few white streaks electrified the atmosphere, heightening the feeling of angst conveyed by the portrait. A just-dried nontoxic linseed oil overlay held it all together. Haesslich put his nose to the canvas and sniffed: there was practically no odor, and what there was would disappear quickly. He looked at the way a spatula had been used to apply the paint in some areas.

"This is it! This *is* Kokoschka!" Haesslich exclaimed, turning to Niki Deschner, whose face immediately flushed with pleasure.

"Now how did you create such convincing craquelure? Oven or sunshine?

"Oh, that was easy. I just let it sun bake in my mother's backyard." He hastened to add: "Don't worry, nobody saw it drying out there, not even my mother. And I had primed the canvas with gesso that I prepared with rabbit skin glue."

Haesslich was so impressed by the boy's work that he doled out an extra five-hundred Euros as he paid him the agreed-upon fee of five-thousand Euros.

After Deschner left, Haesslich immediately placed a call to Theo Papadakis in Vienna.

"I have discovered that the Kokoschka portrait of Constantine Christomanos does exist. It has not been destroyed. Rather, since nineteen-eighteen it has been stored in the Berlin cellar of the house where Georg Lewin—you know him as the art publisher Herwarth Walden—once lived. I now have it in hand, purchased from the family who recently bought the building. They contacted my gallery after discovering it in the cellar."

"This is sensational news, Herr Haesslich, sensational news! May I inquire about the condition of the painting?"

"I wish I could say it is in good condition, but after all these years in a cellar, some restoration work is in order."

"Might I bring my Vienna client to see it?"

"Yes. You may. As long as you prepare your client for the fact that the portrait is not in perfect condition."

"I shall contact my client and inform you of the day we can come."

"Very good. But it is imperative that you inform no one else about this find at this time. I have advised you first, but I do have other clients who would also be interested in acquiring this lost Kokoschka, to say nothing of museums."

"Certainly, Herr Haesslich, certainly."

After they hung up, Helmut Haesslich turned to the canvas on the easel. He carefully removed it from its stretchers, placed it on a long table, then deliberately began to roll it up. Some of the paint could be heard splintering. Haesslich continued rolling.

32

It was Friday and Megan had finished her gallery visits. Her most interesting finds were actually Kokoschka travesties: the excising of the eight plates to his *The Dreaming Youths* book from their binding and putting them up for individual sale at Galerie Hummel, and the questionable Kokoschka gouache sketch for the *Murderer, Hope of Women* poster at the Amadeus Auktionshaus.

She was ready to leave Wien and would enjoy the company of Desdemona on the flight back to Basel. True to her word to let Desdemona pick where they would stay, Megan let her enthusiastic new friend make the hotel arrangements. But she made her own flight reservation, imparting the data to Desdemona on the phone.

It was Saturday afternoon and the Austrian Airlines flight was not completely full. The two women decided to leave the middle seat between them free for their purses. Desdemona was coping very well with her hands in casts, but she was glad to have the extra room.

"Which hotel have you chosen for us in Basel?" Megan asked her fellow traveller.

"Ah, I hope you do not think it is too posh but I have reserved two bedrooms connected by a common living room at the Grand Hotel Les Trois Rois."

"Wonderful! I have never stayed there but I know its terrace restaurant well and I love the view of the Rhine from there."

"I am delighted that *you* are delighted, dear Megan," beamed Desdemona.

"I have asked my friend Hans Tietze to allow us into the museum an hour before it opens tomorrow so that you can enjoy, without interruption, Böcklin's *Isle of the Dead*—your island incarnate."

"How very thoughtful of you, Megan."

On the flight, Desdemona began to speak about the Empress Sisi. "You know, some might call it a fetish, but I am totally enamored of her.

She was such a brave spirit, and experienced such horrible tragedy with the self-murder of her son and his mistress. Also, she was married at such a young age—fourteen—and to such a *wooden* man, Franz Josef. The only thing they seemed to have in common was a love of horseback riding. Of course the people loved her, she was so beautiful, and photographs of her dressed in white, her long hair reaching well past her hips, were circulated by the thousands."

"I've heard her hair was so long it stretched down to her ankles," said Megan.

"Oh, yes. And for the people it seemed to be a fairy story marriage, but in fact life at court was a living hell for her. She couldn't stand the antiquated ritual and conniving politics. When her daughters were born— Sofie, then Gisela—they were immediately taken away from her and put in the care of her domineering mother-in-law. That sparked her years of wandering around Europe. She only found comfort in Hungary, where she made an effort to learn the language, and in Greece, where she traveled with her Greek tutor Constantine Christomanos. Greece meant everything to her. I feel so connected to her because of this."

"I can well understand. And I have been fortunate enough to have visited her Achilleion in Corfu."

"Have you, Megan? How wonderful. Then that gives us yet something else in common."

"And what do you think about Sisi's obsession with beauty, her determination to keep her youthful figure, her anorexia, the hours it took for her to be sewn into her leather corsets, and the hours it took to do her coiffure each day?"

"Well, yes, she was obsessed—after all, she was considered the most beautiful woman in Europe—but Franz Josef made it possible for her to carry out her rigid, hour-long routines. He was smitten by her from the very first glance and allowed for all her idiosyncrasies. A very patient, if dull, man. Devoted to duty and overseeing the immense Austro-Hungarian Empire."

Desdemona shook her head sadly, then asked Megan: "Have you been to the Beau-Rivage Hotel where Sisi was staying in Geneva just before she was assassinated?"

"Oh, you bet I have! And for that very reason. Because the sixty-year-old Sisi stayed there. I was even able to bribe a maid to let me see inside the room she had. It's shut off and marked with a memorial plaque, as you probably know."

"I can't believe this! Another thing in common, Megan! I too have bribed hotel personnel at the Beau-Rivage to let me see her room."

They continued to talk about Sisi as the plane began to make its descent into Basel. About how Sisi did not even realize she had been stabbed in the chest when the anarchist Luigi Lucheni "stumbled" into her path as she walked from the hotel down the lake promenade to a waiting steamer. She actually got up from the ground, thanking those who helped her in French, German, and English, and proceeded to board the vessel before she collapsed and died. And how the rumor grew that her last word was "*endlich*"—"finally!"

Megan and Desdemona were still chatting about the reluctant Empress when their limo pulled up at their hotel after the long drive from the Basel Euroairport. They had invited Hans Tietze to join them for dinner on the terrace at eight o'clock that evening. Both women decided to take naps and catch up on e-mail before getting dressed for dinner, but they met in the living room that joined the two bedrooms for red wine before dinner. Desdemona was horrified that Megan squirted some of her Dasani strawberry-kiwi drops into her glass.

"It's the only way I can drink it," Megan explained. "And I know how healthy one glass of red wine every day is."

"I agree with you there."

Hans was waiting for them in the lobby when they came downstairs and a few minutes later they were sitting on the hotel terrace facing the Rhine.

"And which of the Böcklin *Isle of the Dead* versions do you believe is the first one," Desdemona asked after they had ordered dinner.

"Oh, there is no doubt about that," Hans answered, a proud smile crossing his face. "Ours is. The story is that in eighteen-eighty, the American-born widow of a German diplomat, Marie Berna, visited Böcklin in his studio in Florence where he was at work on his island picture. He already had painted in a lone rowboat with a man at the oars. Berna studied the picture as it stood on the artist's easel, then told him she would like to commission the completed canvas as a memorial to her husband if he would agree to add a white-shrouded female figure standing before a draped coffin. Böcklin complied, and that is the story of the iconography in our picture. The other known versions—in Leipzig, Berlin, Geneva, and New York—all carried over the motif of the coffin and grieving widow. But our *Isle* is the prototype."

"Fascinating. Has Megan told you about my owning the actual island off Corfu that Böcklin portrayed in his painting? Pontikonisi, which I have rechristened Xenia? And that I bought it because it reminded me of an image I had seen in my childhood? An image that she revealed to me was Böcklin's painting?"

"Indeed she has. You probably first saw it in print form, as it was such a popular image that many German and Austrian homes had it on their walls. I can certainly understand why you should wish to see the original painting."

"You mentioned that Böcklin was working in Florence. But I thought he was Swiss," Desdemona said.

"He was," Megan answered, "but he lived and worked in several German cities and in Italy as well—Rome and Florence. He had a studio in Fiesole, which is where that American widow must have visited him."

Hans eagerly took over the story. "His Italian experiences broadened his subject matter and he added riveting mythological scenes to his repertoire. By the time he died, in nineteen-one, he was considered one of Europe's most formidable painters."

"But he was soon forgotten as French Impressionism spread over all Europe," Megan added, thinking of her Danish painter, Anna Ancher.

"I can't wait to see Böcklin in the flesh," Desdemona said as they finished dinner. Hans and Megan smiled at one another. They knew Desdemona had a tremendous treat in store.

33

Jutta Feinstein, curator of Essen's Folkwang Museum, stood alone inside the building's entrance foyer. This is good, she congratulated herself, you can see beyond the entrance straight into the first exhibition room with its two large triptychs. Her *Degenerate Art Revisited* show should grab visitors the moment they entered the museum. Adolf Ziegler was Hitler's favorite painter whereas Max Beckman was one of his most detested artists. The disparity between the two triptychs was chillingly instructive: the one, barren Aryan idealization; the other awash with enigmatic violence—harbingers of life in the Third Reich.

Jutta congratulated herself on the major coup she had brought off in cajoling these two important loans from Munich and New York, respectively. They set the tone for what would greet visitors in the inner rooms of the exhibition. The Nazis had proclaimed that most of modern art was *entartet*—degenerate—and this included art that was Jewish, Communist in slant, or simply "un-German." Jutta's show included all three categories with pictures by Marc Chagall, Ernst Barlach, Franz Marc, Piet Mondrian, Emil Nolde—despite his anti-Semitism—Paul Klee, Paula Modersohn-Becker, Oskar Kokoschka, Ernst Ludwig Kirchner, George Grosz, and Wassily Kandinsky. She had been able to get the loan of Vienna's sixteen-year-old prodigy Max Oppenheimer's 1901 *Sitting Couple*—a painting remarkably prescient in technique and subject matter to his colleague Kokoschka's 1913 *Double Portrait of Alma Mahler and the Artist*. She had placed them in the front room, the Kokoschka to the left of the two triptychs, and the Oppenheimer to the right of them. Stunning, simply stunning, she murmured to herself.

On the didactic label for the Kokoschka she had placed Alma's description of the work in progress: "I was once given a flame-red night gown. I didn't like it due to its overpowering color. Oskar took it from me right away and from then on went around his studio wearing nothing else. He wore it to receive his astounded visitors and was to be found more in front of the mirror than in front of his easel."

The didactic label for Max Oppenheimer's 1901 picture read: "Portrait of Karl and Leopoldine Wittgenstein. Leopoldine Kalmus, a gifted pianist, and Karl, a fine violinist, held one of Vienna's most brilliant salons in the eighteen-nineties. Clara Schumann, Johannes Brahms, Gustav Mahler, and Bruno Walter were frequent house guests. Leopoldine provided her billionaire husband Karl with eight children, two of whom became quite famous: Paul, a concert pianist who, after losing his right hand during World War I, commissioned a number of major composers to provide him with concerti for the left hand, the most famous of which was Maurice Ravel's.

"The youngest son, Ludwig, became a philosopher and, with his *Tractatus Logico-Philosophicus*, is generally considered to have been the greatest philosopher of the twentieth century."

Considering the Jewish background of the Wittgenstein family and the fact that the city of Essen had recently restored its Alte Synogogue, which had survived the bombing of World War II, displaying Oppenheimer's Wittgenstein double portrait seemed to make cultural sense.

It was ten o'clock at night. Jutta Feinstein really should be going home. Tomorrow the whole museum crew would be preparing for the grand opening that evening. She really needed to get some rest. But, she felt, she could be justifiably proud of what she had put together to prick public conscience in this day of renewed anti-Semitism throughout Germany and beyond. Taking a last look at the two triptychs and their contrasting messages, she went to her car and drove home. She hoped the critics would respond favorably to the message for tolerance of her *Degenerate Art Revisited* exhibition.

* * *

Agnes Sauer hated Essen from the first moment she arrived at the airport. The "Krupp" city seemed to be one noisy celebration of soccer, and the traffic was tangled accordingly. Her taxi took her past the city's historic coal mine with its inappropriate Bauhaus exterior. Of course she would have liked going to visit steel magnate Alfred Krupp's former villa, but her mission required her reconnoitering presence at the city's huge Folkwang Museum. She had specifically chosen one of the several nearby hotels as an inside joke that only she and Leo Lang could fully appreciate. It was the

Hotel on the Almastrasse. Delicious irony, considering the task at hand.

After unpacking in her modest room furnished with attractive blond wood bed, chair, and table, she walked the few blocks to the Museumplatz and began to size up the situation. In 2010 the immense U-shaped museum completed a spacious extension built right over one of the older buildings. Agnes circled completely around the vast museum, ending up at the front entrance again. This is certainly no building to attempt getting inside while it is closed, as had been the case in Basel, she thought. No, I'll have to do as I did in Tokyo: enter as a tourist.

Which is exactly what she did. Her capacious purse was subjected to X-ray, but otherwise no further security measures seemed to be in place. Of course there were security cameras overhead. Obviously she would have to use her boots again to carry her syringe and her long-bladed knife into the museum. She checked out the location of the nearest ladies restroom. It was near the gift shop. Good. And now to locate the Kokoschka. She entered the oldest wing of the museum first. French Impressionism filled the walls. Where was the Germanic art? She returned to the central lobby. One arm of the museum was roped off in front of two side screens. A sign on an easel in front read "Closed for Installation Purposes." A second sign on another easel read: "Opening tonight: *Degenerate Art Revisited*." Agnes looked beyond the sign and could see what looked like two triptychs, one agonized, the other saccharin.

"Is the opening this evening open to all, or is it restricted to museum members?" Agnes asked a nearby guard.

"Oh, it's only open to members. We're expecting an overflow tonight."

This was good news for Agnes. A crowded room was just what she needed once she had located her Kokoschka quarry. "And where is the membership office?"

"To the left of the gift shop," the helpful guard informed her. Agnes walked over to a small room next to the gift shop. A metal plaque on the door denoted it as being the *Mitgliedschaft* office. Using a false name and local address—Almastrasse—Agnes acquired a membership card, albeit at a healthy sum, valid for one year.

Now I will have to dress a bit more formally than I came prepared to do, she thought. But looking at photographs on the membership office wall, showing previous openings, she noted that the women were dressed in all manner of styles, ranging from low-necked gowns to blue jeans. All right, I'll wear my rhinestone-studded blue jeans, boots, and camera bag underneath my long silk kimono. Perfect. That decided, Agnes entered what was called the Deutsche Plakat Museum, where an extraordinary presentation of political posters from the late 1930s was on display. She had five hours to kill.

34

Megan and Desdemona were at the Basel Museum early the next morning, an hour before opening time. A smiling guard was waiting for them by the main entry door. He let them in, then called up to the Herr Direktor that his two guests had arrived. Hans appeared a few minutes later, opening his arms wide in cordial greeting. He led his two guests to the Böcklin room. Paintings of centaurs and mermaids playing in great waves of water were on one wall. On the opposite wall, unflanked by any other picture, was the image Desdemona had seen in her childhood and never forgotten, *The Isle of the Dead*.

"Oh! It is *magnificent!*" Desdemona exclaimed. "So haunting, so desolate, so sad. Yes it is assuredly *my* island, my Xenia. The same white water gate and seawall of rocks. Just look at that dense grove of cypress—exactly what is still there in the center of the island today. The same steep cliffs hemming in the island. And how sad, the mourning woman standing in the bow of the rowboat before that white draped casket. What a *mood* of melancholy it evokes.

"You know, Frau Dumba, some of the melancholy comes from Böcklin's own circumstances. His studio in Florence, where the first three versions were painted, was quite close to the English Cemetery, which is full of cypress trees, and where his infant daughter Maria was buried. As you now know, the title did not originate with the artist, although he later used it in correspondence with a patron. He himself referred to it as a 'dream image,' but it was certainly a dark dream image."

Desdemona, her eyes shining with pleasure, continued to drink in the painting before her.

"The American widow who visited the artist in his Florence studio was so struck by his half-completed first version," Megan said quietly, "that he painted a smaller one on wood for her, adding at her request the female figure and the coffin honoring her husband's death. This version on wood is the one now in the Metropolitan. Böcklin then went back to his original and added both mourning widow and coffin to it."

"You might be amazed as to who the owner of the third version, now in Berlin, was," said Hans, with a gleam in his eye.

"Who?"

Megan also asked, "Who?"

"Ach, something you do not know, Megan! Well it was painted three years later and *on copper* at the request of his dealer Fritz Gurlitt."

"Oh, yes, I've heard about him from Megan. He was the 'good' Gurlitt as opposed to the Munich Gurlitt, correct?"

"Correct," continued Hans with a smile. "Well, in nineteen-thirty-three this version was put up for sale and was bought by a very famous admirer of the artist. Can you guess who?"

"Don't tease us, Hans, who?"

"Adolf Hitler."

"No!" Both women exclaimed at once.

"Yes. He took it with him to his beloved Berghof but later it hung in the new Reich Chancellery in Berlin. That's why it's in the Berlin Alte Nationalgalerie now. And by the way, beginning with this version, Böcklin inscribed his own initials—A B—on one of the white burial chambers in the rocks on the right."

"And that's when he began referring to the picture as *Gräberinsel*—island of tombs—right?" Megan asked.

"Yes, quite right."

"Do you know, Hans, there was another famous man who adored Böcklin's *Isle of the Dead*. August Strindberg. His stage instructions for *The Ghost Sonata* specify that the play end with an image of it, accompanied by mournful music."

"I was not aware of that. Thank you for telling me, Megan. But now about the fourth version, which is only known in a black-and-white photograph. It was acquired by Baron Heinrich Thyssen and hung in his subsidiary bank at Berlin, where it is thought to have gone up in flames after a World War II bombing."

"*Thought to have been destroyed?*" Desdemona asked, hope gleaming in her eyes.

"Yes, *thought* to have," Hans smiled. "And don't think every museum director in the world hasn't tried to disprove this perception!"

"So, chronologically, the fifth and sixth versions still exist?" asked Desdemona.

"Yes, one was commissioned by the Leipzig Museum of Fine Arts and is still to be seen there. And the sixth one is safely in Geneva in the private collection of Victor Léman," Hans confirmed.

"Ah! Megan. We have three more Böcklin trips to make together!"

"Had we but world enough, and time ...." quoted Megan.

Desdemona smiled and answered: "But at my back I always hear Time's winged chariot hurrying near."

"Now how do you know Andrew Marvell?" Megan asked in surprise.

"I was taught *To His Coy Mistress* by my English tutor when I was a child."

To memorialize the moment Megan asked Hans if he would take an iPhone photo of them standing beside the Böcklin. "Anything for you two ladies," he smiled, taking her cellphone. Desdemona then took a photo of Megan and Hans in front of the painting.

"And now if you two ladies will walk over to the opposite wall with me, I have a surprise for you."

They turned and followed him obediently as he walked over to a small painting they had not noticed before. It, too, was by Böcklin and it, too, showed an islet. But there was nothing sepulchral about it, no marble tombs cut into slabs of sheer rock. No cloudy sky. No cypress trees in mourning. Instead the small rock of an island rose gently to a soft, crowning green hill below which stood or sat a group of ten young maidens in flowing robes, some of them holding torches. High above could be seen the miniscule figures of a man and woman watching the joyful scene. And below in the blue water a red-bearded Neptune frolicked with a sea nymph while swans paddled about them.

Hans beamed proudly as the women looked wonderingly at the work. "And he called it *Die Lebensinsel*—Isle of Life."

"I never, never knew that Böcklin had done such a thing" said Megan.

"You just never turned around," Hans said, "they have both belonged to our museum a very long time."

"After a few more minutes of watching the women admire the Böcklin, Hans looked at his wristwatch, then asked: "Now that the museum has opened, would you like to see our famous Kokoschka substitution?"

"Oh, yes, I've read that you did have it framed and have hung it in place of the missing one with an explanatory didactic," said Megan.

"It has almost doubled museum attendance, just as you predicted."

Hans led the two women to the room where the ersatz Kokoschka painting hung. It was already filled with people gawking at the work and pointing knowingly to the 'new woman' in the artist's arms. Yet another TV crew was setting up its cameras.

"And you are sure this is not a fake?" Desdemona asked suspiciously.

"Experts like Janette Killar have now come to see it and they have all authenticated it as genuine. Both Megan and I thought it was authentic when we first saw it."

After another half-hour, Desdemona returned to the Böcklin room while Megan went to Hans' office to report her meager Vienna gallery and antiquariat findings.

"And I, too, have really nothing to offer from my Zurich and Geneva sources," mourned Hans.

"It is contemptible the way art dealers are cutting up Kokoschka's *Dreaming Youths* book just to sell the plates individually," he added.

"And you've heard about the defacement of his Alma portrait in Tokyo?"

"Terrible, terrible. So far they have no idea why or by whom."

"And a woman was stabbed in the back as a diversion. Think of it! A *diversion!*"

"It seems as though the world is lighting up with Kokoschka thefts or vandalism—here in Basel, in Vienna, and now Tokyo. What is going on?"

At that moment Hans Tietze's secretary came running to him, a look of extreme concern distorting her face. "Herr Doktor, Herr Doktor! They've just stolen a Kokoschka from the Museum of Fine Arts in Boston!"

35

At his isolated house in Nyack, New York, Bruno Fichte had just received a long-awaited delivery from the three men whom the fanatical organization *Remove Nudity From Museums* had assigned to the confiscation job. Silently they removed the large painting from its crate. Few words were exchanged as Bruno paid the $15,000 charge for "home delivery." But he could not contain his curiosity.

"How did you do it?"

"Not difficult," said one of the men. "We used our own storage van and an auto painted like a New York state trooper's car. We intercepted the moving company's van on Highway Ninety at the turnoff for Lake Onondaga. Jack, over there, was dressed as an officer, and he went up to the stopped van on the service road and pointed a gun to the driver's head. He had him release the locks on the back door of the van. Then the two of us jumped from our van, removed this crate, loaded it, and took off down the service road. Jack followed us for about a mile, we both stopped, then he ditched his car and joined us in the van. It was a clean getaway. We passed several police cars speeding in the opposite direction. Yeah, a neat caper. Really awesome."

Bruno wondered whether he was in danger now that these three tough characters knew where his house was. But his fears were put to rest when Jack, apparently their leader, asked him to join them in a prayer of thanks to God for having removed one more piece of nudity from public gaze. The four men knelt and Bruno bowed his head, barely containing his hilarity. After solemn handshakes were exchanged, the men drove off. Bruno wouldn't be surprised if they were now singing hymns.

At last he could turn his full attention to Kokoschka's *Two Nudes: The Lovers.*

"Felix!" he called to his son who had remained upstairs during the delivery, a rifle pointed at the three men in case anything went wrong.

"Dad?"

"Come on down now. Everything's all right."

Felix clamored down the stairs and stopped in front of the canvas. "Golly! It's big!"

"It is also beautiful, son, truly beautiful. Perhaps his greatest portrait of Alma."

"If you say so. To me it's just embarrassing that they're standing there both naked."

"But they are not just standing there. They are moving in a slow dance, a slow love tango perhaps, she facing us, he with his back to us. Alma tenderly cups his head with her hand, turning his face back toward us. Just look at his poignant expression. Their arms, their bodies are interlocked. Forever, he seems to be saying."

"Yeah. But to me he looks real sad, worried you could say. And Alma looks like she's far away, dreaming or something."

"But that is it, don't you see? He is sad because he knows this moment won't last forever; she is thoughtful because she fears their relationship is too frenetic, too riddled with arguments, with accusations. They may be going along separate paths in spite of everything. That's why each is stepping in a different direction."

"Okay, but why do they have to be naked?"

"Because Oskar was trying, literally, to get down to the naked truth of their togetherness."

"Where are you gonna keep it, Dad? At our New York place?"

"Good Lord no! No one must ever know about this, Felix. The painting must stay here. It is safe here. No one knows I have this house in Nyack and we never have visitors out here. You may not like the portrait now, Felix, but this is your legacy. One you must keep safe and keep secret. Do you understand?"

"Okay, yes, Dad. But I still don't *like* the painting."

"You have to live with it. The day will come when you will appreciate it, you'll see. In the meantime, how does it feel to have a life-size portrait of your own great-great grandmother?"

"Good, Dad. Good. But I still wish she wasn't naked."

"Son, she is not really naked, she is *nude*. There is a huge difference."

Felix shook his head in silent exasperation. Sometimes his dad just didn't seem to be living in the real world.

36

Five hours in Essen. Agnes Sauer had spent three of them slowly touring the rest of the huge Folkwang museum, the name of which, she learned, derived from the meadow where the dead spent their afterlife, the *Fólkvangr*, ruled over by the Norse goddess Freyja. In the Deutsche Plakat Musem, which had been cleverly incorporated into the Folkwang, Agnes examined at length the radical political posters from the years of Hitler's rise to power. She kept her eye out for possible exits from the building other than the main entry.

Finally she walked back to her hotel and had dinner at a nearby Indian restaurant before changing into her costume for the evening. She removed a blonde wig from her suitcase and settled it tightly on her head. Gingerly she placed her loaded syringe in one boot and her long knife in the other, then she fastened her Gucci belt so that its empty pouch was along her back. Later, in the museum's ladies restroom, she would effect the transfer and wear the pouch in front. Just as she had done in Tokyo.

At a quarter to eight in the evening Agnes presented her new membership card, passed uneventfully through museum security, and entered the Folkwang Museum. People had been assembling there since seven o'clock and she could see that the triptych room was packed to the point of bursting. Just what she had hoped for. But impossible to get to the bathroom. The Kokoschka double portrait with Alma had to be either in that first room or in one of the rooms behind. How many rooms behind she did not know. But how to get through the crowd quickly? The answer came from an unexpected, sudden source.

A furor was taking place at the museum entryway. Voices were raised, there was shouting, and a couple of guards were rushing to the scene. There, bypassing security altogether, was a dense swarm of loud young men all dressed in black shirts with swastikas on their sleeves.

"Destroy degenerate art!" they were yelling. Hearing the ruckus, museum visitors from the back rooms crowded into the packed first room. Agnes was the only person pushing deeper into the room. Everybody else was trying to get out into the lobby to see what was going on. Neo-Nazis? Here in Essen?

Agnes elbowed her way deeper into the room. Now she caught a glimpse of one of the two triptychs she had spotted the day before. And to the right of it she saw the Kokoschka double portrait. She pushed her way to the front of the gesticulating images and, stooping down, managed to ease the syringe from her boot. In another second she had squirted its toxic contents directly on Alma's disagreeable face. Now all she had to do was mingle with the crowd as it surged toward the lobby. Another five minutes and she was out the door. Mission accomplished.

Agnes had to catch her breath. She decided to take a walk around the long exterior of the museum. But there was too much pandemonium to circle the building as police cars, sirens blaring, began to pull up. And now a television crew was on the scene. As she stood in the crowd watching events unfold she was suddenly knocked into by a powerful man who tried to wrest her purse away from her. "No you don't," she cried, holding on to it and giving him a punch in the face with her free hand. He backed away and disappeared in the crowd.

But now Agnes was unnerved. She had stayed calm during the Neo-Nazi invasion of the museum—glad of its unexpected cover—but now she was trembling all over. Certainly, right now she was not steady enough to walk back to the hotel. Finding an empty bench in the middle of the gathering crowd, she sank down in gratitude. The next thing she knew a microphone was thrust into her face, a bright floodlight aimed at her, and a TV reporter was asking her: "Did you *see* the riot?" "No, no, I didn't" Agnes lied weakly, vaguely aware that her face was being broadcast to the world. Thank god for the wig she was wearing. The reporter turned away and the flood light changed direction. After resting for another ten minutes on the bench, Agnes slowly walked back to the Alma Garni Hotel. Why did this successful caper not fill her with the same thrilling sense of accomplishment as had the Tokyo one?

31

Herr Moser of Moser's Art Security and Storage Company could hardly believe his eyes. The mail had brought him a lawyer's notice that he was being sued by one Karl Palkovska of Geneva for "negligence in the theft of fourteen crates of painter Oskar Kokoschka's personal belongings." As the nephew and heir of Olda Kokoschka, née Palkovska, the claimant was legal heir to the crates. He had learned about the robbery in the newspapers and now he was taking legal means to ensure that Moser's insurance company pay up for the loss involved.

But what *was* the loss involved? Moser only had the sizes of the fourteen crates on file, not the contents. The crates had never been opened. He would have to hire his own lawyer now, damn it! He realized that his company's own insurance policy would be unlikely to make good on a loss when it was unknown as to what the loss was. He was in a fix, and his mood became blacker by the minute.

***

After his father's early death, Karl Palkovska had lived on dole-outs from his aunt all his life. It had been she who had financed his studies at King's College London, but also she who told him what his two specialties should be—studio art and chemistry. He had done well in both, but could hardly make a living by painting, although he had proven adept at copying museum pieces. After several unsatisfactory jobs with pharmaceutical firms, resulting in dismissal because of missing drugs, he had made a fair living for himself as a pharmacologist at Harleys Pharmacy in South Kensington.

He was much more at home in Europe however—Prague had been his father's and Olda's hometown—and when his aunt asked him to help out with her ailing husband's business matters, he had not hesitated to join her at Villeneuve, renting an apartment in a nearby house. Twenty-three years old at the time, he much preferred Switzerland to his dreary life in London. After Kokoschka's death he had spent months helping Olda sort through the massive material of artworks, books, letters, and original works for the theater the artist-playwright had left behind. Karl had occasionally filched an item or two of interest probably only to him. He also developed a talent for accurately sketching each Kokoschka painting as it came to light. Photographs could tell only part of the story. The touch of the brush, the particular hue, here was where copying was at an advantage. And Olda was so complimentary of his prowess.

Eventually the holdings all went into the *Fondation à la mémoire de Oskar Kokoschka* founded by Olda in 1988 in the neighboring town of Vevey. When she died in 2004, Karl was named as the only beneficiary in her will. All of her Kokoschka material had, of course, gone to the Foundation. Recently a newly acquired painted fan by Kokoschka, done for Alma Mahler eons ago, had been stolen from the Foundation and the night watchman and his dog murdered. The inept local police could shed no light on the crime.

The fact that such a specific robbery occurred at his aunt's Foundation had started Karl thinking. The small inheritance he received from his father and then from his aunt had been large enough to enable him to move to Geneva, if he lived on a shoestring there. Still single at fifty-five, with receding hairline and yellow teeth, he adored the French-speaking city, had made a few friends there, and was thinking of marrying a local well-off widow. But he needed more money of his own as his tastes were becoming increasingly more and more costly. And his dependence on crystal meth didn't help.

38

What with the Neo-Nazi demonstration inside the museum and the crowds pushing to get out, Agnes Sauer had not been able to send her employer a cell phone photo of the damage she had inflicted on the Kokoschka double portrait the night before.

But this morning, after sleeping late, she decided to give Leo Lang a call. He answered almost immediately, sounding a bit anxious, and when he learned who it was he threw a fit. *"How could you have done such an idiotic thing? Why did you do it?"*

"What are you talking about? I don't understand."

"And *I* don't understand. Why didn't you eradicate the Kokoschka?"

"But I did, I did. I just wasn't able to e-mail you a site photo last night because there was too much bedlam going on around me."

"I've seen the site photo! Have you not turned on your television this morning?"

"No."

"Your stupid blunder is on all the news!"

"What blunder? I squirted acid on the painting from just one foot away."

"You sprayed the wrong painting!"

After Leo Lang slammed the phone down with a couple of expletives, Agnes turned on the television in her hotel room and waited for the top of the hour newscast. There it was, item number two after the continuing German economic gloom forecast: "Neo-Nazi intruders vandalize picture by Jewish painter." A close-up shot showed the damaged canvas. The woman's face was completely eradicated while the man's face had been left intact. The announcer's voice continued: "The object of the Neo-Nazi intruders was this double portrait of Karl and Leopoldine Wittgenstein by the Jewish painter Max Oppenheimer."

Max Oppenheimer? Who the hell was *he?* And where was the damn Kokoschka? The camera backed off and showed two triptychs with the Oppenheimer on the right and on the left…. Wait a minute, *that* has to be the Kokoschka over on the left beyond the second triptych. Well, no wonder she made a mistake in all that rush. She'd had just a few moments and it was only natural that she would think a double portrait of a man and a woman was the Kokoschka double portrait. An understandable mistake. Herr Lang should have been there to experience the crazy crowd and demonstrators, then he would understand why I presumed that was the Kokoschka. So I made an honest mistake. No need to bawl me out like that.

Agnes beamed up the Kokoschka painting on her laptop. It was painted with swirling brushstrokes and palette scrapings just like the Oppenheimer picture. And Alma was wearing a red dress similar in color and style to the one Leopoldine was wearing. No wonder it was confusing! Herr Lang should understand. I hope I haven't lost this lucrative client for good. Such a temper!

39

The call came in for Desdemona at the Les Trois Rois as she and Megan were dressing for dinner that evening.

"Gnädige Frau! It is Theo Papadakis. I hope I am not disturbing you but I have stupendous news."

"Yes, Theo, what is it?"

"May I inquire whether you are alone?"

"Yes, for the moment."

"My Berlin contact just called me. He has *found* Kokoschka's missing portrait of Constantine Christomanos!"

Desdemona took a deep breath and sat down. Could this be true? Was it possible that this link with Sisi still existed after all?

"Tell me what you know, Theo."

"First let me assure you that my source is the owner of one of Berlin's most prestigious galleries. The *Am schwarzen Schwan*. It is he—Helmut Haesslich—who, after many decades of research, has acquired the Kokoschka."

"Acquired? Was it in a private collection all this time?"

"No, quite the contrary. It has been in a basement cellar all these years since nineteen-eighteen. The cellar belonged to Kokoschka's art critic and publisher friend Herwarth Walden, and he left it there when he fled Hitler's henchmen and moved to Russia. Walden was a Jew and he was a Communist. Nevertheless, in nineteen-forty-one he died in a Soviet prison because the Stalinist regime considered his avant-garde ideas dangerous."

"So he never went back to Berlin to get the Christomanos portrait?"

"Never. Not while Hitler was in power."

"But how did your Herr Haesslich know that it was in a cellar?"

"He didn't. The people who recently bought the building the cellar was in had begun to modernize it, starting with the basement, and that's how they came across it. They weren't art people at all, had no idea what the painting was worth. They brought it to the *Am schwarzen Schwan* because they had heard of the gallery. And Herr Haesslich bought it from them."

"This is indeed momentous news. Were you told what condition it is in?"

"I'm afraid the condition is not the very best after basement storage of so many decades."

"I suppose it was rolled up?"

"Yes. That was common in those days. Now, because Herr Haesslich knew I was representing you, gnädige Frau, he gave me first offer on the portrait. Subject, of course, to your seeing it."

"Arrange it for day after tomorrow, please, for ten o'clock in the morning, Herr Papadakis. I shall fly to Berlin tomorrow."

"And I shall meet you at the gallery, gnädige Frau."

Megan, who had just entered Desdemona's room, looked at her friend inquiringly. Desdemona signaled her to keep silent, then concluded her conversation with Papadakis. She looked up at Megan, a broad smile on her face.

"What is it? What has happened?"

"You'll never believe this, Megan. I didn't at first, it seemed so improbable. Here, sit down."

Megan sat in the chair indicated and stared at her friend whose face was flushed with excitement.

"Constantine Christomanos's portrait by Kokoschka *has been found!*" Desdemona related the details of her phone call to Megan.

"In a cellar all those years? What must be the condition of it now?"

"That's what you are going to find out with me, Megan. I leave for Berlin tomorrow and you must come with me."

Megan did not need much persuasion. She loved Berlin and one of her favorite former students, Ehrengard von Gemmingen, a gifted cellist, lived there with her American physician husband and their two boys. It would be grand to see them again, especially since the boys were growing at such a fast pace.

She looked affectionately at the still-excited Desdemona. "Yes, I will come with you to Berlin. And do you realize, Desdemona, that while there we can go to the Alte Nationalgalerie and look at the copper Böcklin *Isle of the Dead*?

"Oh, my god!" Desdemona jumped up, throwing her hands up, "I hadn't even *thought* of that! We will have *two* errands in Berlin."

"Yes, but I really am going to have to call Dallas and arrange for my dog to be kept longer by the friend who is babysitting him for me."

"By all means do so, Megan. And then let us have a big celebration dinner at our own hotel's terrace restaurant. The Rhine is sparkling tonight!"

4O

It was one of Bruno Fichte's several personality quirks that he posted a blog every day. It was something he had originally learned to do from one of his techie students at Hunter College. A verbose man when alone online, and a contentious one, he was apt to argue with the whole world on points he considered obvious, overlooked, or important.

This evening in his Nyack house, after Felix had driven back to Manhattan, Bruno had a "conversation with a nude lady" online. Although she remained anonymous, a few cognoscenti who read the blog that night might have guessed he was talking about Alma Mahler. The description of the noble sad look that illuminated her countenance went on for several paragraphs as did Bruno's defense of her nudeness (heroic) versus nakedness (erotic). He refrained from mentioning the pose or that she was in the company of a male companion, but should a Kokoschka *Kenner*—a knower of Kokoschka—surf the net that evening or in the future, an educated guess might very well be made.

41

"Yes, you can sue for loss if you know exactly what the loss is," Karl Palkovska's Geneva lawyer had told him. Karl caught on instantly. From having helped his aunt Olda sort through Kokoschka's papers and artworks after his death, Karl had a good idea what the subject matter of paintings fitting into fourteen small crates might possibly be. He also had a fertile imagination. He had already shown the lawyer the will drawn up by Olda on her death bed, naming him heir to her small estate.

"What exactly the loss is? Oh, yes, of course, I know. The fact is that each crate contained a still life. They were unusual in that each was painted in a different city the artist had visited, from his youth to old age. So each one, therefore, contained a view of a city across the back plane with flowers or fruit pertinent to its climate in the front. Truly exceptional and original. It would be a tremendous loss if the paintings are not found."

"And yet I understand the police are getting nowhere in their investigation?"

"Yes, this is correct. That is why I am here. Restitution is what I mainly hope for, of course, but as the artworks—incredibly valuable—have not been found, I think it is high time to hold the storage company liable."

"Are you able to supply exact information and possibly *photographs* of the artworks?"

"Yes, I am," Karl said without batting an eye. He now knew what task was ahead of him but he also knew that he was up to it.

42

Agnes Sauer was not a person who gave up easily. An hour after her agitated phone call with Leo Lang, she was back inside the Folkwang Museum, her blonde wig in place and her tools tucked into the camera bag on her belt. She had placed an additional item in the canvas container.

Entering the first room of the now heavily attended *Degenerate Art Revisited* exhibition, thanks to the stir in the press, she passed by the Kokoschka double portrait feigning indifference and instead paused before one of the three colorful Chagall paintings on the opposite side of the room. An armed guard stood next to it. Agnes listened to a guide instruct her large tour group as they slowed down in front of it.

"We have posted an armed guard by these Chagalls because of the Neo-Nazi demonstration that took place here last night. The destruction of works by Jewish artists was their objective and, as you know, they did manage to harm one of them: a double portrait by the Viennese artist Max Oppenheimer." She pointed to the wall where the painting had hung.

Everyone looked at the empty spot on the wall. Agnes moved quietly into the next room which was full of works by Kandinsky and Marc. No guard on duty here. Quickly she produced the tool she needed first. It was a 120-decible keychain alarm.

Agnes chose her moment. Just as the tourist group was about to enter the room, she bent down, pushed the switch and in the same motion scuttled the screeching alarm across the floor to the far wall. "What's *that*?" she yelled, wheeling to join the entering group. The armed guard came running as did all the other occupants of the first room. Agnes moved backward into the oncoming phalanx of people and within seconds was facing the Kokoschka, syringe in hand. People passed her as they rushed into the inner room where the siren with its ungodly shriek was still blasting and people were yelling. Agnes pushed the plunger and two ounces of sulfuric acid hit Alma's face directly. Dare she take an iPhone photo? She did. And, in the chaos around her, she even had a chance to whip off her blonde wig, hiding it under her jacket arm.

A minute later a tall brunette woman took refuge in the museum gift shop, waiting for events to quiet down. She made several purchases and stuffed her wig down into the bottom of one of the two bags, both of which proclaimed in huge, cheerful font FOLKWANG MUSEUM ESSEN GIFT SHOP.

Agnes had a gift for Leo Lang.

43

On the plane to Berlin Megan and Desdemona spoke at greater length about the reluctant Empress Sisi.

"I suppose I'm drawn to her because I—and don't you laugh now—I look a bit like her. I have her height—five-foot, seven-and-a-half inches—her slenderness, and her long chestnut brown hair."

"However, I bet you don't wash your hair with cognac and eggs, nor do you go on starvation diets," Megan ventured to their mutual amusement.

"Nor do I have Sisi's bad teeth. But I do have her same melancholy spirit."

"And you are beautiful," Megan supplied.

Desdemona smiled self-depreciatingly, spreading her two cast-encased hands out in front of her. "Well some people think so. Did you know Sisi wrote poetry? That's another thing we have in common."

"No, I didn't know she was a poet. What sort of poems?"

"Oh, very sad, short ones. I know some of them by heart."

"Oh, do recite one!"

"All right. This is my favorite:

> I wander lonely in this world,
> Delight and life since long averted,
> No confidant to share my inner self,
> A matching soul never asserted."

"That is indeed touching. Especially when you consider how smothered she felt at court, with her bland husband, her domineering mother-in-law, and all those competitive ladies-in-waiting."

"But she never found a true confidant. That is Sisi's tragedy. Christomanos came the closest to it. After Sisi's death, he published moving memoirs of her."

Their talk turned to other matters.

"Do you know anything about Helmut Haesslich and his *Am schwarzen Schwan* gallery, Megan?"

"Not much. I have been told by one of my Vienna gallery contacts that it is amazing, almost suspicious even, how lucky Haesslich seems to be in locating artworks that disappeared in World War II."

Desdemona's face clouded over. "Well, couldn't that just be a case of envy?"

"Perhaps. After we've landed and checked into our hotel let's do a bit of Internet research on the gallery."

"Fine. But I'll have to be looking over your shoulder since the one thing I cannot seem to do with these dratted casts on is to type on my laptop."

"And it's all my fault," said Megan apologetically.

"On the contrary! Remember, you *saved my life*! If I weren't a touch deaf I might have heard that streetcar approaching, but as it was, I had no idea it was there."

"Didn't the doctor tell you that in three weeks you could have the casts off and switch to elastic, self-adhesive bandages?"

"Yes, and I cannot wait for that day!"

Desdemona had booked a suite again for them and this time in a hotel that Megan knew well from previous visits to Berlin, the Kempinski Hotel Bristol, right off the Kurfürstendamm. She could imagine some of Kirchner's splintery night stalkers wending their crowded, frenetic way down the Ku'damm.

"After lunch we have all afternoon and evening to ourselves before we meet with Herr Haesslich tomorrow," said Desdemona after they had unpacked. "Shall we first go see the Böcklin?"

"Absolutely! And I know a health food café—if it's still there—just across the street where we can get a quick lunch."

The health food café, Funk You, was in business no longer but a vegan café had taken its place. Although neither Megan nor Desdemona cared for the vegan idea they shared a vegan margherita pizza with a small light beer each.

And then they were off by taxi to the stately Alte Nationalgalerie on the Museum Island—speaking of islands, they laughed. The unavoidable equestrian statue of Friedrich Wilhelm IV greeted them as they mounted the steps to the museum entrance. Megan remembered where the Böcklin was and they made a beeline to it, passing wonderful works by Caspar David Friedrich and Adolph von Menzel.

"Oh!" But this one is so much whiter than the Basel one," Desdemona exclaimed. It was obvious that she was, at first glance, disappointed in the Berlin version.

"Keep looking," advised Megan.

"Well, the cliffs look more chalky and the cypress trees don't seem as tall. The water is bluer, less threatening, the sky too."

"What else do you see?"

"Ah ha! Now I see. The initials A B carved into the rocks on the right."

"I think it's just a case of your getting used to the lighter palette. The more you look the more the 'tomb island' as it's called sometimes, the more ghostly, literally sepulchral it appears. In some ways it comes across even more as an isle of the dead."

Some five minutes passed.

"Yes, now I'm beginning to like it. It is so like the image I saw in my childhood. Shall we take a selfie together in front of it?"

"Why not," Megan tried to smile engagingly at the guard who was watching them.

"*No flash!*"

"Right, no flash."

On the way back to the front entrance they stopped to admire Gottfried Schadow's poignant marble ensemble of the two Prussian princesses. There was always an admiring court of museum visitors milling around the charming young duo.

They exited the museum at a little after three in the afternoon. "We still have time for another museum," Megan said looking at her watch.

"Your choice," invited Desdemona.

"If you give *me* the choice I'd like to have us go pay homage to the statue of Käthe Kollwitz in the park of her old neighborhood out in Prenzlauer Berg. It's in what was called the Wörther Platz in Kollwitz's day, but is now, appropriately, named the Kollwitz Platz."

"Prenzlauer Berg? Wasn't that an impoverished section of Berlin in Kollwitz's time?"

"Yes. That's why her physician husband Karl settled the family there, to be near his patients. His calling was to minister to the poor."

"I see. So his patients naturally became *her* subject matter along with the neighborhood workers she depicted with such pathos."

"Yes, she thought such people were beautiful and, in her words, they 'had guts.'"

While they were on the subway out to Prenzlauer Berg, Megan told Desdemona about the funny adventure she had decades ago, when that district was still under Communist rule. She wanted to get into an apartment that overlooked the Wörther Platz so she could photograph the same balcony view that the artist had had for the fifty-two years she lived there. Kollwitz's corner apartment building had been destroyed during World War II so Megan had entered the apartment house next to it and worked her way up to the third floor. There she had the temerity to knock on the door of an apartment that probably gave out over the Kollwitz square. A child's voice answered from behind the door. Megan explained that she had come all the way from Texas to look out her window and see the same view that the famous artist Kollwitz had seen.

"Who is Kollwitz?"

"But you *live* on the street named after her!"

There was a long pause. Then Megan was asked if she were *really* from Texas, did she know what was going to happen next in the television series *Dallas*?

Megan quickly affected a Texas accent: "Natürlich!"

The door opened a crack and Megan could see a large window with balcony across the room facing the Kollwitz Platz. Inventing some astonishing incidents in J. R.'s devious dealings, she worked her way past the door and to the balcony. There she took photographs of the triangular park upon which seven streets converged—Kollwitz's microcosm in the macrocosm that was her Berlin. Larry Hagman had been responsible for the success of her mission that day.

When the two women arrived at the Kollwitz Platz, which now contained a children's playground, they went up to the bronze statue of Kollwitz seated. Just as had occurred on Megan's previous visit, children were climbing up the statue to sit on the lap of the motherly effigy of Germany's most committed pacifist. "*Nie wieder Krieg!*—Never again war!" had been her battle cry—she who had lost a son in World War I and a grandson in World War II. This had been an admonition—ignored by the world—that Megan had tried to convey to her classes across the decades.

It was restful being in a park and both women enjoyed relaxing for a time. Megan suggested that they visit the nearby Jewish Cemetery, most of which had escaped Nazi desecration in the 1938 November pogrom, and where the artist Max Liebermann and the composer Giacomo Meyerbeer were buried.

Then, at Megan's suggestion, they walked over to the nearby Senefelderplatz where an impressive marble statue of the inventor of lithography—one of Kollwitz's mediums—stood, Alois Senefelder. They saw the way his name on the statue was carved in mirror-reversed lettering, as it would look on a lithographic stone. One of the two sculpted children at the base of the statue was looking at the lettering with a hand mirror in which the name appeared correctly.

"How appropriate for a lithographer," Desdemona said admiringly.

"Yes, I thought you might enjoy this cheerful ensemble with its wry sense of humor."

When the two women returned to the Kempinski they went upstairs and tended to e-mail and phone calls for about an hour. Megan's sister Tina had e-mailed her a photo of Button with one of her own dogs, assuring her that all was well on the home front and that her friend Claire was taking good care of Button.

Desdemona suggested that they eat at Reinhard's im Kempinski, a very decent restaurant just downstairs and in the hotel. Megan was glad not to have any more walking to do. There were times when her body reminded her that she was eighty. Over dinner they studied the six different Böcklin *Isle of the Dead* images on Megan's laptop—the lost one in black and white only. Then they got down to discussing the exciting prospect of seeing Kokoschka's portrait of Constantine Christomanos the next morning, regardless of the poor state in which it most likely was. Desdemona's eyes sparkled with pleasure and anticipation.

"Tomorrow is *the* day!" she smiled as she bid Megan good night.

44

In his remote-from-Manhattan Nyack house over the weekend Bruno had spent most of his time sitting and communing with his new and greatest Alma treasure. What was the inner vision that saddened and held her eyes? Was she of two minds about Kokoschka? Had the newness of being so adored begun to wear? Had the artist's jealous tantrums finally dismayed her?

Bruno recalled what Alma had written about that jealousy: "I was not allowed to look at anyone or talk to anyone. He insulted all my visitors and was always lying in wait for me. My dresses had to be closed at my neck and wrists: I was not allowed to cross my legs when I sat down."

The longer Bruno studied the painting, the more protective he felt of his great-grandmother. And he had good reason to. Recent incidents of willful damage to images of Alma in various museums were being sensationalized in the press and on the Internet. The travesty in Tokyo, the willful damage in Essen, to say nothing of the actual kidnapping of *The Tempest* from Basel!

Of course, his own noble redirection of Boston's Alma was a daring act of protection. She must be kept safe from a mad, unpredictable world soiled by vandalism and theft.

But as Bruno pondered the Alma happenings, he began to see a master plan. Someone out there had a Kokoschka-like fanatical sense of revenge or possession and would stop at nothing to eradicate or acquire images of Alma. Too much had happened in the past ten days. And then there was that strange story of the thievery of fourteen crates of unidentified Kokoschka artworks from a Vienna storage vault. The robber must have known what was in those crates. Oh, how he, Bruno, would like to know what the contents were. Could they be more images of Alma? Sketchbooks, perhaps? From various galleries in Europe he had been able to acquire some dozen chalk drawings Kokoschka had made of them together and he knew the artist had created more than 400 images of her.

One of the online Vienna newspapers mentioned the fact that an American art historian and expert on Kokoschka was in Europe at the request of the Basel museum's director. Her name was Megan Crespi. This was a name Bruno instantly recognized. He had never met her but she was a person he automatically despised. How could you live in a godforsaken place like Texas and be an "authority" on things Viennese? It was he who was an authority on things Viennese and who had a blood connection with Wien. He looked Crespi up online and read she had taught at Columbia University for ten years before changing to Southern Methodist University where her mother had founded the Italian Department. Both she and her mother had attended Barnard College and Crespi had recently curated exhibitions for Canadian and East Coast museums. Okay, so she was keeping her hand in the game, but, still, really, *Texas*?

If she were making progress, however, with her Kokoschka investigation in Europe, actually *finding* things, then perhaps it would be wise to set Felix on her trail. Who knows what Crespi might turn up that could be useful to them? Yes, he would fly Felix to Vienna and have him drop in on the Christian M. Nebehay Antiquariat with which he had done business over the years. They could probably give him an idea of where she was. Who knows, perhaps even effect a face-to-face meeting?

45

Karl Palkovska had been able to create fourteen decent "Kokoschka" oil paintings in his home lab with the help of sketches he had made while helping his aunt Olda categorize Oskar's estate. Each wildly articulated picture showed just what he had described to his lawyer: a still life, usually of flowers, but sometimes of fruit, set in front of a different city landscape— Naples, Rabat, Prague, Vienna, Athens, Paris, London. He then took color photographs of them and mailed the impressive results to his lawyer. On the basis of Olda's will designating him as her heir and the photographs, Herr Moser of Vienna had been informed that he was being sued for the loss of fourteen Kokoschka crates of irreplaceable paintings.

Now, his lawyer informed Karl, he needed to show his photographs not only to the police, of course, but to various galleries, auction houses, and museums to ascertain the probable value of each painting. After consulting the latest auction catalogues, he had attached a tentative total value of seven million Euros. This was based on his own purview of the present-day market value, but it was entirely possible that Karl could document some of the individual paintings as being worth far more than the average sum of five-hundred-thousand Euros each.

Karl decided to act on his lawyer's advice and go to Vienna where the Kokoschka gallery action was. The hotel where he made reservations was on the same street as the first gallery he would visit. The hotel was named Römischer Kaiser.

46

The photo of the acid-eaten Alma face Agnes Sauer had e-mailed to Leo Lang from Essen's Folkwang Museum had made Leo's day. "Sorry I lost my temper with you yesterday," he texted her immediately. "Well-earned payment awaits you."

Leo sat down with his missions photograph album full of further Kokoschka depictions of Alma that might be possible targets. A number of European museums had examples of Kokoschka chalk drawings pertaining to Alma: these would be almost impossible to get at as they were seldom displayed. Better to continue singling out paintings belonging to museums. There were three Leo was particularly interested in eradicating: one in Berlin, one in Stuttgart, and the third in the small Austrian town of Klosterneuburg. All three were of the ersatz Alma: the life-size doll Kokoschka had had made and kept in his Dresden studio. The earlier Stuttgart image of 1919 showed a partially reclining Alma doll, the raised right hand supporting her head, the left lying along her hip with fingers splayed. She wore a blue dress that exposed both plump breasts. A dreamy expression animated the cloth face.

The 1922 Berlin version of the doll also included a prurient, clothed Kokoschka pointing to the naked doll's genitals. Both faced the viewer with solemn expressions that were neither challenging nor immodest.

But the most unusual of the Alma-doll paintings was the Klosterneuburg one. Kokoschka showed himself with an upright Alma, both clothed, in a dense pine forest, and with a small boy walking between them—the child Kokoschka had so desired to have with Alma. The fact that she had aborted the child she would have had by him never left the painter's mind.

The final pages of Leo Lang's mission album were devoted to the group of fans Kokoschka had painted for Alma. Their imagery dealt with the couple in fanciful situations and surrounds. Seven of the fans were in Hamburg's Museum für Kunst und Gewerbe. The eighth fan was the one recently stolen from the Kokoschka Foundation in Vevey.

Which Alma image to set his bulldog Agnes onto next? One of the Alma dolls or the seven fans in Hamburg? Leo decided on the fans although he was aware that difficulties possibly even greater than damaging single images were involved. He remembered that the fans were displayed along the wall of one of the museum corridors. They had been placed at eyelevel in a long, narrow, recessed, glass-protected shelf. The glass would have to be shattered without harming the fans. Was Agnes up to the challenge?

47

Tomorrow had come for Desdemona and Megan. Their appointment to see the Kokoschka portrait of Constantine Christomanos at Helmut Haesslich's gallery was for ten o'clock that morning. They had tea and breakfast in the room, dressed for the warm day outside—Megan wearing her Google glass—and took a taxi out to Charlottenburg Palace and the gallery *Am schwarzen Schwan* on Spandauer Damm, almost directly across from the Palace.

Exuding cloying charm, a smiling Helmut Haesslich stood up to greet them. At his side was Theo Papadakis, freshly arrived from Vienna, and the welcoming smile on his face one of possessive pride.

Desdemona stopped dead in her tracks as she spotted the picture on the wall behind Haesslich's desk. Megan stopped too, gazing in wonder at the painting.

"But, but you have one of the Böcklin Isles!" Desdemona exclaimed in disbelief.

"Ach, would that I did, Frau Dumba, but it is merely a copy of the Böcklin we have in our Alte Nationalgalerie here in Berlin. A very good copy, but a copy."

" Is it for sale? If you say yes, I buy it on the spot!"

Megan was a bit perturbed by Desdemona's spontaneous outburst. This eagerness to acquire might jack up the price of the Christomanos portrait, if she knew anything about gallery owners and their psychology of selling. Her fears were confirmed by Haesslich's answer.

"Oh, dear, no, I don't think so. It is my own private possession. A sort of memento mori, if you will. I commissioned the copy to be made—you notice, perhaps, that it is not as large as the one in our museum—for my own meditations."

"I too am desirous of a vanitas. Oh, dear Herr Haesslich, please do consider allowing me to buy it."

By now Megan was cringing at her friend's naïve display of vulnerability. She put a restraining arm on Desdemona's arm, but to little avail.

"Couldn't you just have another very fine copy made for yourself?"

"Unfortunately the elderly man who made this uncannily close copy died recently," Haesslich lied easily, "and I do not think there is another copyist in Germany who could repeat what has been done so successfully here."

Theo Papadakis, anxious to initiate the groundwork for the commission he was expecting, intervened. "Perhaps, gnädige Frau, we should turn our attention to the Kokoschka?"

Megan cheered silently, but she was sorry Desdemona had come across as such an impulse-buyer.

"Come with me to my back office," Haesslich invited the group. "I have not, of course, exhibited the Kokoschka since I promised Herr Papadakis, on behalf of you, his client, first refusal."

They walked to the back of the gallery and entered a spacious work room in which one wall was outfitted with painting racks filled to the bursting point. A large easel stood in front of them and a velvet cloth was draped over it.

"If you will stand back a little to get the best view, I shall show you the Kokoschka," directed Haesslich dramatically. He stared at his visitors for a moment, then whipped the cloth off the painting.

All three visitors exclaimed at once. Constantine Christomanos, his arms protectively around his torso and his face wrinkled with anxiety against a churning El Greco-like background, seemed to be physically present in the room. The canvas had been placed on stretchers and stood squarely on the easel.

Haesslich let the moment play out. "Yes," he said, "it is a most commanding portrait."

Papadakis added helpfully: "And the measurements, one-hundred by seventy-five centimeters, are the same as the artist's famous portrait of Karl Kraus, Vienna's carping feuilletoniste."

As she photographed the painting with her Google glass, Megan did the conversion to inches in her head: that's about forty inches high and thirty inches wide. Sounds right. Then, as she always did when looking at a painting for sale, she went right up to the canvas without asking, surreptitiously sniffed it—no discernable odor—then stepped quickly around to the back of the canvas to examine it. Looked like a close wove canvas of about a hundred years ago, she conjectured. Going to the front of the painting again, she noticed a few places where miniscule chips of paint were missing—most likely from its having been rolled for decades.

Desdemona had been in an ecstatic trance since her first look. The missing paint chips meant nothing to her. *This was Christomanos! This was Kokoschka's Christomanos!*

"Extraordinary!" she proclaimed.

Megan did not chime in. Something about the ensemble did not bond in her mind. What it was, she could not say, but it just seemed that there was, how to phrase it, there was *too much* Kokoschka standing before her on the easel.

48

Vienna was not new to Felix Fichte. He had been there many times with his father over the years. They had both had business cards printed indicating they were art history professors at Hunter College in New York. Bruno's were legitimate, Felix's not. These cards had proven very useful for getting into private collections and print rooms of museums. Unlike his father, however, Felix didn't care about staying at the fancy Hotel Sacher opposite the Opera House. He preferred the modest but comfortable Pension Suzanne on the Walfischgasse, also near the Opera House, but also much closer to the kind of late night life he preferred. When he checked in at nine that morning Felix noticed that the pension now boasted of having Freud's consulting couch in its lobby. Not likely, Felix thought, but a neat idea, for sure. Up in his room he stuffed a few sheets of paper into a blank envelope, sealed it, then wrote in particularly large hand, "Frau Doktor Professor Megan Crespi." He was now equipped to make the rounds of inner city hotels enquiring for her, pretending he had an urgent document she must receive.

He decided to try his father's Sacher Hotel first and was informed at the reception desk that there was no Frau Doktor Megan Crespi staying there. Then he walked down the Ring to the Hotel Bristol, same answer. Maybe the Texas woman stayed in a more modest hotel. Wouldn't it be ironic if she was at his own pension? He doubled back and asked the receptionist. No such person. Felix decided to work his way down hotels off the Kärntner Strasse, left and right, until he got to the Stefanskirche. Leaving the Ring back by the Opera House, he walked over to the Annagasse first. At Number 7 was the Mailberger Hof. No luck there. He walked further down the street to Number 16 and went up to the reception desk, holding his envelope out in front of him. Same routine. "I have an important document to deliver for Professor Doktor Megan Crespi."

The Römischer Kaiser desk clerk looked at him with interest. "You have missed her. She was here and she is returning in a couple of days, but right now she is out of the country—Basel and Berlin, I think. Shall I hold the envelope for her?" The woman smiled at Felix.

"Oh, that's all right. I'll come back. It's a dated document, so I'll have to amend it for the day she's back." Pleased with his instant prevarication, he went back to his hotel and e-mailed his father the good news. He had found Crespi's hotel. She was out of the country at present but would be returning to the hotel in a few days. Anything he should do in the meantime?

Since it was eleven in the morning there in Vienna and five in the morning in New York, Felix knew his father wouldn't have a chance to respond to his e-mail until later. He decided to work out at a fitness place he knew of, the Holmes Place Fitness Club at Wagramer Strasse 17. In the UNO City. An old timer at the club actually remembered him. Felix attacked the barbells for some thirty minutes, then jogged around the club's outdoor track for another thirty minutes. He finished by doing aerobic exercises in the small indoor pool maintained by the club. But the best part was yet to come—a fifteen-minute massage by a young woman with powerful hands. He tried to interest her in a date that evening but got nowhere.

Refreshed and ready for action Felix checked his cellphone. There was a terse text from his father. "Call." Felix left the building and called his father from the street.

"First, you've done very well locating Crespi's hotel, and it's our luck that she will be returning to Vienna. You've got to keep close watch on that hotel."

"Yeah, Dad. For sure."

"Secondly, I want you to scan very closely each day's papers from Vienna, Basel, Essen and Tokyo's English edition online to see if there are any arrests or breaks concerning the Alma damages and Basel theft. I'll be doing the same thing from here, but four eyes are better than two."

"Okay. Will do."

"Thirdly, start chatting up different gallery owners to see if you can get any enlightenment concerning how the police are doing on that fourteen crate theft.

"Yup. Anything else, Dad?"

"Yes. One more thing. And this is important. Go to the Albertina Museum and ask to see Kokoschka drawings from nineteen-twelve through nineteen-nineteen. Don't mention Alma's name, but let's see how easy or difficult it is to for you to get access to them. Some thirty years ago I had them all brought out to me and laid on one of the tables for me to go through."

"Got it. I'll call you tonight, then."

"And if you have any news before then be sure to text me, all right?"

"Okay."

Felix took a streetcar back to the Pension Suzanne and flung himself on his bed for a half hour. Then putting on his sport jacket to "dress up," he walked over past the Opera House to the Albertina, Vienna's great museum devoted to the graphic arts and possessor of one of the greatest collections in the world.

On the basis of his business card, he was admitted to the Studiensaal where he filled out and submitted his request to see Kokoschka drawings and lithographs from 1912 through 1919. He took a seat at one of the long tables and waited. He noticed that there were several other people at different tables around the long room, all of them scrutinizing monitors in front of them and transferring information onto laptops. When Felix's monitor was uploaded with his requested material he noted that the images were impeccably scanned. He could zoom in on a pencil stroke. He went through the motions for about twenty minutes, then closed down his monitor and stood up. Enough of museums for one day.

He had discovered what his father wanted him to find out: there was easy enough access to Kokoschka images, but only on monitors, not the originals, as his father had remembered. And in a room full of other people and at least one guard. He hoped this would deter anyone hell bent on damaging Alma-related imagery.

Back on the street again, Felix decided to go to the nearest gallery, the Christian M. Nebehay Antiquariat on the Annagasse right next to Megan Crespi's hotel, to see what he might learn about any police developments in the fourteen Kokoschka crates robbery.

"Well! What are you doing in Vienna?" asked the gallery's director Dr. Hanskarl Klug, who happened to see Felix enter his shop. "And how is your father?"

The Fichtes, both father and son, had been regular customers of the Nebehay Antiquariat and Dr. Klug was well aware of their blood tie to Alma Mahler. He had notified them of any number of graphic works relating to Alma and they had been excellent customers over the years. He much preferred the sophisticated father to his somewhat coarse son.

"My dad is fine, he just couldn't come this time. But he says hi." Felix was to the point. "He wants me to find out from you if the police have made any progress in finding out who stole the fourteen Kokoschka crates and what was in them."

"We'd *all* like to know that! But no, there has been no further progress on the case, at least none that I know of."

"And they haven't even been able to find out *what* was in the crates? Wouldn't you think there was a manifest of some sort?"

"What has been established is that they were deposited by the painter himself, decades ago, and that the firm has been receiving yearly payments from the artist's estate ever since. But the storage company—Moser by name—claims that no list of contents had ever been submitted by the artist. Makes finding out the contents of the crates even harder."

"I guess the art world will just have to wait for a bunch of Kokoschka works to suddenly appear on the market."

"Unless they were stolen for a private collector. And in that case it may be many, many decades before they are heard of again."

"Well, so what else is going on in the Kokoschka world?"

"Of course you've heard about the terrible vandalizing in Essen and Tokyo, and the downright thefts in Basel and Vevey."

Felix could feel his ears burn at the mention of the town Vevey, where he had so recently liberated the Alma fan for his father's collection.

"Yes, I've been reading about all that. Do people think it was done by one person or several?" he asked with vested interest.

"General consensus is that the European incidents were by one and the same person. But the Tokyo damage perhaps not. Who knows! Nevertheless this spate of Kokoschka capers or whatever you want to call them, has made one of my clients extremely edgy. She has an extensive collection of early allegories by the artist, and is afraid her house, where they all hang, might become the next target."

"Oh? Who is that?"

"Surely you can guess? She is one of the doyennes of the European art world."

"I think I know who you mean, but can the old gal still be alive? How old is she now, a hundred?

"She will be one-hundred-and-three next week."

"Come on! You're kidding?"

"No, not at all. And I would have informed your father about her very soon. Except for a few minor pieces which she is placing with me, she is about to give her entire collection of Kokoschka allegories to her hometown and the Wien Museum."

"Margareta Nussbaum! One-hundred-and-three! And about to give away all those Kokoschkas?"

"Yes, it's true. And the Berlin museums are furious at her decision to leave her collection to Vienna, since she has lived in Berlin for so many decades now."

"Is that where she got to know Kokoschka?"

"No, no. They met in London during World War II and she bought many of her artworks directly from him. Mostly allegories. She also owns the large wall mural at Haus Mahler."

"Does the old gal still have her daily Bloody Mary?"

"That, and wine later."

"Secret of long life, I guess."

"Possibly."

"So do you think I should go visit her?"

Dr. Klug looked at Felix with a mixture of surprise and contempt. "Absolutely not, Felix! Your father might, but you, you don't have the, how can I put it, the *class*."

"Hell, that's exactly what my dad says! Okay, okay, I just wanted to anticipate what I think he might want me to do next."

"I truly doubt that Frau Nussbaum would be interested even in seeing your father right now, given all the recent sensational Kokoschka happenings. And be aware, please, and this goes for your father as well, that my gallery is the exclusive purveyor of works she might wish to sell."

"Yeah. Well thank you, Mr. Klug. I guess I'll be going now."

"And it's *Doctor* Klug."

"Oh, yeah, well, whatever."

Back at the Pension Suzanne, Felix called his father and related the events of the day. He left out Hanskarl Klug's assessment of his suitability to call on Frau Nussbaum. He was surprised to hear his father become so interested in the pending Margareta Nussbaum gift to the Wien Museum.

"Don't you realize, boy? This means that Kokoschka's Haus Mahler fireplace frieze—with Alma in it—might soon be on public display in Vienna? And therefore in danger!"

49

Helmut Haesslich watched Frau Dumba in silence. She was still staring at Kokoschka's portrait and it was obvious she was enthralled by what she saw.

Not so with her companion, an older woman who had had the nerve to go right up to the portrait, sniffing at it like a dog. She even stepped around to the back of the painting, looking at the canvas. Who was she? A restorer, perhaps? Her accent in German sounded Italian and she had been introduced as Doktor Megan Crespi. It was clear that Frau Dumba was taken in by the "Kokoschka." What was not clear was whether or not Frau Crespi was.

At last Frau Dumba spoke. "And what is your asking price, Herr Haesslich?"

Without hesitation Haesslich answered: "We have done the research on present prices for early Kokoschka works. As you know they are extremely rare to come by and this is a unique opportunity. The gallery can go no lower than one hundred and twenty-nine million Euros."

Megan shot Desdemona a warning glance but she took no note of it. Instead, Desdemona looked questioningly at Papadakis who responded with an enthusiastic nod of the head.

"That seems a correct figure," he said to her. "I too have explored the market for like pictures and they are exceedingly difficult to find."

Now Desdemona looked at Megan who, unbeknownst to any of them, had been taking Google glass photographs of the work. Megan cleared her throat. "Um, there is some serious restoration work to be done, I think, before acquisition of the painting can be considered seriously."

"But naturally the gallery's price includes restoration," said Haesslich, improvising right on the heels of Megan's comment.

"Well in that case, and upon Doktor Crespi's approval of the restoration work, I am inclined to meet your price, *provided* you include the Böcklin."

Haesslich looked at Megan Crespi with new interest. Who *was* she? Did she work for a museum? Her next remark was infuriating and caused him some alarm.

"I also think it would be worth your while, Desdemona, to bring over the Kokoschka expert Janette Killar so she can take a look at the painting."

"Oh, no. I don't believe that is necessary, Megan. I know, I *feel* this portrait is by Kokoschka."

"But…" Megan was interrupted by Papadakis.

"If you compare the painting with Killar's photograph of it in her oeuvre catalogue, it is absolutely identical."

"Yes, but…" Haesslich interrupted Megan this time.

"It's the brushwork that counts. That you cannot determine in a black and white photo. As you can see, the handling of the brush and the occasional use of a spatula are pure Kokoschka for anyone who knows his early work." Haesslich looked meaningfully at Megan as he said this.

Desdemona turned to Haesslich. "Your price of one hundred and twenty-nine million Euros will be acceptable to me. I will not haggle as long as you have the restoration work done promptly—I leave for Greece next week—and *if* you include the lovely Böcklin that hangs on your front wall."

Megan was flabbergasted. Desdemona was far too impetuous. And she said she wasn't haggling but she was. She understood what having the portrait of Sisi's Greek tutor meant to Desdemona, that it was a unique link with the Empress Sisi for her. But Megan could not understand her friend's imprudent haste to acquire the Böcklin copy. Haesslich's next words only made her more suspicious of the dealer.

"All right, Frau Dumba. The Böcklin *Isle of the Dead* copy, and please realize it is only a copy, can be part of the price. Although I shall miss it terribly. And I certainly do not mean to rush you, Frau Dumba, but I do have a prominent client who has an enduring interest in all things Kokoschka. I have not notified her of this Christomanos discovery yet, but I do feel obligated to do so if we have not come to an agreement today."

"Ah, but we *have* come to an agreement, Herr Haesslich, so long as the restoration is conducted right away and, of course, Doktor Crespi and I have the opportunity to pass on the quality of the restoration."

"But of course you will have the final word about the quality of the restoration," Haesslich said, regretting every word. What if this skinny woman gets it into her head that the restoration is unacceptable? What if her companion, the old hag in dark glasses, talks her out of buying the thing?

"I must tell you that I will have to offer this stunning portrait to my other client quite soon, restoration or not."

"I'm curious. Might I ask, Herr Haesslich, who your other potential client is?" asked Desdemona.

Haesslich drew himself up with great dignity. "Madam, I cannot betray the confidentiality of a client, just as I would not betray yours."

"Oh, of course. I understand. That was thoughtless of me. I was merely curious, that's all." Desdemona blushed.

Megan could hardly wait to get her friend alone. She certainly needed a few pointers in what could be called gallery etiquette, to say nothing of caution when considering buying. Desdemona was charming in her enthusiasm, but Megan could see how she might easily be taken advantage of. And something about this dramatic Kokoschka, admittedly with *his* style of brush application, just didn't feel right.

Papadakis left the gallery with the two women. When they had walked a few steps down the street he held up his hand, motioning the women to stop.

"*I* can tell you who the mystery client is, gnädige Frau," he said excitedly, turning to Desdemona. He had decided to apply pressure for what he hoped would be a quick sale with no reservations about restoration defects.

"Who?"

"*Frau Margareta Nussbaum. And she lives right here in Berlin.*"

50

Armed with color photographs of the fourteen "Kokoschka" still lifes he had creatively brought into being back in Geneva, Karl Palkovska exited his hotel on the Annagasse and walked down to the Christian M. Nebehay Antiquariat.

He was greeted by a smiling receptionist who, when Karl said he had photographs of some Kokoschka works to show to the resident expert, motioned him to a seat at a small table and went in search of her boss. Within a few seconds Dr. Hanskarl Klug appeared and took a chair opposite Karl.

"So! You have something to show me, I am told."

"Yes. I thought I would come to you first as you represent Vienna's most esteemed gallery and antiquariat."

"Indeed, that is what people say."

"Let me introduce myself. I am Karl Palkovska, nephew of Kokoschka's wife Olda Kokoschka-Palkovska. I am her legal heir. When I learned that fourteen crates deposited by Kokoschka decades ago had been stolen here in Vienna, I thought I had better come and help the police sort out things."

"Ah. You have visited with them?"

"No, not yet. I wanted to speak with you first. And to show you photographs of what was in those crates. I would appreciate your giving me an evaluation of what you think these works would now command on the open market so that I can work with the insurance company representing the Moser storage vaults from which the crates were stolen. And, of course, show them to the police as well."

Karl Palkovska laid out the photographs in front of Dr. Klug, who did not hide his growing astonishment.

"But these are remarkable. *Fourteen* unknown still lifes with cityscapes as backgrounds. I am certain they are not in Killar's oeuvre catalogue. But how is it that these paintings are not in the Kokoschka Foundation at Vevey?"

"Because they were no longer with Kokoschka when he moved to Switzerland with my aunt in ninety-fifty-three. He did not wish to sell them because, as you can see, they represented his travels, cities where important events had transpired for him. So he placed them in storage. I doubt that my aunt ever gave them much thought. It is quite likely that she even forgot about their existence, she had so much on her hands when Uncle Oskar died. I helped her sort through the estate, by the way. Certainly when she opened the Kokoschka Foundation thirty-five years later, she made no mention of them."

"Well, it is good that you are now making the contents of the stolen crates public to the art world and to the police. That way no legitimate business would sell or auction the works, and no honest collector would pay for them. Whoever stole the artworks would be stuck with them. This is not to say there would not be buyers for these works. But that is where the underworld of art begins and the police have their task in front of them."

"Makes me shiver. But tell me, Doktor Klug, what do you think chances are that the police will find the thieves who stole the crates? And will they find the crates?"

"Impossible to predict. But with *fourteen* paintings on their hands, you'd think they would make some mistake when trying to palm them off, sell them, hide them."

"Well, it's Moser's insurance company that will have to deal with that, when and if it happens. But in the meantime I would very much appreciate you telling me just what you think each of these still lifes might be worth."

"I would have to see them in the flesh, of course, to give you a true figure, but merely on the strength of these photographs, I would imagine each one to be worth roughly in the neighborhood of seven-hundred thousand Euros each."

Karl managed to suppress his glee. This was twenty thousand more Euros more than his lawyer had estimated.

51

Once again Agnes Sauer wondered why her host and employer Leo Lang had commissioned a copy of the life-size Alma doll be made for his solitary Vienna villa. They were seated at the table in his private study looking at his missions album and the gynoid-Alma seemed to be watching them. She had been moved from the straight-backed chair in the corner of the study to his desk. Her hands were no longer tied together in front of her; they lay palms up on the desk, a book placed between them. Agnes wished she had the nerve to see what the book was. But Leo, his album open to photographs of the seven fans on display at Hamburg's Museum für Kunst und Gewerbe was talking to her eagerly.

"Your main problem will be gaining access to the museum at night. There is always something going on at the Steintorplatz, since it's so close to the south railroad station. And I don't think you could get to the fans in the daytime—too many visitors during museum hours. I recommend you give yourself plenty of time during the day to locate and study the fan layout as well as evaluating the security setup as much as you can."

"Let's see if we can find the ground plan on the Internet," Agnes suggested, pulling a small laptop out of her purse.

A minute later they were staring at photographs and the closed-E-shaped ground plan of the huge old four-story building which had been badly damaged during World War II but totally restored since. A number of glass panels gave out onto a very large inner courtyard which was divided into two smaller ones by a broad, three-level crossing topped by a skylight in the center. A modern staircase as well as an elevator gave access to the three floors of exhibits.

"As best as I can recall," said Leo, "the fans are on the top floor of the crossing."

"If they are still there it looks as if entry might be made via the skylight."

"Ah ha, I see. Looks encouraging."

"What are some of your other Alma missions," Agnes asked, wondering how long the golden crop of Leo's commissions might be harvested.

"See this copy of Kokoschka's Alma doll here at my desk?"

"I certainly do. She's rather hard to ignore."

"Well, I've spoken with you before about the three outlandish images of the doll painted by Kokoschka. I mean to have them demolished."

"So, not just the face, as before, but the whole picture?"

"Yes. One of them, the doll in a blue dress about which I told you, is in Stuttgart another, the one of him dressed with the naked doll, is in Berlin. And the third one is in Klosterneuburg."

"Yes, I remember your telling me about them and the 'pudendum.' All three doll pictures sound doable but I gather you first want me to get the seven fans."

"Yes, and, this is important, *do not destroy them*. Bring them to me. I want to review their disgusting imagery before I set them on fire. Who knows, I might even cut out the features of my grandfather and save them, even if they do show him crazed by that witch of a woman!"

Agnes gave one last look at the Alma doll as she left Leo's study. The man himself was a study. Why did he live with the Alma doll—and that's what he was doing actually—if he so hated Kokoschka's images of her? After all the artist was responsible for commissioning the doll in Alma's image, "including all orifices."

Perhaps that was the answer. Leo Lang wanted to be able to do to his doll what Oskar Kokoschka had done to the original doll. Penetration. For one, the act would be done with love, for the other, an act of pure hatred. Rape, if you will. Yes, Leo Lang who lived alone with his life-size doll was indeed a madman.

52

Megan was relieved when Theo Papadakis left her and Desdemona's company after they exited the *Am schwarzen Schwan* gallery. "It is necessary that I return to Vienna immediately," he had told them, wringing his hands with urgency.

"I know a lovely Russian tea room just up the street to the right of Charlottenburg Palace," said Megan.

"Oh, I am so excited that it would be wonderful to quiet down with a lovely cup of tea."

"This place even has samovars and, of course, it won't be cups but glasses of tea. The pastries are really good too."

Once the women were seated and had selected the pastries offered them, Desdemona turned to Megan and asked: "Do you know who Margareta Nussbaum is? My potential rival?"

"I do. In fact I know her and would like to pay her a visit while we're here in Berlin. She is an absolute dear of a person and extremely sage. At one-hundred-and-three she has all her wits about her. She's confined to a wheelchair now and is very hard of hearing, but otherwise she's as fit as you or I."

"Tell me about her."

"Well, she worked as a journalist in her early years and didn't marry until she was thirty-seven, when she met one of the Thyssen steel works family members. They were both passionate about collecting art. He left her an extremely wealthy widow when he died, in the seventies, and she has continued collecting. She has a special interest in Klimt, Schiele, and Kokoschka. That's why I know her. To avoid public attention she goes by her maiden name, Nussbaum."

"If you visit her do you think I might come along?"

"Frankly, I am not sure. You two are potential rivals, as Haesslich took such delight in pointing out."

"Oh, dear, there I go being indiscreet again."

"Never mind about that, Desdemona. What we really should discuss now is whether or not the Kokoschka Christomanos is genuine."

"Oh, Megan, *please* don't tell me that you have doubts about it."

"I can only tell you quite frankly that I just don't feel right about it. Something doesn't quite jell."

"But Papadakis was so enthusiastic about the painting!"

"How long has Papadakis been your agent?"

"For years and years. He has managed to turn up so much from the original Dumba household—books, paintings, including Klimt's *Schubert at the Piano*, and even the old Bösendorfer piano you played at my flat."

"Even so, I would advise that you not let his enthusiasm blur your judgment."

"But, Megan, I really must have the Christomanos."

"You *do* care about its being by Kokoschka, don't you?"

"Good god! When you put it in *those* terms, yes, of course, I do."

"Well, then here is my advice. Let the restoration be done, but in the meantime see if you can fly Janette Killar over to authenticate the painting. Agreed?"

"All right. I'll have my secretary contact her immediately."

"You could always offer to buy the Christomanos as an acknowledged 'painting in the style of Kokoschka,' just as you've agreed to purchase the Böcklin copy."

"But do you think Haesslich would agree to such a proposal?"

"That I can't predict." Megan poured out a second glass of hot tea for them both. The two women sat silently for a few minutes.

"I'll tell you what," Megan said at last, taking out her iPhone. I'm going to give Margareta Nussbaum a call and see if we can both visit her, provided we tell her about the Christomanos portrait for sale." Megan knew how stable a person Margareta was and that she would by nature be extremely dubious that the lost Kokoschka portrait of Christomanos had miraculously surfaced. Her doubts might get through to Desdemona in a way she, Megan, was unable to.

Desdemona eagerly agreed and Megan made the call. The secretary she spoke with put her on hold while she informed Frau Nussbaum who was calling. Then she heard several background noises as the phone was handed to an eager Margareta who immediately said: "Megan, dear. Where are you?"

"I'm here in Berlin. Only for a short time, but I'd love to come out and see you."

"Can you come *now*?"

"Yes, I can. But I'm with a friend, an art collecting friend. May I bring her with me?"

"What did you say?"

Megan raised her voice. "I said yes, I can come now. But may I bring my friend with me? Like you she is an art collector, and of the same period—Klimt, Schiele, Kokoschka."

"Yes, yes. Bring your friend. Can you both come this afternoon, say four o'clock?"

"Wonderful! We will come at four." Megan hung up and nodded to Desdemona. "We can both come."

"Where does she live?"

"Ah, you'll like it. She lives in Babelsberg. We can take the S Bahn out there and get off at Griebnitzsee. That's what I did before. Then her villa is not too far away, although we should definitely take a taxi there. We ought to make up a song to sing to her, now that she's reached one-hundred and three. To the tune of Honey Bun from *South Pacific*. She thought for a moment. Then sang:

A hundred-and-three
Golly gee,
She is older than you or me,
She's an inspiration to us all.

Desdemona laughed appreciatively, then said: "Babelsberg. Babelsberg. Now why does that ring a bell?"

"Probably because the old UFA film studios were out there. It's the oldest big movie studio in the world. That's where Marlene Dietrich made *The Blue Angel* and Fritz Lang's *Metropolis* was filmed. And more recently, *The Grand Budapest Hotel*."

"Oh, of course. But I remember it for its dark days during Nazi times when Goebbels took over and began making propaganda films by the hundreds."

"Yes, and Leni Riefenstahl's super propaganda spectacle *Triumph of the Will*. I used to show that one to my students."

"To your students?"

"I wanted them to see how Nazi Germany utilized even sports to vaunt itself in the minds of the impressionable. I devoted an entire lecture to the rise and fall of Hitler, using his degenerate art show as the art history lead in. You have to remember, these younger generations have little knowledge of recent history."

"I feel that way about children growing up in Austria these days. They should learn about their country's embracement of Hitler and the Third Reich."

Megan looked sharply at Desdemona. This was the first time she'd sounded as though she had a level head on her shoulders since she lost it over the suspicious Kokoschka portrait.

53

In New York, Bruno Fichte-Mahler was beside himself with concern. His apprehension was over the possibility that Kokoschka's Haus Mahler frieze was destined for the Wien Museum where it would no doubt be put on public display. He had a poor color reproduction of the seven-foot-long, two-foot high work. On the far left a white-gowned Alma gestured upward, urging Kokoschka, engulfed by flames and specters of death, to follow her heavenward.

Bruno also knew who the present owner of the mural was. Margareta Nussbaum. A Viennese by birth, she had lived in London for a period during the war and finally settled in Berlin's affluent outlying suburb Babelsberg. Her house had been written up in *Der Spiegel* once and he had kept the magazine in his Alma file. Bruno had tried contacting the old lady once, asking if he might view the Kokoschka works in her collection. Her letter back was most gracious but she turned him down, saying she was a recluse and treasured her privacy. He wrote her again, revealing his blood relationship to Alma Mahler—he was her great-grandson—and his understandable desire to see any images of his great-grandmother that might be in her collection. This time he received no answer at all.

Chagrined, Bruno had put the rejection on the back burner for many years, but perhaps now, with Felix in Europe and Nussbaum's desire to leave her artwork to the Wien Museum, a bold maneuver needed to be initiated. After all, Frau Nussbaum must be a hundred or so years old by now. She might go to her reward any day. Time was of the essence.

When Felix next reported in by phone, Bruno asked if he had been able to get any idea of when Crespi was expected back in Wien.

"I've checked the Römischer Kaiser every afternoon, but so far I've pulled a blank, Dad."

"And the hotel management can't give you any information about her projected return date?"

"Nope."

"And you say Dr. Klug told you Margareta Nussbaum is about to donate her collection to the Wien Museum?"

"That's right, Dad."

"All right. Now here is what I want you to do, Felix. Buy a wide duffle bag; it doesn't have to be longer than two feet and a couple of inches, just plenty wide, say two and a half feet, then take a flight to Berlin and go out to Babelsberg where Margareta Nussbaum lives. Stay at the Lili Marleen Hotel; it's near her villa which is at the edge of Park Babelsberg. Write the address down: Mühlenstrasse seventeen. Got it?"

"Yeah, Dad."

"Now I want you to take a look at the house from every angle and without your being noticed. All right?"

"Sure, Dad."

"Really case it out. See how many people go in and out; staff and visitors."

"What for, Dad?"

"Son, I want you to figure out how to enter the house without being seen. There could most likely be a burglar alarm if you enter at night, so you would have to contend with that. But once in the house you're to go straight to the 'long gallery' as the *Der Spiegel* article called it. Go directly to the Kokoschka frieze—in all likelihood it is backed by canvas—and slice out the image of Alma. She's on the left, you can't miss her, but I'll e-mail you a photo. You'll have to roll it up and put it in your duffle bag. Bring it back to Vienna with you and keep it under your bed at your hotel until you fly back home. Got that?"

"Yeah, Dad. This sounds real exciting."

"Never mind about the excitement. You're going to have to keep a cool head, boy. Just as you did at Vevey. And remember, Felix, this is for the *family*. We have to keep as many Alma images as we can save from public scrutiny."

"I'll go buy that duffle bag right now, Dad."

"Excellent. And call me after you've checked into your hotel in Berlin."

"Will do, Dad."

Bruno hung up feeling elated. Why hadn't he thought of this important venture earlier? Especially after receiving that letter of rejection from the old lady? Well, he was still teaching then and Felix was too young for such a caper. But now the time was ripe. Another Alma would be saved. And she could join her counterpart in Nyack.

54

This police station has a very noticeable stink, Karl Palkovska thought to himself as he exited the building at Brandstätte 4 in Vienna's inner city. His meeting with one of the station's detectives had gone well. Playing the role of concerned victim to the hilt, Karl had left the detective with photographs of the "stolen artworks" that had been stored in the fourteen crates stored at *Kunst Sicherheit und Lagerung Firma Moser*.

"We shall notify you as soon as there is a break in the case," Detective Versteckt had assured him.

Karl was quite sure he would not be hearing from the solicitous man, but his "loss" was now registered with the police as well as with Moser's insurance company. Now all he had to do was sit back and wait for payment.

There was one other person in Vienna he wanted to contact with his color photographs of the stolen Kokoschka still lifes: the Greek art impresario Theo Papadakis—known for his ability to ferret out long-lost works of art. He, too, might have a good idea as to what the Kokoschkas would fetch on the market.

Back on the Brandstätte street and a discreet distance from the police station, Karl inconspicuously snorted some crystal. His nose began to bleed, but he had never felt more alert.

55

Desdemona was of two minds. Megan had several times referred to the break-in at Moser's art storage facility and she herself had, of course, seen the news on television right after the Kokoschka theft occurred. But Desdemona did not see it as a theft. She saw it as a liberation. Allowing the precious artworks—the subjects of which would be revealed at Xenia—to be admired as they ought to be, rather than languishing in a vault. Of course she would direct in her will that the artworks be left to Vienna's Leopold Museum. But during her lifetime she would and must act as their caretaker. This was her sacred duty. *Ein muss.*

She wanted so much to share her good news with Megan, who was so likeable, so like-minded, and so helpful. She had, after all, saved her life when she pushed her out of the way of the oncoming streetcar. And now she was watching out for her concerning the authenticity of the Christomanos portrait on which Herr Haesslich had offered her first refusal. In fact, she had persuaded her to fly Janette Killar over from New York to take a look at the Christomanos portrait.

But would Megan, open-minded as she seemed to be, understand the redemptive purpose underlying the liberation of those fourteen crates from the prison of a vault? Enthusiasm and the joy of sharing propelled Desdemona to confide in her friend, but something held her back. A cautionary feeling she could not suppress. Well, perhaps the day would come when she could reveal to her friend just what she had done for Kokoschka, for the extraordinary artist they both so admired.

56

Yes, one could truly describe the architectural layout of Hamburg's Museum für Kunst und Gewerbe as a closed E shape, Agnes thought. Wearing her blonde wig, she paced through room after room of the vast museum. It was ten o'clock in the morning and this was the second time she had walked through the museum arms. She had arrived at the bustling port city on the Elbe the night before. A search online for the hotel closest to the museum had come up with the small Alt Nürnberg, on the Steintorweg that led directly into the Steintorplatz where the nineteenth-century museum proudly stood. Security was minimal at the museum entryway; in fact not even her purse was questioned. A good omen.

Leo Lang had remembered the Kokoschka fans as being on exhibit in what would constitute the middle corridor of the E-shaped museum and Agnes had gone to it first. Sure enough, there was a grand staircase and an elevator going up to the third level. She decided to climb the stairs, casing the walls for fire alarm stations and surveillance cameras. She found both. There were no recessed display shelves lining the corridor on the second floor. Instead, the space was given over to a variety of old wooden keyboard instruments, all of them roped off from the public.

Agnes climbed up to the third floor. There, close to the center of the corridor and not far from the skylight, were the seven fans. They were spread out to their full width and stood in one continuous line along a lengthy recessed shelf. A thick pane of glass intervened between viewer and object—probably a polycarbonate sheet which, Agnes knew, was practically unbreakable.

But there they were, all seven of the, apparently, precious fans. Agnes did not care for the scenes—they were too hard to make out and the colors were far too bright for her taste. In other words, they certainly did not look like those sophisticated fans from the Orient. Well, to each his own taste, Agnes thought, shrugging her shoulders and feeling slightly irritated that

Lang would not want her to destroy the fans on the spot. It would be so much more difficult to slip them unharmed out of the museum.

She studied the skylight. Yes, it was conveniently close to the fans, but it was very, very high. She would have to have a harness and be able to lower herself to the floor without setting off any alarms or being observed by security cameras. This was fine in action films but not in real life, she told herself. And a night break-in did not seem realistic either. There were simply too many rooms, too many offices, and very likely too many guards making the rounds.

A distraction, like the fortuitous one in Essen with the Neo-Nazi demonstrators, is what was needed, Agnes decided finally. After a last check of the locations of women's restrooms on all floors, she left the building and headed back to her hotel room. She had some Internet research to do. In the meantime she would have lunch and listen, amused, to the local Hamburg-isch dialect, doubly funny to a German-speaker from Basel.

Perfect! Agnes had located a nearby Bauhaus superstore on the Unterer Landweg. She walked to the store and headed for the house paint section. There she selected two containers of paint thinner. Next on her list was a large steel hand wrench. Paying for them in cash, she placed them in the cloth bag she was carrying. Then she walked over to a department store and bought two cotton skirts, a bottle of *Vent de Folie* perfume, and a Bic cigarette lighter. Back at the hotel she cut the two skirts into strips and soaked them in the paint thinner cans. After they had partially dried she sprayed them with the strong perfume she had bought to mask their powerful odor. She stuffed the rags into her cloth camera case then put the cigarette lighter into her right boot and the wrench into her left. She donned her wig, blue jeans, long boots, and kimono, and slid the camera case around her belt to the back underneath the kimono. After another ten minutes she was back at the museum and entered just ahead of several large groups of noisy school children. All the better.

She headed straight for the second floor and the ladies restroom farthest from the keyboard instrument display and waited in a booth until the room was empty. It was a long wait. Finally she was alone. With her cigarette lighter she set the paper towels over the sinks on fire and then threw several of her paint-thinner soaked rags on the floor. She ignited one. Flames burst out immediately and she barely missed being burned herself. She ran out of the restroom shouting *"Feuer, Feuer!"* and startled museum visitors took up her chant, pointing to the restroom from which clouds of smoke were already pouring. Several guards ran toward the restroom, cell phones to their ears, and talking excitedly. Two more appeared brandishing fire extinguishers. The museum was filled with shouts of people crowding around the restroom to see what was wrong. A teacher was vainly trying to herd his group of curious school children down the stairs to the exit.

Unobserved, Agnes reversed her path and came back to the keyboard display. Quickly she threw her remaining rags onto the instruments, igniting each one with her lighter. The wooden pianofortes and harpsichords immediately caught fire. Now the whole second floor was threatened by flames and, as crowds scurried to get down the stairs, Agnes ran up the stairs to the third floor display of the fans. No one was around. Not even guards. The bleating sound of a fire alarm had emptied the floor. The security camera was aimed toward a pottery exhibit across from the fans. Agnes pulled out the wrench from her boot and held the cigarette lighter's flame right up to the rim of glass separating her from the fans. Much to her surprise it began to liquefy almost immediately. So this was *not* polycarbonate! A few instants later enough glass had dissolved for Agnes to carefully push the wrench through. It only took a minute more to shove the glass pane outward and onto the floor. Agnes grabbed the fans, closed them, and stuck them into her belt. Not bothering to retrieve the wrench, she whipped off her wig, stuffed it into her purse, and bolted over to the stairs where, one floor lower, she joined the panicked throngs of people pushing each other to get down to the museum exit. A brunette again, she exited the museum and joined the gaping crowd, her work accomplished.

57

Early in the morning Felix had taken up his stance across the street from the driveway entrance to Margareta Nussbaum's villa in Babelsberg. The short drive was lined with red maples and Felix could see the yellow villa at the end. But getting down the drive in the daytime could be a problem. He decided to stay at his post and check what service vehicles might appear, if any. Perhaps there was a delivery service of some sort, maybe for a newspaper? His observation point was an ideal one: there was a bus stop opposite the villa and he was glad to be sitting on the convenient bench. His duffle bag securely underneath the bench, he began to play Spiderman games on his cell phone.

* * *

The taxi Megan and Desdemona had taken from the Griebnitzsee S Bahn station turned down the Nussbaum driveway at exactly four in the afternoon. Its arrival was duly noted by Felix, who saw that the vehicle contained two female passengers. Hope they don't stay till after it's dark, he thought to himself, settling back on the bench.

As soon as Megan rang the front doorbell a smiling young man dressed informally in Hawaiian shirt and shorts opened the door and greeted them. A very old German Shepherd barked a wary welcome.

"Frau Nussbaum is expecting you," he said, indicating that they enter a book-lined room to the right. At the far end of the room, seated in a wheelchair at a round wooden table, a half-full glass of white wine in front of her, was a tiny woman, weighing perhaps not even one-hundred pounds. She was dressed elegantly in a long embroidered white dress that complemented the white of her short hair. Margareta beamed a welcome to her two guests and listened attentively as Megan introduced Desdemona.

"Do sit down," she said, waving her hand at two of the table's three chairs.

"Now, Megan. Tell me why you are in Berlin. The last time I saw you was ages ago."

"Ages ago, yes, but I've never forgotten our wonderful visit or getting to look at your marvelous collection."

"And may I say that I've never forgotten how you asked if you could make quick drawings of each work."

"Well, there is something about hand to eye to brain that triggers memory in a way no mere photograph can do. I still do it today. Just like Bernard Berenson. Very useful in detecting forgeries."

"I am not surprised. But tell me. Why are you both in Berlin?"

Megan and Desdemona looked at each other and broke out laughing. "It's a long story..."

"First of all, Megan saved my life!" interrupted Desdemona, explaining about the streetcar incident and holding up her cast-encased wrists.

"And I was in Vienna because of the spate of crimes concerning Kokoschka paintings, both here in Europe and in Japan."

"Ah, yes! I've been reading about that in the paper. Dreadful. But these criminals seem to be targeting museums, not private collections, God be praised. I had been worried about that." Margareta looked apprehensively around the room, the walls of which were hung three deep with black-framed drawings by Klimt, Schiele, and Kokoschka.

"I hope you have a burglar system, Frau Nussbaum," said Desdemona fervently.

"A burglar system? No, never! Friends tell me they are always going off at the wrong time—either they have them turned on and forget and walk where they are not supposed to, or the alarm goes off all by itself. No thank you. I've managed just fine so far and I'm a hundred-and-three. Anyway, my faithful Nero here is a wonderful guard dog."

"I certainly hope so," Megan said with emphasis. She decided it was time to bring up the topic of Kokoschka's so-called portrait of Christomanos.

"Margareta, the reason Desdemona and I are in Berlin is that Kokoschka's lost portrait of Constantine Christomanos has, supposedly, been found. It is being offered for sale by the gallery *Am schwarzen Schwan*."

"Say no more! I know Herr Helmut Haesslich personally. Several times now he has approached me with drawings described as being by Kokoschka. In each case I was not able to convince myself that they were genuine and I told him so."

"Very interesting," Megan said, looking meaningfully at her companion.

Desdemona spoke up. "Now it's an oil portrait he has at his gallery, and Megan and I saw it this morning. I loved it the moment I saw it, but Megan has counseled caution. Wants me to bring Janette Killar over to determine its authenticity."

"I think Megan was absolutely right to reserve judgment until Killar pronounces her verdict. After all, she is the author of the Kokoschka oeuvre catalogue. You could engage no greater or more up-to-date authority."

What you say is very wise and, I must say, convincing, Frau Nussbaum."

"If you get to be my age and are still not wise, then there's no point to it."

"Well, I've heard tell that one hundred is the new ninety," laughed Desdemona.

"I hear, Margareta, that the Wien Museum is going to receive a major gift from you," said Megan, changing the subject.

"Yes indeed. How could I ever forget my own hometown?"

Megan softly sang the chorus of *Wien, Wien, Nur Du Allein.*

Margareta and Desdemona happily chimed in. Then Megan spotted an old guitar standing in a corner of the room and asked if she could look at it. Permission was granted. The strings were sagging, but as soon as Megan had tuned them up she announced: "Desdemona and I have a birthday song for you, Margareta."

They both rose to their feet, the guitar on Megan's hip, and performed the little ditty they had made up earlier. It was a huge hit. Margareta laughed and laughed. Then she asked if they would like to see the Kokoschka wall painting in the long hall.

"What a treat!" Megan exclaimed. "I've told Desdemona about it, and how the new Haus Mahler owners had gone through the arduous strappo technique of having the frieze transferred to a canvas backing."

Margareta picked up a book that was on the table and hit the wooden table with it a couple of times. Instantly Bruno and the young man who had answered the door appeared.

"Adrian, take these lovely ladies to the long hall and tell Patti to come get me."

Megan and Desdemona obediently followed the smiling Adrian to a long hall that took up most of the left side of the house. As they came around the corner Desdemona gasped. Although only about twenty-five inches high, Kokoschka's frieze extended some thirteen feet across the west wall. The two women examined it in silence. Margareta, her dog Bruno in tow, joined them as Adrian pushed her wheelchair into the room.

"Overwhelming, is it not?"

"It's so much more vivid than the photographs show," Desdemona said.

"I remember the story that Alma's little daughter Anna told when she saw Kokoschka working on the frieze in the Semmering house. Anna had asked him if he couldn't paint something other than her mother all the time," Megan supplied.

They all laughed, and once again Megan made a few quick sketches in her notebook. "Every time I see it, and I grant you this is only the second time, I see something more," she murmured in explanation.

"Oh, draw away to your heart's content, Megan, dear. But I daresay that Frau Dumba would like to join me for white wine and some Saint Angel triple-crème cheese now." She and Desdemona went back to the front room and Megan joined them a few minutes later. The talk revolved around how Margareta had become friends with and a patron of Kokoschka in London. Both of them had lived through Hitler's blitz campaign and both of them had become British citizens after the war.

"Well, it is wonderful having you here," said Margareta suddenly. Megan knew from her previous visit that this was the dear lady's way of signaling it was time for her guests to leave. She got to her feet and picked up the guitar to return it to its corner.

"Oh, do play and sing that song you made up for my birthday again, please!" begged Margareta.

They complied with their hostess's request and at the end of the song Margareta raised her wineglass to thank and toast them. She took a sip then gasped. The wine had gone down the wrong way. She began coughing violently, with great heaves. Megan went up to her and carefully patted her delicate back. Margareta began gasping for air, aspirating, her body jerking with the effort. She fainted in her wheelchair, a wisp of a woman, her frail figure now twisted like a double S.

"*Adrian!*" Megan screamed. "Call an ambulance, call an ambulance!" Patti, the petite Hispanic caregiver ran into the room. "Oh, I do it, I do it!" she cried, picking up the landline phone and dialing 110. This must have happened before, thought Megan.

Within minutes an ambulance pulled up at the front door, its siren wailing. Two attendants jumped out and immediately provided Margareta with lifesaving intravenous fluids, placed her on a gurney, and wheeled her to the ambulance. After Margareta was settled inside, both Adrian and the caregiver clamored into the ambulance as well. "I go too, I go too!" Patti cried.

"Can we ride with you as well?" Megan asked the ambulance driver.

"If you don't mind sitting in the back," he answered. Both Megan and Desdemona climbed into the back of the ambulance, one on either side of Margareta.

"It is just like last time," moaned Patti.

"We will bring her home again, do not worry," Adrian comforted her.

Felix Fichte had jumped up from his bench across the street and watched, open-mouthed, as an ambulance, its siren blaring, raced down Margareta Nussbaum's driveway. A few minutes later the ambulance, its siren still on, sped out in the direction of Babelsberg's St. Josefs Krankenhaus.

Felix's mouth was still open. "*This is my lucky day!*"

58

"You are extraordinary," Leo Lang told Agnes Sauer when she called him to report the Hamburg success. The television that evening had reported that the museum fire had been set by an unusually tall, blonde woman in a kimono.

"We're just lucky the panel was ordinary glass and not polycarbonate, which is three hundred times stronger than glass."

"What is the condition of the fans?"

"They are in near perfect condition from what I can tell."

"Do you want to fly to Vienna now and deliver the fans or would you rather complete the three other missions we've discussed first?"

"I think it is best that I carry out the other three jobs first, Herr Lang."

"All right then. It's your choice as to which one you'd like to tackle first. The Alma doll painting in Stuttgart, or Berlin, or Klosterneuburg.

"After all this excitement I think I'd like to take on the Klosterneuburg mission first. It's a sleepy little town outside Vienna, isn't it?"

"That's right. It is known to art historians as the town young Egon Schiele went to school. Otherwise there's an abbey. Not much else."

"It would be a downright vacation for me, compared to Basel, and Tokyo, and Essen, and Hamburg."

"Shall I send you the image you saw in my missions album?"

"Yes. It would be helpful to have it so I can study it closely."

"All right. Call me when it's done, and good luck, although you don't seem to need it."

"Oh, yes, I do," countered Agnes. She felt a bit suspicious about her run of luck and whether it could continue.

Back in her Hamburg hotel room she made plane flight reservations for Vienna and then beamed up on the Internet all that it had to offer about the abbey town of about 26,000 souls. The abbey had a little museum.

Agnes decided to memorize the Kokoschka painting. No more mistakes like the one I made in Essen! She pulled up the image in her e-mail. There was the Alma doll, and clearly it was the doll in its blue dress, "walking" in a pine forest with Kokoschka, who was wearing a dragoon's uniform and curving helmet. Between them was a little boy, perhaps three, perhaps four years old. The colors were those of a dense pine forest. The path through the forest was streaked with ominous spatula strokes of black. Oskar and Alma's expressions were the same, determined and serious. The child smiled a sad smile as he looked up at his doll mother. Certainly not a controversial picture, Agnes thought. Unless you realized that the mother was a doll made in the likeness of a woman who, in the eyes of Kokoschka, had betrayed her lover by aborting his child. Ugh. Complicated. But at least she didn't have to remove or destroy the entire painting. A squirt of her syringe on the doll's somber face would do the job.

The next morning Agnes was on the eight o'clock flight to Vienna where she checked into the Ingram Hotel off the Kärntner Ring. It was near the Hertz car rental she had used before and she liked its convenient location. By eleven she was on her way north on Highway B 14 to hilly Klosterneuburg in a gray Opel Astra sedan. It was a glorious June day and she was looking forward to driving through the green countryside. She was still smarting over the laugh an American clerk who took her order at Hertz had had at her expense. "Fräulein Sauer? Why, did you know that 'sauer' in English means acidic?"

Yes, a drive in the country would be a welcome hiatus.

A hill separated the two main squares of Klosterneuburg, the Niedermarkt and the Rathausplatz. Agnes chose the latter and followed the street signs pointing to the Essl Museum for Contemporary Art. She approached a very new and modern building. Could the Kokoschka be here? She went inside. A ridiculous exhibit of large bobbing forms and colored balloons pivoting in the air above the lobby was entitled *Fräulein Atlantis*. It made no sense to Agnes as she looked into the smaller rooms. Everything was very contemporary. Nothing that could go back as far as 1914. She sat down next to the small gift shop, knocking balloons out of her way, and brought up the Internet on her cell phone. The only other possible museum was the abbey museum. Could Kokoschka, with his wild imagery, be at the abbey?

She retraced her steps and passed the Kierling sanatorium where a sign marked the death of Franz Kafka there in 1925. She climbed the steep hill to the Augustinian monastery with its twin turrets and remnants of the high city walls. A sign inside read "To the Verdun Altar." Not very promising for a Kokoschka display, and she really was not a fan of church art, past or present. She stopped a monk who was passing by and asked if the abbey museum contained any modern works.

"Certainly not!" was his shocked answer as he stared at his tall, blonde interlocutor standing there so brazenly in her low cut blouse, rhinestone-studded blue jeans and high boots.

Agnes could not wait to exit the abbey. Perhaps she should go to the little city tourist office she had noticed right on the Rathausplatz. A friendly young woman returned her greeting and to her question as to where a famous Kokoschka painting might be in Klosterneuburg, she received a knowing giggle.

"You are not the first person to ask where the Kokoschka is. Despite its contemporary thrust, the Essl does have a small permanent collection that is kept in the director's office. He would be happy to show it to you, I'm sure."

Agnes thanked the helpful girl and returned to the Essl building. Irritated, she batted one of the huge balloons out of her way as she entered.

"Oh, no," cried the show's artist who was standing next to her. "You're supposed to put your arms around the Atlantis bubble—embrace it—and follow it wherever it leads you. Remember, Atlantis is sinking, sinking into the ocean, never to rise again."

"Oookaaay," Agnes parceled out the two syllables, deciding that her balloon would lead her directly to the director's office. She let herself seem to be guided by the oversize bubble and slowly gyrated to the back of the building. She saw a thin man in shirtsleeves talking outside an office to a group of school children. The office was marked "Direktor" and the door was open. Agnes floated past the group, murmuring "Where it leads, I do but follow." The director smiled, stepped aside, and said, "Please, please, just float in. Make yourself comfortable with art of the past." He continued talking to the children as Agnes swept inside, following her balloon's bidding. *And there, to the left of the director's desk, was the Kokoschka.*

She had just seconds to act, but the director's back was to her and he was drawing out the children with inane questions. She whipped the syringe out of her shoulder bag, aimed it straight at Alma's face and pushed the plunger. The face disappeared as she watched the instant effects of the concentrated sulfuric acid. Then she whirled back around with her balloon and followed its trajectory as it led her past the children who were now asking the director questions. At the front door she handed her balloon to the artist and thanked him for the rewarding journey to Atlantis. Minutes later she was in her Opel headed south on Highway B 14.

59

In his hotel room back at the Römischer Kaiser, Karl Palkovska was taking a snort. He needed to have his wits about him now. A visit to the Amadeus Auktionshaus, with his color photographs of the fourteen "stolen" Kokoschka still lifes had proved to be potentially lucrative. Cornelius Weber, the director of the online auction house had expressed keen interest in the subject matter of the missing Kokoschka canvases. He wanted to know whether there were any more of this row of small still lifes with city views behind them, or had they all been lost during the robbery?

"No," Palkovska had lied immediately. "There are a few that slipped through the grate. Not even Killar's catalogue raisonné documents them. But they exist. I have seen them."

The lie had had its desired effect. "If you ever can persuade the owner or owners to part with any of them, I should be most interested in placing them on my monthly auction list," Weber had said.

Palkovska was encouraging. "I think that might be possible. At least for one of the still lifes. The owner, whose identity I can not reveal to you, lives right here in Vienna. I shall inquire on your behalf." Another quick-witted lie. In the meantime, international publicity relating to the shocking theft was raising their value daily.

Kokoschka's "heir" had gone straight from the Amadeus Antiquariat to Boesner's art supply store out in Simmering. He bought what he needed, including brushes, isopropanol and acetone. He also asked a kindly restorer working in the back of the establishment if he could have the old cotton swabs he had been using to remove the aged natural resin varnish from the painting he was working on. Request granted.

While Palkovska was in the Simmering district he went online and answered an ad for a furnished room to let near the Central Cemetery. The owner met him at the apartment house door. Karl took one look at the room and rented it on the spot. It would be a perfect place for his creative endeavors in the name of Kokoschka.

He then headed back to the center of town on the U-Bahn Line 3. There he visited two antique stores and in the second one found what he required: an old painting from the early 1900s measuring about two feet by three feet. He bought it for all of seventy-five Euros, and headed back to Simmering with the painting and all his "restoration" materials.

The painting was a portrait of a child. Karl first gently sanded off an initial layer of the paint, taking care to leave some tooth to the surface. His eyes needed a rest from all the residual powder in the air, but the canvas was beginning to look ready for the two layers of acetone that would remove the rest of the paint.

What cityscape should he place behind the still life of grapes, cheese, and wine glasses he had planned to paint in the front plane? Venice. Yes, Venice was a city Kokoschka had visited and painted a large view of—that would be perfect! He would beam up a view of San Marco and its vast piazza on his laptop and get to work. And now his head was working at highest capacity—the meth had kicked in nicely.

He opened a window for ventilation and began applying isopropanol to remove the varnish, then acetone to remove the old paint. After that, once dry, he would prime the canvas with gesso prepared with his favorite rabbit skin glue. It would take several days for the gesso to cure. Then it would be ready to absorb Kokoschka's Venice.

He would show the finished product not only to the Amadeus Auktionshaus but also to the Vienna-based Greek art dealer Theo Papadakis. The Viennese grapevine had it that the man had located a lost Kokoschka portrait of the court reader to Sisi, Constantine Christomanos. Surely Papadakis would also be interested in his newly discovered Kokoschka still life with a view of Venice.

60

As soon as the noise of the ambulance's siren had faded away, Felix Fichte made his move. Grabbing his duffle bag he crossed the street where he had been observing Margareta Nussbaum's house and boldly walked up the driveway to the front door. In his hand he held a lightweight Taser with a lithium power magazine capable of some fifty applications.

He rang the front door bell. The sound of a large barking dog greeted his ears. He heard a woman's voice, calling to "Nero" to be silent. Margareta Nussbaum's secretary, Barbara Screib, opened the door a crack and Felix could see the barking German Shepherd straining behind her.

"I have a controlled medication delivery for Frau Margareta Nussbaum," Felix said, holding up his duffle bag.

Over Nero's unceasing barks the woman asked, "Would she have to sign for it? The house is in an uproar right now, as Frau Nussbaum has been taken to the hospital."

"Is there anyone else in the house who could sign for it?"

"There is no one else here right now. But I am her secretary. I could sign for her."

Without a moment's hesitation Felix thrust the door open violently, knocking the woman down with a body slam. Nero's barking became deafening as he confronted and lunged at the intruder. Felix aimed his Taser directly at the dog, who fell instantly to the ground whimpering from the electroshock. The secretary, screaming for help and struggling to get up, was Felix's next target. He beamed her twice for good measure, gave the god dammed dog another shot, slammed the front door shut, locked it, and began searching the house.

He turned first to the right and ran through the connecting rooms. Art on the walls, yes, but no Kokoschka. Arriving at the empty kitchen he bolted back to the front of the house and started down the left side. Awesome! There it was: the long hall. And there opposite him as he entered was the Kokoschka frieze. Yeah, Dad was right, you sure couldn't miss Alma. Taking a package slicer out of his duffle bag Felix went to work gingerly slitting the figure of Alma out of the mural. Just as Dad had said, the thirteen-foot long strip of canvas was only a little over two feet high. After Felix removed the Alma part he rolled up the image and placed it snuggly into his open duffle bag and closed it. A perfect fit.

He returned to the front door where the secretary was still writhing on the floor. The dog, for the moment at least, lay motionless. For good measure Felix zapped the dog one more time, then walked rapidly up the drive to the bus station across the street. Within five minutes he was on board a bus heading back to his Lili Marleen hotel. Dad is gonna blow a gasket, he'll be so pleased.

61

Megan and Desdemona had finished breakfast and were waiting in the hotel lobby for Janette Killar to arrive. They had been discussing Margareta Nussbaum's miraculous recovery, thanks to the quick-thinking doctors at St. Josef's Hospital. The two women had stayed with Margareta until nine that evening. She would need to be hospitalized for a few more days, the attending physician informed them. But they were not to worry. Unless something unforeseen happened, Frau Nussbaum would be back home by the middle of the week. She was one tough lady.

But of course something unforeseen had happened: the vandalizing of Margareta's Kokoschka wall painting in which the figure of Alma Mahler had been cut out of its surround. Megan had enjoined Margareta's staff not, under any circumstances, to mention this shocking incident until their elderly employer was back home. The fact that Margareta's dear old dog had died during the attack would only make things worse for Frau Nussbaum. In the meantime Megan and Margareta's secretary had conferred with the Babelsberg police. Barbara Schreib had been able to give a detailed description of the man who had forced his way into the house.

Megan's iPhone rang, sounding out the Méditation from *Thaïs*. It was

Janette Killar: her taxi had just turned off the Ku'damm and was pulling up in front of the hotel. A few minutes later the three women were talking excitedly as Janette checked in.

"You're on the same floor we are," said Desdemona after introductions had been made, "and just one door down from Megan." She looked at the Galerie St. Sebastian owner with approval and anticipation. Janette was a slender woman with a head of voluminous short blonde curls that fell around her face. In fact she looked rather like Klimt's portrait of his muse, Emilie Flöge, thought Desdemona.

"Thank you, so, so much for being willing to make this blitz trip to Berlin."

"I am happy I could squeeze it in. Actually, I can get some other business done while I'm here and in Hannover as well. And the possibility of looking at a genuine, let us hope, early Kokoschka portrait is quite a draw."

Megan suggested that, after Janette had unpacked her few items, they have an early lunch at the hotel and then walk up the Fasanenstrasse to the Käthe Kollwitz Museum before their three o'clock appointment with Herr Haesslich at the *Am schwarzen Schwan*.

"I'm game," said Janette. "Haven't been there in a couple of years now."

"And for this evening," announced Desdemona happily, "I've taken the liberty of booking us three tickets to a Berlin Philharmonic concert. Among other goodies, they're playing Tchaikovsky's *Swan Lake*."

"How wonderfully appropriate," murmured Janette. "We'll have a black swan two times in a row today."

Lunch at the Kempinski was excellent, if not greatly varied. At Megan's suggestion they decided to have coffee and dessert at the Literaturhaus, which was invitingly connected to the Kollwitz Museum by a passageway. "It is considered one of Berlin's most 'civilized' cafés," she pronounced knowingly. Her friends agreed after sampling the desserts and enjoying the quiet ambience. The latest newspaper and magazine issues were available on several racks along one side of the large room.

Then, methodically, they went through all four floors of the Kollwitz Museum with its permanent collection of graphics and sculpture by the artist.

"I wonder why they put the heavy sculpture on the top floor," Desdemona felt impelled to comment. Megan and Janette had no explanation.

They spent the longest time in front of a charcoal and chalk self-portrait of 1892 in which the twenty-five-year-old artist showed herself on her balcony, silhouetted against the row of apartment houses on the far side of Wörther Platz, a view she would contemplate for over half a century. She partly stood, partly sat on the balcony, precariously and unceremoniously raising her left knee up to her chest so that her foot rested on the railing.

For Desdemona's benefit Megan asked, then answered several rhetorical questions. Will she fall? No, certainly not. Frau Kollwitz is not contemplating suicide; she sits in the fading evening light, her attention directed outward across the square as lights begin to appear in the windows opposite. This was now her Berlin. What would she be able to contribute? How could she live up to her grandfather's axiom, "every gift is a responsibility"? Her husband Karl was already becoming involved with his medical practice. But of what would her work consist? How could she pursue the separate callings of artist, wife, and mother?

The answer, Megan told Desdemona, was in front of her: Wörther Platz, with its teeming cast of characters, its daily human comedies and tragedies, its insistent pulse of life. Wörther Platz, her microcosm within the macrocosm that was Berlin. The confines of Wörther Platz, decades later to be renamed Kollwitzplatz, would become her world village from which she would extract her blunt, concentrated images of universal suffering.

"I think I must begin collecting Kollwitz," murmured Desdemona, appreciatively.

"Hey! It's about time we got out to Charlottenburg," warned Janette suddenly, looking at her watch. The trio hurried out of the museum and up to the Ku'damm where they hailed a passing taxi. They pulled up to Haesslich's gallery a few minutes before three o'clock. Megan had said nothing to Janette of her misgivings about the Christomanos painting, not wanting to influence her in any way. And Desdemona was equally discreet, at Megan's urging.

Helmut Haesslich was not nearly as welcoming as he had been on the previous occasion of Megan and Desdemona's visit. Wasting no time in small talk after Janette Killar had been introduced, he led the women back to the room where the Kokoschka portrait of Constantine Christomanos stood on its easel.

Janette took in the painting silently. It was quite something. The hunchbacked man emanated nervous energy, and the painter's brushstrokes followed suit. Just as Megan had done, she went up close to the canvas and sniffed for any giveaway odors of fresh paint or varnish. Nothing. And, as Megan had done before her, she stepped quickly to the back of the canvas, taking in the close weave texture. She returned to the front and stepped back for a whole view of the portrait.

Her face expressionless, she asked Haesslich for the provenance. He explained that it had just been discovered in a cellar that had once belonged to Herwarth Walden. New owners of the building, which had changed hands several times, were instituting renovations and the painting had been discovered in the basement. They had brought the artwork straight to him.

"Um hum," allowed Killar, her face still expressionless. She became silent again, studying the picture. Desdemona and Megan waited in suspense. Finally she spoke.

"Herr Haesslich. This painting is not genuine. I base that judgment on its execution which, although in a knowledgeable-enough style, is very obviously a copy of Kokoschka's brushwork. It has been applied from above, you might say, and not built up as we would expect Kokoschka to do. It is inspired by the black-and-white photo in my oeuvre catalogue and the copy is good enough, but that is exactly what it is. A copy."

She refrained from saying that it was an outright forgery; a phony pure and simple.

"But, but…" Haesslich sputtered.

"Thank you for allowing me to examine the artwork, Herr Haesslich," Janette said as she and the other two women turned to leave. Haesslich followed them down the hall to the front room, blustering protests.

As they left the gallery, Desdemona said with great dignity to the furious owner, "I no longer wish to acquire your copy of the Böcklin. It could be by the same hand that created the Kokoschka."

Megan beamed with pleasure at Desdemona. Finally her friend was beginning to show some deliberate judgment. It must be the influence of discerning Janette Killar and her measured manner in front of the hoax.

When they were out of earshot, Janette exploded. "Why, that guy had the nerve to show us an outright *forgery*! I really ought to publish an oeuvre catalogue of phony Klimt, Schiele, and Kokoschka artworks.

"I must tell you, Janette," Desdemona confessed, "that Megan warned me against buying the canvas. She had a *feeling* that something was wrong. That's why I begged you to fly over from New York. I'm so very grateful to you. I guess the idea of having Kokoschka's portrait of Sisi's Greek tutor was so overwhelming that I simply lost my head. I so *wanted* it to be by Kokoschka."

"Don't feel bad. You have to realize, Desdemona, this is something I meet with all the time: passionate collectors who lose their judgment when offered something that passes as a work by the artist they are interested in."

"What should be done now that we know the painting is a forgery?" Megan asked, hoping Haesslich could be stopped from offering the portrait for sale.

"Unfortunately, nothing. Haesslich will find an 'expert', probably a local guy, who will testify that the work is legit. And in Europe you can always find someone who is willing to write out an 'authentication' document."

"How about crossing over to the Charlottenburg Palace?" suggested Megan, eager to distract Desdemona. "We could visit Queen Luise's mausoleum with its sculpture of her in a gentle sleep atop her sarcophagus."

"Oh, who did that? Rauch?" asked Janette.

"Right. Christian Daniel Rauch. Luise was only thirty-four when she died. And Rauch didn't have to idealize her. She was—like Sisi—Desdemona, considered to be one of the most beautiful women in Europe."

"Oh, yes, I know about her. She tried to use her beauty to persuade Napoleon to go easy on Prussia after its humiliating defeat by him."

"But it didn't work," added Janette.

"In more modern times she was used by the Nazi propaganda machine to inspire schoolgirls as the personification of womanly qualities they should emulate," volunteered Megan.

They had reached the mausoleum and went inside. There lay the white marble effigy of Luise, recumbent on her casket, her hands crossed and her lovely face turned slightly on her pillow, asleep for all eternity.

After a sufficient period for silent admiration, Desdemona suggested they go to Megan's Russian tea room. They all looked forward to the evening's musical experience and merrily talked away about different concerts and performers. Desdemona's mood was lifted.

On their way back to the Kempinski after exiting the U-Bahn, they passed an antique store on the Ku'damm. Megan glanced at the display, then put a restraining arm on Desdemona's.

"Stop! Look what's in the window!"

Desdemona and Janette looked. There, leaning against a large vase, was a small oil painting. It was a very decent copy of the Leipzig Böcklin's *Isle of the Dead*.

"So I do buy *one* of my two desiratas today!" exclaimed Desdemona as she hurried inside the shop.

62

Another woman was staying at the Hotel Kempinski in Berlin. Agnes Sauer had decided to treat herself to some efficient German luxury after her country escapade at Klosterneuburg. She had laughed all the way back to Vienna's Hertz rental. The job had been ridiculously easy, once she had located where the Alma doll effigy was. She had been almost tempted to keep the balloon that had fortuitously 'led' her to it.

But now, in Berlin, getting access to the second gynoid-Alma was going to require all her skills. The large double portrait, with a clothed Kokoschka pointing to the naked doll's private parts, was housed in Mies van der Rohe's solemn glass and steel Neue Nationalgalerie on Potsdamer Strasse. It faced, on the other side of the street, the Berlin State Library. Agnes had taken up temporary post there, making an initial assessment of the comings and goings of people during the day and during the early evening hours. This was no place to break into during the wee hours of the morning. There was simply too much automobile and pedestrian traffic. And with its glass walls the building was all too public.

It was time to go inside the museum and investigate the options. At the entrance a long line of people were placing backpacks, briefcases, and purses onto the belt of a very modern scanner. Backpackers and briefcase carriers were directed to the cloakroom where they had to leave their loads, and women with oversize purses had to check them. A surprisingly large number of guards were on duty, even in the lobby. Not much chance for a Neo-Nazi demonstration here.

Even before she bought her entry ticket, Agnes saw something that would have brought her deeper into the museum under any circumstances. A large overhead sign announced the special exhibition: *Kokoschka's Women*. The whole interior left side of the museum was taken up with images of women from every decade of the painter's career. *The Dreaming Youths* was displayed in a cabinet at the center of the room, opened to the page showing the girl Lilith and boy Kokoschka. Also from the year 1908 was the artist's somewhat wooden portrait of the young Lotte, her body silhouette edged with an ominous dark shadow. The bloody 1909 *Murderer, Hope of* Women poster was also on display. From the year 1910, the year in which Kokoschka definitively found his spastic application of paint, there was the portrait of Else Kupfer, a demure woman with soulful eyes and an alert small dog in her lap.

The second room was devoted to some one hundred lithographs and drawings devoted to depictions of Alma Mahler, often with Kokoschka. An eye-catching didactic read:

> This exhibition was planned before the recent spate of outrages against Kokoschka works showing his lover Alma Mahler. For that reason some of the paintings intended for the show are not available. We present instead this series of drawings and lithographs that feature Alma Mahler.

As Agnes approached the third room of the exhibit what she saw stopped her in her tracks. Not only was the museum's own Alma doll portrait on display, but, right next to it, *the one from Stuttgart had been loaned to the show!* The one featuring the life-size Alma doll recumbent and clothed in a blue dress, her bared breasts popping out at the beholder.

What amazing luck! Two Almas for the price of one.

63

Kokoschka never looked better. Karl Palkovska congratulated himself as he studied the still life with view of Venice he had concocted in his rented room. The painting was now dry and ready for brush application of the discolored varnish he had extracted with isopropanol from the discarded cotton swabs given him by the amiable restorer at Boesner's. Even under ultraviolet examination the varnished surface of the painting would give off a light green-yellow glow, just as the aged varnish on an old oil painting would do.

Karl was now ready to visit two potential takers. Theo Papadakis, just back from Berlin, and the Amadeus Auktionshaus. He would tell both Papadakis and Cornelius Weber that he had been able to persuade the Venice still life owner—who wished to remain anonymous—to place the painting with him for sale. As agent for Herr Anonymous, the funds acquired from the sale would be paid directly to him, to his Geneva bank account. And, Karl would intimate, there were a few more still lifes like the Venice one he might be able to dislodge from their owners.

It was stimulating for Karl to realize he was capable of extending, repeatedly if finances required, Kokoschka's oeuvre. How right dear old Aunt Olda had been to insist he major in studio art and chemistry when he was at King's College.

64

It was a long shot, Theo Papadakis knew. But if the impetuous Frau Dumba could be fanatically interested in acquiring Kokoschka's portrait of Christomanos to the point of almost accepting a forgery, she might—when not under the influence of her nosy friends Megan Crespi and Janette Killar—just possibly fall for a "Kokoschka" rendition of Böcklin's *Isle of the Dead*. Witness her eagerness to acquire the small copy of it hanging in Helmut Haesslich's gallery. She must still be regretting that she had not acquired it.

Given that, after her return to Vienna from Berlin any day, Frau Dumba would be leaving for Greece and her beloved Xenia island almost immediately, Theo had devised a bold plan. Earlier that morning he had met with a Karl Palkovska of Geneva. The intense man with yellow teeth who appeared to be on a drug high, had shown him photographs of fourteen Kokoschka artworks stolen recently in Vienna. He had also shown him a fifteenth work, a still life in the flesh—fruit with a view of Venice behind. The young man maintained he was Kokoschka's heir, via his aunt Olda Palkovska-Kokoschka.

Well, Theo thought to himself, either the still lifes were executed when Kokoschka was slightly tipsy, or, at least to the practiced eye, they were enthusiastic forgeries. He suspected the latter. If this Palkovska had concocted fourteen Kokoschkaesque paintings, fifteen counting the Venice one, perhaps he could fabricate a sixteenth one. This one would be an admitted copy of Böcklin's *Isle of the Dead*, but done with Kokoschka's nervous brushwork. The combination of Böcklin *and* Kokoschka would be irresistible for Frau Dumba. She would just *have* to take it to Greece with her.

65

Agnes Sauer was sure her ingenious plan would work. She had remained in the Neue Nationalgalerie room for some twenty minutes, studying the layout. The two Kokoschka Alma doll paintings hung next to each other in an inner corner, one on each wall. Mounted above them in the same corner a security camera faced away from them. Between the two pictures, on a tall black pedestal that must have measured some eight feet high was the agonized self-portrait bronze head the artist had done of himself after Alma had broken up with him for keeps in 1914. The head was twice the size of a normal one and there was nothing normal about it, with its popping eyeballs, long, smashed nose, and open, screaming mouth. It was covered with streaks of red, blue, and yellow paint. Kokoschka's own take on Munch's *Scream*. How appropriate to place it between two images of the woman who had driven him to near insanity. From its high perch the head could look down in defiant disdain on both Almas.

This third room of the exhibition was only partially filled. Apparently the display of graphics in the second room demanded longer attention, as did the first room with the artist's earliest outrageous work. One of the early paintings displayed, for example, had prompted Archduke Franz Ferdinand in 1911 to exclaim "Kokoschka ought to have every bone in his body broken!"

A plan was beginning to form in Agnes's mind as she left the museum. Back in her hotel room she phoned her sister Rita and asked her to fly to Berlin immediately. Fifteen years younger than Agnes, Rita and her husband Emil Luge had occasionally helped her older sister with her shady undertakings and daring escapades. And now, after telling her about Leo Lang of Vienna and his bizarre fixations with Alma and the gynoid-Alma doll, Agnes promised her a handsome sum for helping her with this, her newest caper. Rita made flight reservations immediately and would arrive in Berlin that very evening.

Agnes then went out to the Invacare supply store at Alemannenstrasse 10. Twenty minutes later she left seated in a luxury Invacare wheelchair with heavily padded armrests. After thoroughly mastering the manual technique required for maneuvering the chair, Agnes entered the U-Bahn station again and assessed what she would need to do to go down to the trains by escalator.

Finally she was ready to go. She backed onto the escalator's down stairs, with the large back wheels on the lower step and the front wheels on the upper step. Leaning far forward she lifted her body slightly and held onto the escalator's handrails with both hands. So far so good. She was slowly descending. Then she awaited the bump that would come when she rolled off. When she got to the bottom step she let the handrails pull her off, then wheeled smartly around and faced an incoming train. Enjoying her new mode of transportation, as people made way for her to board the train, she actually wheeled herself all the way back to the Kempinski after exiting at the nearby U-Bahn stop.

Once inside her hotel Agnes stored the wheelchair in the lobby cloakroom. She still had some supplies to purchase before putting her plan into action the next day. First she took the U-Bahn out to Charlottenburg's Friseur Hohenschild where she bought herself a short, very white wig. Then to Modulor's art restoration and supply store where she purchased two glass syringes and four ounces of concentrated sulfuric acid.

Back at the hotel she relaxed with a good meal, then waited in the lounge for Rita to arrive. She watched indifferently as a pair of women stood talking at the checkout counter—the one middle-aged, slim, tall, and aristocratic looking, the other older, short, and just bordering on the plump side. Both had brown hair but it was clear that the short one dyed hers. As they began to make their way out to a waiting taxi she heard the desk clerk call after them: "Auf Wiedersehen, Frau Dumba, auf Wiedersehen, Frau Doktor Crespi. Do visit us again."

After a full day in Berlin, Megan and Desdemona had caught an early evening flight back to Vienna. The *Isle of the Dead* copy, wrapped with brown paper and masking tape, was tucked carefully in the overhead bin. Desdemona was trying to persuade Megan to accompany her to Greece.

"Oh, do come with me, Megan. I will show you my beloved island. You would be my first visitor ever, as Xenia is my retreat from the world."

"I'm intrigued and would love to go, but first let me see how things are percolating in Vienna and Basel. I'm supposed to be helping in the investigation of all these terrible Kokoschka incidents."

"I guess the Christomanos forgery we encountered at Haesslich's gallery counts as one."

"You bet it does. And it's most worrisome because it may not be the only Kokoschka forgery out there being offered to potential buyers."

"Do you think Basel's stolen *Tempest* is being offered on the black market?"

"It's entirely possible. That's where the international police come in. They pool their intelligence and occasionally a sale is detected while in progress. Sadly, more often, just *after* a collector has bought one and the seller has disappeared from the planet."

"I've heard of some paintings being cut up and sold for their various parts as though the parts were complete artworks in themselves."

"Quite so. And then there are cases of paintings being passed off as original when in fact they were copies made by students at their teacher's instigation. Take for example, Rembrandt. There used to be some ninety self-portraits assigned to him, but modern scholarship has shown that part of his training of students was to have them copy his own self-portraits. So now there are only about forty self-portraits actually ascribed to Rembrandt."

"That's quite a shrink in numbers!"

"I know of one case in which a Jackson Pollock was cut up into three pieces and each piece was sold separately as a genuine Pollock, which indeed it was—partly."

"Now I begin to see why some lawyers become specialists in art cases. Plenty of opportunity out there."

"Yes, one of my favorite former students, Jim Soar, now a top New York lawyer, has resolved several fraud cases for the Metropolitan Museum."

Desdemona sat a long time in thought, then asked very seriously: "Megan, do you think it could be wrong if someone were to *save* art that hadn't been seen for decades and decades?"

"How do you mean, 'save'"?

"Well, let's say rescued from oblivion."

"Would depend on the circumstances. In principle, I should think it would be something positive, just so long as the artworks aren't then sold from underneath the original owner or as being by another artist."

Desdemona was silent for awhile, mulling over what Megan had said and wondering if she could ever show her the contents of the fourteen Kokoschka crates. Contents neither she, nor Theo Papadakis, nor anyone living knew the nature of yet. Whether they were artworks or books or what have you. That, she would only know when the crates were opened by her in the privacy of her Xenia. Oh, but it would be so grand to share them with someone!

Taking a taxi to Vienna's inner city, Desdemona dropped Megan off at the Römischer Kaiser, then proceeded to her own flat atop the Dumba palais. She hung the Böcklin *Isle of the Dead* copy over her bed, thrilled to have the mystery of her childhood memory of it reified.

67

"If you can return to my office, I should be interested in offering you a commission," Theo Papadakis said to a surprised Karl Paldovska who had just answered his smart phone. He had left Papadakis his business card after showing him photographs of the fourteen Kokoschka artworks that had been stolen from Moser's storage. And he also showed him the newly unearthed original still life with Venice in the background. Now he was on his way with it to the Amadeus Auktionshaus.

Curious, however, he retraced his steps to the building on the Graben where Papadakis's office was. It faced the famous Vienna Pest Monument. Karl wondered if that might be a sign.

"Ah, there you are again, Herr Palkovska. Good. Come sit down a minute," said Papadakis, beaming a welcome. He was at his desk and waved a hand toward the chair next to it.

Palkovska smiled his yellow-toothed smile. "Have you changed your mind about buying one of the Kokoschka still lifes should they be found?" He held up his wrapped package. "Or perhaps this recently unearthed one I showed you with fruit and a view of Venice?"

With a scowl on his face, Papadakis looked silently at the man. At last he spoke. "Do you really think you can pass phony Kokoschkas off on me?"

Palkovska looked as though he might bolt for the street. "What?"

"You know exactly what I am talking about. But forget it. I appreciate the talent involved in what you showed me and I would like to commission the person responsible to create something for me."

Karl felt a flood of relief. "Oh? And what are you thinking of?"

"To put it precisely, what I want is a same-size, nine-by-five-foot rendition of Arnold Böcklin's *Isle of the Dead*, the one that's in Geneva. It is in a private collection but you can find excellent color reproductions of it online. I want one detail altered however."

"What would that be?"

"The rowboat that approaches the island. I want it to be *leaving* the island and with only the oarsman in it. No standing figure, no coffin."

"I don't doubt that could be accomplished. Makes for a less spooky picture after all."

"And there is something else I would want done. This is why I have approached *you*. You, or your contact, seem to have a decent enough 'Kokoschka touch—for the uninitiated at least. I would stipulate that the Böcklin be painted, agitated brushstrokes and all, *in the style of Kokoschka*."

"Hm. I suppose such a thing could be done. I would have to consult my contact, however, who must remain anonymous. And the asking price would likely be substantial."

Karl could hardly believe his good luck. His finances were running low and the fact that he needed more meth emboldened him.

"I would have to have a good faith down payment now."

Theo nodded agreement. "There is one other requirement. It would have to be done *immediately*."

"I believe I could guarantee that." Karl remembered that, at the second antique store he had visited, there was an old painting from around the 1920s of the same dimensions Papadakis had specified. He could go buy it right away. Remove the varnish and paint, prime it, dry it, then apply the new paint and old varnish. He would have to go back to Boesner's for more isopropanol and acetone. And beg more discarded cotton swabs of removed varnish from the friendly restorer who worked in the back of the store. But all this was possible for the right price.

Papadakis was looking at him intently, questioningly.

"If you give me one thousand good-faith Euros now, I can guarantee you delivery in four days," Karl said, sounding unusually confident.

"All right. And, one more thing. Under the initials 'A B' on the right cliff be sure to place, as prominently as he would have done, the initials 'O K.'"

"Done."

68

Agnes looked appreciatively at her younger sister Rita. Like her, Rita was six feet tall, and also like her, had a head of luxurious brown hair. With fifteen years separating them, they could easily pass for mother and daughter, which was exactly what Agnes was counting on. The white wig she had bought was for herself; her regular blonde one was for Rita. Agnes had carefully sliced the wheelchair's padded armrests, and inserted the two loaded syringes and sealed them back with duct tape. They had rehearsed their museum scenario several times last night, and now, after a delicious breakfast in their hotel, they were ready to roll.

Roll was the right word, as Agnes, her white wig in place, was wheeled by Rita out of the hotel to a waiting taxi. At precisely ten o'clock, the museum's opening time, they were in front of the Neue Nationalgalerie with its low glass front facade. On the right side of the seven entry steps was a ramp for handicapped visitors, and Rita carefully rolled her sister up to the entry door.

They were among the very first visitors to arrive. In fact the museum was quite deserted. Clearing security—their purses riding through on the scanner belt—Rita pushed Agnes through the first two rooms of the special Kokoschka exhibit and directly into the third room. They had passed only one guard, and she was in the first room.

Once in the third room, with the wheelchair pulled up in front of the two Alma doll paintings, the two sisters parted company. Agnes quickly reopened the arm pads on her wheelchair and removed the two syringes. Rita strolled into the second room, apparently lost in contemplation of the Kokoschka graphics on display. Back in the third room Agnes sat upright, waiting, ready to leap up from her chair, a loaded syringe in each hand.

A few minutes later, entering the front room where the guard was stationed, Rita suddenly emitted a horrendous gasp, then fell to the ground moaning, her body convulsing with jerking movements, her eyes rolling upward. A very convincing epileptic seizure was being staged. The lone guard ran toward her, calling for help.

Upon hearing the sounds of Rita's "attack," Agnes jumped up from her wheelchair, syringes at the ready. But she had forgotten to fold back the foot rests. Her left foot became entangled with the front wheel and the chair tipped heavily to one side. Agnes fell against the black pedestal supporting Kokoschka's heavy bronze head. It fell directly on her, shattering her face and forehead. She died instantly.

69

Back in his Pension Suzanne room Felix Fichte did exactly what his dad had told him, placing the duffle bag with the Alma cutout under the bed. No more rolling or unrolling. Keep it as intact as possible, he had said. And continue to monitor the Römischer Kaiser to see if that Texas scholar Crespi had returned to Vienna yet.

Two mornings later he was successful in ascertaining that Crespi was now back in Wien. The desk clerk pointed her out to him. She was seated, her back to the street window, at the far end of the hotel breakfast room. Rehearsing in his head what he would say, Felix, dressed in beige shorts and a red T-shirt, approached the lady who was methodically mixing fruit and yogurt into her cereal.

"Dr. Crespi?"

"Yes?" Megan looked at the casually dressed young man, a bit too casual for the Römischer Kaiser.

"My dad is Professor Bruno Fichte of Hunter College, and he asked me to look you up. He heard from the Nebehay Antiquariat people that you're in Vienna."

"Well, as you can see, I am indeed right here in Vienna. Just got back last night as a matter of fact. Why did your father want you to look me up, and what is *your* name?"

"Oh, I'm Felix. Do you know who my dad is?"

"I'm afraid his name doesn't ring a bell."

But as soon as she said this, Megan recalled that she had come up with his name and institutional affiliation when in Basel she and Hans Tietze were looking up Fichtes and possible Fichte-Mahlers online. In fact this particular Bruno Fichte was the only one they had found in the age group that could possibly boast a great-grandson of Alma Mahler. So perhaps this Felix Fichte in front of her was a great-great-grandson of Alma Mahler's? She decided to let that go for the moment.

"Wait a minute. Yes, now I do remember noting that your father is, or was, connected to Hunter. What is his field?"

"Mesopotamian art and archaeology, especially ziggurats."

"No wonder our paths didn't cross when I was teaching at Columbia," Megan laughed. "But why would your father want you to look *me* up?"

"Yeah, well, it's a kinda long story."

Felix had memorized the misleading lines that now came from his lips. "It's like this, see. Dad has a thing for Oskar Kokoschka." Megan winced at his pronunciation of the name Kokoschka, with the stress on the second "ko," whereas it should have the accent on the first syllable, being a Czech name.

"He's collected Oskar's graphic works for decades," Felix continued, oblivious of the slight frown on Megan's face. "Now, back in New York we heard about all these bad Kokoschka happenings in Europe and even Japan, and Dad's really worried because he thinks Kokoschka, and anyone who owns Kokoschkas, are now the objects of Neo-Nazis."

"*What?*"

"Yeah. Well you know how the original Nazis called Kokoschka a degenerate artist and took all his pictures down from museums. Well, don't you see, the Neo-Nazis are hunting down Kokoschkas as degenerate art again. And *owners* of Kokoschka too. Did ya hear about the slashing of a Kokoschka wall mural in Berlin?"

Sadly, Megan knew all about the shocking discovery in Margareta Nussbaum's home. She wished she had been able to stay in Berlin longer to try to solace her 103-year-old friend who must be devastated by the vandalism.

"Yes, I have. And it is terrible."

"So don't ya see why my dad is so worried? I mean they're attackin' Kokoschka not just in museums but in private homes. And, like I said, Dad has a *huge* collection of his graphics. You can see why he's so worried."

"He lives in New York City, correct?"

"Yeah. Manhattan and Nyack too. So?"

"And there have been no Kokoschka—Megan emphasized the first syllable of the artist's name just in case the garrulous fellow caught on to the correct pronunciation—incidents of vandalism or thefts reported in New York City or Nyack, correct?"

"Yeah, that's true. So far. But, you see, my dad is just so suckin' worried.

You wouldn't believe it! And he was excited to learn from the Nebehay folks that you, a Kokoschka expert, are here in Vienna at the same time I'm here. So he wanted me to try and talk to you about what was being done by the police."

"I'm certain the police are at work not only here in Vienna, but in all the cities where Kokoschkas have been attacked or stolen. But I can't tell you any details."

Megan was beginning to wonder if she would ever be rid of her un-invited interlocutor. And her green tea was getting cold. But now she had a pressing question to ask the man and this was the moment to do so.

"Are you and your father related by any chance to Alma Mahler?"

"Oh, yeah, well sort of. Dad is actually her great-grandson, but she never acknowledged him and that sort of pissed him off. So we haven't paid much attention to that connection. After all, the woman has been dead for over fifty years."

Megan had fished out what she needed to know. The Fichte-Mahlers were related to Alma. And they were eager to talk to her so they could find out what was happening vis-à-vis the Kokoschka crimes. Perhaps they were even involved in these crimes. After all, one of the most important thefts had taken place in upstate New York when the Boston Museum loan never reached the Albright-Knox Museum.

Almost as though he felt her growing interest, Felix turned to leave saying: "Well, I'm stayin' real close to your hotel, so maybe I could talk to you again about the situation. Those dirty Neo-Nazis are really scary and my dad is just so upset about what's happening to Oskar."

"Yes, well perhaps we will talk again," Megan said in what she hoped was a strong sign of dismissal for the day.

It was not.

"It sure would help if I could go with you on your errands here concerning Oskar. You know, like kinda be your partner."

Megan could feel her toes tensing in irritation. She uttered a small lie: "I am here to authenticate Kokoschka artworks, not to be a detective."

Finally it seemed as if Felix caught on. He turned again to go, then looked back and said with a happy smile, "Boy oh boy, you sure made that Amadeus Auktionshaus man angry, didn't you!"

"What do you mean?" Suddenly Megan realized this Felix character had another dimension to him.

"Oh, um, when you told him he ought to get some Kokoschka drawing he has authenticated."

"That is common practice. I don't see why that should have angered him."

Felix held up his hands helplessly. Now Megan decided to be the interrogator.

"And why were you at Amadeus?"

"Oh, Dad told me to check out all the galleries and such while I'm here, so I had a long talk with Herr Weber about the Kokoschka mess. He told me that somebody on the inside must have been in on that robbery of Kokoschka crates."

Megan was tempted to ask if Herr Weber had also told him how to pronounce the name Kokoschka, but decided to hold her tongue.

"I would imagine the police have already explored that angle," she said instead.

"Sounded like a neat idea to me—an inside job."

Actually, Megan was glad to be reminded of such a possibility. She too had wondered about its being an inside job.

"Well, Mr. Fichte, perhaps our paths will cross again," she said, turning to her stone cold tea.

"Oh, yeah. I'll stop by tomorrow morning for sure."

Megan wondered if her face showed her exasperation. Tomorrow morning she would now either have to go to breakfast horribly early or eat breakfast out somewhere—all this nosy man's fault, damn it!

"And I'll tell my dad that we talked," Felix said as he turned and finally left the breakfast room.

Back upstairs in her room Megan called Claire in Dallas to assure her that she was all right but needed to stay on for a few days. Was Button behaving himself, she hoped? All was well in Dallas and Megan's sister Tina was checking her house daily for any important mail. She should feel free to stay as long as she was needed. Claire had given Megan's symphony ticket to her son John.

After Megan got off the phone she thought about the Fichte-Mahlers, father and son. She had never heard of a major collection of Kokoschka graphics being in New York, not that it couldn't be so, but still, it made one think. Bruno Fichte's expertise in Mesopotamian art did not immediately suggest a hunger for Kokoschka's work.

On the other hand, the Fichte's conviction that Neo-Nazis were responsible for the Kokoschka happenings might not be so wacky. The only problem with their theory was that it assumed, without exception, that images of Alma, not Oskar, were being damaged or stolen. Not that some of the pictures didn't contain Oskar's image as well, as presumably the stolen fan from Vevey did. But his face had not been damaged in the vandalized paintings, whereas hers consistently was. And yet, Alma was not Jewish. True, she married two Jews—Mahler and Werfel—but she herself, especially in later life, had demonstrated a surprisingly anti-Semitic attitude. So she didn't seem to qualify for Neo-Nazi opprobrium.

Far more likely was the possibility that the Fichte father and son duo had had something to do with the Kokoschka happenings. At least in America, where the double portrait of Oskar and Alma nude, and in lockstep, had been hijacked in upper New York state.

Nevertheless, she would keep the Neo-Nazi theory in mind when she met with Detective Versteckt at Vienna's main police station. Hans Tietze in Basel had asked her to visit the police in person in order to coordinate information and to emphasize the possible relation of the Basel *Tempest* switch to the Vienna heist of fourteen Kokoschka crates. She would ask the detective what he thought of a possible Neo-Nazi connection.

10

Rita Sauer's epileptic convulsions had miraculously subsided amid the frenetic goings on at the Neue Nationalgalerie. The clattering sound of a great crash had brought guards, including the one solicitously bending over her, rushing into the museum's third room. A horrendous sight greeted their eyes. The body of a woman lay crumpled backward over her tipped and still spinning wheelchair. Kokoschka's bronze bust lay squarely on her face—the features smashed beyond recognition. A white wig had been knocked several feet away and on the floor by the body lay two syringes.

As the guards absorbed the scene, their compassion for the dead woman turned into disbelief as her criminal intentions were revealed by the presence of the loaded syringes.

Attention turned to the woman's blonde companion who was struggling to get to her feet. The museum director had joined the guards. Rita instantly feigned a dazed state, clawing at the guard who had been bending over her for support.

"Who are you and who is your companion?" the head guard was asking her.

"I am Rita Luge," she said breathlessly, "and I don't have any companion. I'm here alone."

"Then who was the woman you wheeled into the museum and is now lying dead in there?" said the director, pointing to the third room which was being roped off from curious eyes.

"I don't know who she is. When I arrived at the museum she was approaching it in her wheelchair and asked if I would mind pushing her in through the door and through security. I did so. But we never exchanged names."

"Then you have no idea who she is?"

"None."

One of the museum guards spoke up. "I did see this lady here wheel the woman toward the far room but then she left her and was on her way back here when she was overtaken by convulsions that sent her to the floor."

"Yes, I suffer from epilepsy, and the seizure came on suddenly. This nice guard was helping me when the sound of something falling occurred."

"So you have no relationship to the dead woman at all?"

"None at all," lied Agnes's sister, stooping as she spoke in the hope that no one would notice her tall height was the same as that of the dead woman.

The director spoke up as the police and an ambulance arrived. "Nevertheless we will have to ask you to stay and give a statement to the police."

"Of course," said an unruffled Rita. In her mind she was cursing their employer Leo Lang for having gotten her and her poor sister into such a situation. Well, as soon as she extracted herself from this mess at the museum she would pay the man a visit. So far she had been successful in putting off comprehending the full impact of her sister's death. She had been in such a merry mood just the evening before. She would try to remember her that way. And she would avenge her death.

11

Theo Papadakis had been more than pleased with Karl Palkovska's so-called contact's work. Just as he had promised, Karl brought him the finished, dried, and even discreetly framed "Kokoschka" copy of Arnold Böcklin's *Isle of the Dead*, Geneva version. Theo had to admire not only the excellent copy of Böcklin's *Isle*, but also the Kokoschkaesque handling of the surface with its sprawling bursts of paint and insistent spatula thrusts. How could Frau Dumba not want to acquire this glorious find? Especially after the Christomanos disappointment. A disappointment which he too had shared, not having suspected that what Helmut Haesslich would show his valued client was a forgery.

But this, this doubly endowed painting combining both Böcklin and Kokoschka, this was an absolutely brilliant work of art. And it was all his idea. Yes, he, Papadakis, knew how to tweak a client's innermost desires. Put yourself in your client's place. This was the true secret of his renowned successes.

And now Frau Dumba was back in Vienna. He would invite her to his office right away. And tell her to come alone. He certainly did not want the Texas woman to be there with her. What a fiasco that had been in Berlin. The way that woman went up and actually sniffed the Christomanos! And studied the back of the canvas. And then that interfering expert from New

York, Janette Killar. No, he needed to have Frau Dumba come to him. She would see the Kokoshchka-Bocklin *Isle* the moment she walked in and she would fall totally in love with it.

Things went just as Papadakis had envisioned. Frau Dumba came to his office that very afternoon. He had placed the framed painting on an easel facing the entrance door of his office on the Graben. Frau Dumba arrived at four o'clock. She neglected to close the door behind her when her eyes met the commanding three-by-four-foot painting. She gasped.

"This cannot be possible!"

"Yes, Frau Dumba, it is."

"Kokoschka painting a copy of Böcklin's *Isle*?"

"But as you know, gnädige Frau, Kokoschka traveled all around Greece, painted different sites there, and wrote about his experiences there. Perhaps he even saw your Xenia. We do not know. His letters and autobiographies make no mention of the isle. What we can know is that he wanted to have his own memento of Böcklin's image of Greece, and so he painted a copy for himself."

"Of course. He would have known Böcklin from reproductions if not in person. And his love of Greece found a responsive chord in the artist's *Isle of the Dead*. I see, I see," murmured Desdemona, half to herself.

"I have researched the six known versions of Böcklin's *Isle* depictions and this is the one in Geneva, in a private collection. Because Kokoschka lived in Switzerland so long he might well have seen and copied the picture in the flesh, if he became acquainted with the owner."

"That seems reasonable. But how interesting that he has the rowboat *leaving* the islet, empty of woman and coffin—only the rower. I wonder what that means?"

"Yes, I see. How interesting." Theo had learned to let his customers find things in the works he offered them.

"And look how boldly he signs the painting 'O K' right under Böcklin's own initials on the right hand cliff."

"I must warn you, gnädige Frau, this painting is not in the Killar catalogue raisonné."

"What does that matter? It is Böcklin *and* Kokoschka all at once! I love it. And I must install it at Xenia, yes, Xenia. What is your price, Herr Papadakis?"

"I have it on commission for a client who wishes to remain anonymous. He is asking one-hundred-and-forty thousand Euros, but I told him that since it was only Kokoschka's copy of another painting, he could probably not get more than one-hundred-thousand Euros. I am afraid he will not take less than that. I talked him out of offering it at auction. But he has only given me a month to move the painting. Otherwise he will indeed place it for auction at the Dorotheum."

"No, no. I cannot let that happen. I shall write you a check here and now." Desdemona was almost beside herself with excitement. Her face fairly glowed.

"Now express ship it, please, to my warehouse in Greece where the other fourteen crates await me. My trusty handyman will then ferry them all over to Xenia. I shall be going there myself in a few days."

"Exactly as you wish, gnädige Frau, we shall do exactly as you wish."

12

"She said she was here only to authenticate Kokoschka works, but after we talked in her hotel breakfast room I followed her and she went straight to the main police station."

Felix was reporting in to his father after a morning of shadowing Megan Crespi. Upon exiting the police station she had returned to the Annagasse but not to her hotel. Instead she entered the Nebehay Antiquariat, probably to confer with Dr. Klug there. Felix had kept watch from across the street and witnessed, without being seen, Crespi's exit about twenty minutes later, at which point she did in fact return to the Römischer Kaiser.

"I guess the old gal needs her rest for the day," Felix concluded.

"Not necessarily," said Bruno. Continue to be on the watch. From everything I hear about her, she has the energy of a much younger woman.

Did you have a chance to dangle the Neo-Nazi element before her?"

"Oh, yeah. She seemed kinda interested."

"And you told her about my fear of having my so-called Kokoschka collection attacked?" Felix noticed his father pronounced the crazy painter's name the same way Crespi had.

"Yeah, I sure did. She tried to point out that there had been no robberies or vandalism in Manhattan or Nyack."

"In Nyack! How the hell would she know about Nyack?"

"Oops. I guess I slipped there. Just let it out, ya know. Sorry, Dad."

"Just let it slip? Are you crazy? No one knows I have a house in Nyack. You know how hard I've tried to keep that a secret. And here you go blabbing to someone like Megan Crespi! Whatever is the matter with you?"

"Dad, I said I'm sorry."

"Sorry isn't enough. What if she mentioned us and Nyack to the police there? Surely she went over all the Kokoschka incidents with them. And whatever the Vienna police know, the New York police will know soon enough. They exchange information, especially in an international crime situation."

"Well, wadda ya want me to do now? *Kill* the old dame? Like I did with the night watchman at Vevey?"

"You say that in jest, Felix. But I am thinking this might actually be a necessity. Especially now that you have blurted out the fact of our second home to her."

"Jeez, Dad. How do you figure I can do that? She's always surrounded by people."

"But she has to get from one place to the next, and in the inner city there, she'd hardly take a taxi. She'd walk. You will simply have to be on watch, all the time."

"Let me be sure I've got this straight, Dad. You actually want me to *eliminate* Crespi?"

"Don't put it that way, son, just make sure she is put out of commission. And soon. Perhaps she has not yet blathered to the police about the Kokoschka disappearance in America. But we can't know. As I said, these police departments exchange information when different countries are involved."

"Okay, Dad, whatever you say."

"And, Felix, don't take any unnecessary risks, all right?"

"All right."

After they hung up, Bruno felt sick with worry. All he could do was hope the Nyack slip had made no impression on Crespi. But he could not be sure. It was best that she be silenced.

13

Rita Sauer-Luge, after being interrogated by the police at the scene of Agnes Sauer's death, had returned to her hotel without being detained further. She was filled with anger. Anger that her sister had met with such a horrible accident when the caper should have been so easy, and anger at her sister's Viennese employer Leo Lang.

She could do something about the latter. She pulled up Lufthansa on her smart phone and made a reservation for a nonstop flight to Vienna leaving later that day. After checking out of the Kempinski, she remained in the lobby researching Leo Lang on her laptop until time to take a taxi out to Berlin's Tegel airport.

An hour and twenty minutes later her plane touched down in Vienna. Rita rented a car. She had reserved a room at the Penzing district hotel An der Wien, not far from Leo Lang's villa. Before checking into her hotel she circled the Art nouveau villa, observing the layout and the fact that there was a balcony over the ornate front door. When it got dark she would return and check the grounds around the house as well as the back and any side entrances. She was encouraged that the house had many windows and two more balconies at either end of the front façade.

Night had fallen and after passing the Church am Steinhof from which Rita could see part of the Lang villa, she parked a block down from the building. She was dressed in black and equipped with a heavy duty flashlight, a multi-tool Swiss knife, a pepper spray, and a garrote wire.

Going around the left side of the house on her way to check out the back entrance, she looked into one of the brightly lit windows and observed a solitary diner at a long dinner table. He was a thin man—in his late fifties, most probably. He had a long-boned face, gray stubble on his chin, and a receding hairline. Just as her sister had described him. Rita pressed her face against the window and saw further into the room. At the opposite end of the dinner table sat a second diner clothed in a blue dress, her breasts totally exposed. But this diner was not eating. In fact she could not eat because she was not human. She was a life-size, stuffed doll. Again, just as Agnes had described to her. The madman and his erotic partner.

Immediately Rita decided that Lang's death must be an ironic one. One that would include his gynoid-Alma. If her sister had died an ironic death because of a Kokoschka bronze head falling on her, so would Leo Lang die a paradoxical death. She would wait several hours to make sure her proposed victim was in bed asleep. In the meantime, while he was still eating dinner, she would enter the house and acquaint herself with the layout of rooms.

The backdoor lock turned as soon as Rita had inserted the third of her Swiss knife's blades. There was no one in the kitchen. Stealthily she entered the rooms on the ground floor one by one, avoiding the dining room where the meal was still in progress. Up on the second floor she came across several book-lined rooms, the largest of which appeared to be a den. She climbed to the third floor and entered what had to be Lang's bedroom. It contained a king-size bed with a wooden valet in front of the closets on either side. On one was hung a pair of men's pajamas; on the other a long white nightgown. Obviously the doll "slept" with him. Taking a position behind the velvet curtains that were drawn closed across the French windows, Rita bided her time. Sooner or later Leo Lang would retire for the evening with his doll. Rita would be ready.

Leo Lang had drunk more than usual of his favorite Johnny Walker Platinum Scotch whiskey with his dinner. He was hugely upset by the evening television news. Apparently an attempt had been made at Berlin's

Neue Nationalgalerie to damage Kokoschka paintings on exhibit there. The would-be perpetrator of the crime had been found dead, hit by a large bronze bust that had fallen on her. The wheelchair she had been in had tipped over sideways and two syringes loaded with acid were on the floor by the victim's hands. It was a freak accident. No one else had been involved.

"Damn that Agnes Sauer and her botched job!" Leo had exclaimed aloud, addressing the placid Alma at the other end of the table. Sauer still had the seven Kokoschka fans with her. Where were they now? In her hotel room? How soon would that room be searched? How quickly would the discovery be made that it was Agnes Sauer who had stolen the fans from the Hamburg museum? There was no chance that Leo could lay his hands on them now. The fans, with their despicable images of the woman for whom Kokoschka had jilted his grandmother, would go back on display for all the world to see. Rebarbative!

It was getting late. Leo was exhausted emotionally and physically. He had drunk far too much. Better to forget about things for now and go to bed. He picked up the Alma doll and slowly climbed with her to the third floor. In his bedroom he first changed into his own pajamas, the top only, then carefully undressed the doll and slipped the white negligee over her body. He placed her on her back on the bed with her legs spread wide apart. He knelt astride her. It was then he realized he was too besotted to perform. He rolled over on his back and within seconds was sound asleep, snoring loudly.

Rita's moment had come. She emerged from the concealing drape, flexed her garrote, and approached Lang's side of the bed. He gave a loud moan and, still snoring, turned fitfully on his side toward the doll. Rita quickly wrapped the wire around his neck and pulled. The man never had a chance to wake up: he was conscious only of increasing, suffocating pain. Then he was dead.

His murderer's work was not yet done. She picked up the Alma doll and positioned her atop Leo's body, her hands wrapped around his throat. It was thus that the dirty old recluse would be found, if anyone should even wonder about him.

Rita's sister was avenged.

14

After her breakfast had been interrupted by that dreadful Felix Fichte-Mahler, and after she had made her call to Dallas, Megan walked to the central police building for her midmorning appointment with Detective Peter Versteckt.

"Please to sit here, Frau Doktor," an amiable but obviously high strung Detective Versteckt said to her.

"Thank you for seeing me. My colleague, Dr. Hans Tietze in Basel, is most eager to learn, as am I, of any new developments in the Kokoschka crate robbery case, as well as in other cities where destruction or theft of Kokoschka has occurred."

"Of course. I can understand that you are both greatly concerned. So far this is what we have learned. In regard to the fourteen crates theft, we are now interrogating a certain Sibyl Speros, one of the employees who has access to all the Moser company records. So far we have learned nothing from her, but if the robbery was an inside job, which we think it had to be, she is the only person at the firm responsible for data that would have enabled such a heist."

Megan interrupted. "Sibyl Speros? That's a Greek name, isn't it?"

"Yes, I suppose so. The Moser firm is quite integrated: they have a Japanese and a Pakistani working there as well. Why do you ask?"

"Oh, no reason. The name just struck me, that's all."

"Well let me ask *you* a question, Doktor Crespi, since you are American. What do you know about the theft of that large Kokoschka oil from the Boston Museum while it was being transferred to another museum? Have the police made any progress with that case?"

"Not to my knowledge, but then I've been in Europe for the past week. However, I have come across something strange that may be of use to both you and the American police."

"And what is that?"

"Does the name Bruno Fichte or Bruno Fichte-Mahler mean anything to you? Also Felix Fichte or Felix Fichte-Mahler?"

"No."

"Well, they are father and son, live in New York *and* Nyack, and apparently have an extensive collection of Kokoschka graphic works, not oils, but works on paper. Bruno Fichte's son is here in Wien and he contacted me this morning while I was having breakfast at my hotel."

"Yes," said Detective Versteckt, starting to take notes.

"He told me that they fear their collection might be in danger, given what's been happening to Kokoschka works in Europe and Japan. In danger because of the rise of the Neo-Nazis."

"The Neo-Nazis? They are behind all sorts of violent demonstrations lately. Just look at how they took over Essen's Folkwang Museum a couple of days ago. They attacked two paintings, one by a Jew and one by a degenerate artist, if you go back to Hitler times."

"Just so."

"So you think these Kokoschka crimes are the work of Neo-Nazis?"

"Not exactly. It's just something to keep on the table. For instance, I suppose one could read Neo-Nazi involvement in the substitution of a blonde, 'Aryan' woman in the *Tempest* painting that was left in the Basel Museum in place of the painting that was stolen. It showed a dark-haired woman, Alma Mahler."

"Well, there are no Neo-Nazis in Japan, I don't think, so the damage done to the portrait of Alma Mahler there certainly doesn't seem to be a political act."

"I agree with you. But what we keep coming back to is that the recent spate of vandalism concerns either the defacement of a Kokoschka depiction of Alma Mahler or the theft of a painting in which she is portrayed, such as the Boston Museum's *Two Nudes: Two Lovers*. And don't forget that this pertains to the two Alma doll paintings at Berlin's Neue Nationalgalerie. They were the obvious intended victims there."

"Ah ha. So you are saying we should keep our eye on a Mahler connection. Perhaps this Fichte-Mahler father and son duo you have mentioned."

"Yes, I think it would be wise to confer with your New York police contacts and see if either father or son has ever been arrested on charges related to art."

"Colossal! I shall get to work on that today. Here is my card and might I have your card as well, Doktor Crespi?"

After a few more exchanges Megan left the police station, pleased over the exchange with Detective Versteckt. She had no idea that she was being followed by one of the persons she had mentioned to the detective.

15

Desdemona had returned to the intense, sad state usually so characteristic of her. Her "Sisi" state, she called it. Gallivanting around Berlin with the energetic but prudent Megan Crespi had, in spite of the Christomanos disappointment, lifted her spirits and prompted a rare spontaneity in her. She realized that she longed to have a close friend like Megan. And she yearned to share her Xenia with someone. Perhaps she could convince Megan to fly with her to Greece.

She had just come back from her doctor's office with her wrists newly wrapped in plaster casts. She was healing nicely, her physician had told her, but the casts must stay on for another five weeks. Now she was awaiting Megan for lunch and what she hoped would be a successful invitation to travel with her to Greece for a few days. She had decided to take the plunge. If Megan came to Xenia with her, she would reveal her most recent acquisition to her. They would go together to her island. They would watch as her handyman opened the crate. And Megan would see the remarkable copy Kokoschka had made of Böcklin's isle portrayal—*her* isle.

As for the contents of the fourteen other crates awaiting her at Xenia, she had not yet decided whether or not to share them with Megan. That is, if she could persuade Megan to accompany her there. Heaven knows she could do with some help while her wrists were still in casts. But how wonderful it would be to look at the Kokoschka *Isle* copy with an expert on the artist.

As Megan walked up the Ringstrasse to Desdemona's apartment atop the Dumba palais, she was unaware that she was being followed. Felix Fichte remained some fifty paces behind her, but it was easy to spot the nimble walker because she wore a red woven cap with a small brim, even though the weather was warm and sunny. Just one of the senior citizen's many quirks.

Lunch with Desdemona was delightful. The usually somber woman was full of enthusiasm because she would soon be leaving for Greece. And truly, Megan must come along as her guest. Try as she might to defer the invitation to another time, her hostess was insisting upon *now*. After lunch, when they had settled in the music room for tea and to admire Klimt's Schubert, she ceremoniously handed Megan an air ticket.

"It's open ended," Desdemona declared, her dark eyes sparkling. You can return whenever you like, but please, please leave with me day after tomorrow."

Megan gave up. "All right, I'll try to get most of my business done in time to leave. But I'll have to call Dallas and tell my doggie that his human won't be home when she thought she would be."

"I've often thought of having a dog companion, but I do too much traveling from Wien to Greece and back to make it feasible."

"They are such wonders, dogs. Every time you come home they give you a standing ovation. Why don't you at least consider it. If you did get a dog, what breed would you like?"

"Guess, Megan, guess."

Megan eyed her hostess, remembering that it was a proven fact that people were often drawn to dogs that reflected them, often even looked like them. So certainly not a bull dog. Possibly a collie? But no, a more exotic breed. Finally she stated her guess.

"An Afghan Hound?"

"Yes! But how could you guess?"

"Well, there is something aristocratic about them, and they are long-limbed and long-haired, like you."

"I appreciate the compliment. Perhaps it is in the cards that I add an Afghan to my life."

"I hope so, Desdemona. But now I really must go. Duty calls. Especially if we are to leave for Athens in just two days. That only gives me today and tomorrow."

Her guest looked at her thoughtfully. Would she dare to show Megan her Kokoschka trove?

Felix Fichte had failed to see Megan exit from the side of palais Dumba, but he spotted her red cap as she turned to walk along the Ringstrasse toward the Opera House. He fell in step behind her, wondering what on earth her mission had been to take so long inside the British Kookshop, the store near the corner she must have entered. She had not come out with any packages.

Megan, speaking on a smart phone, led him past the Kunsthistorisches Museum in the Maria-Theresien-Platz and on to the Museumsplatz where she entered the Leopold Museum. Felix selected his post across from the museum, which he knew was devoted to works by Klimt, Kokoschka, and Schiele, and impatiently took up his watch again.

Inside the Leopold, Megan took the stairs to the director's office where Johannes—"Hannes"—Ohm stood waiting for her.

"Come in, come in. What is the latest on the Kokoschka front?"

Megan told him about her conversation with Detective Versteckt and that she had suggested a background check on the Fichte-Mahlers, father and son. She also mentioned to Hannes the Neo-Nazi element and was glad to hear him poo-poo any such connection with the Kokoschka incidents.

"Why would Neo-Nazis carefully replace *The Tempest* in Basel with another version by Kokoschka? Why wouldn't they just destroy the original? And why was Tokyo's Alma Mahler portrait as Mona Lisa attacked? She wasn't Jewish after all. No, I don't buy that theory. Who suggested it to you?"

"You might be surprised to learn that it was the son of Alma's great-grandson, Felix Fichte-Mahler. And even more surprising is that neither he nor his father, Bruno, use Mahler in their surname. It's as though they do not want the connection to be known."

"Did you tell the police that?"

"Yes, I did. I suggested that they contact the New York police about them, since they both live in New York. Although right now Felix is here in Vienna. He importuned me at breakfast this morning. Wants to be my 'partner' in exploring the Kokoschka crimes. You can imagine what I said to him about that!"

"Indeed I can," said Hannes fondly, remembering what a private person Megan usually was. But sometimes the Italian half of her heritage emerged and she could become unexpectedly animated and expansive. This usually culminated in making music of some sort, even if it was only singing. But the Megan he saw today was in the throes of her Scotch-Irish half, and she was tenaciously pursuing the Kokoschka happenings, speaking in a clipped, serious manner.

"Do you think your Kokoschkas here in the museum are safe from attack?"

"The moment the news about Basel reached us we enhanced our security here. I think everything is safe. Unless some lunatic tries something. And even then, we have well-trained, alert guards. Also our security cameras are some of the best on the market. No, I am not overly worried."

After a few more minutes of conversation Megan left Hannes and visited the gift shop on the way out. There were always new publications to leaf through and interesting souvenirs. One of the best museum shops in Vienna, she thought.

Felix spotted Megan as she finally left the museum and followed her back toward the Ring and ultimately to the Annagasse and her hotel. He wondered whether he might take a break from watching Crespi's movements. The old biddy was probably taking a nap. Reluctantly, he took his stance opposite the hotel. Forty-five minutes passed and suddenly Crespi exited the hotel. Good thing he had waited. He did not have to follow her very far. At the end of the Annagasse she crossed one street over to the Walfischgasse—*his* hotel street—and entered an Italian restaurant, Il Tempo Bistro.

Ah ha! Maybe he could get a bite to eat as well at the nearby sushi bar. He could still keep an eye on Crespi's restaurant. Eventually she did indeed appear, exiting Il Tempo and walking purposefully back up the street. Felix, his meal long since devoured, fell in behind her. Perhaps he could jump her from the back and break her neck. But there were too many pedestrians, both on the Walfischgasse and then on the Annagasse, where she turned in for the night, obviously.

Now I can do something *I* want to do, Felix thought, envisioning his favorite red light district. But first he had to report the day's activities to his father.

Bruno was not at all pleased by his son's accounting of the day.

"You've got to get her alone somehow. As long as she's walking around the inner city it's going to be difficult. Too many people. What if you were to catch her in the hotel as she leaves her room for breakfast? Or on her way back to her room? As I recall the hotel staircase winds around the single small elevator.

"Yeah, that's a good idea, Dad. But how am I gonna find out what floor she's on and which is her room?"

"*Shadow* her, boy, shadow her!"

"But she's bound to spot me. Especially in a such a small hotel."

"That's where you have to use your ingenuity. Do you know if she goes back to her room after breakfast, or does she go straight out on her errands?"

"This morning she went back to her room."

"All right then. Early tomorrow morning linger in the lounge until you see her take the elevator up. If you take the stairs you can easily tell which floor it stops at. Then you can make your move."

"Okay, Dad, I'll try."

His duty call over, Felix headed over to the Naschmarkt area for what he hoped would be a pleasant night's activities.

16

Olda Palkovska-Kokoschka's nephew had been busy in his Simmering rented room. He had created two more "lost" Kokoschka still lifes, one with a view of Delphi, the other with a panorama of Jerusalem. Both were excellent, with an arrangement of different fruits in front. He had two likely customers: Cornelius Weber of the Amadeus Auktionshaus and Theo Papadakis, for whom he had concocted the copy, supposedly by Kokoschka, of Arnold Böcklin's *Isle of the Dead*. He had placed his previous Kokoschka still life with a view of Venice with Weber for the next Amadeus auction, but he hated to wait all that time.

A new plan began to engage him after he had taken another dose of meth. What about contacting that renowned Graz collector of Kokoschka, Kallias Andriopoulos? Yes, he was a recluse, but he was an obsessive hoarder of all things Kokoschka. Karl had located the man's e-mail address and could write him that he had two Kokoschka still lifes with cityscapes in the background for sale and that he was planning a business trip to Graz. He could jump on a railjet to Graz and be there within two hours and a half. Simple. Why wait for an auction when he could reach a potential buyer directly?

Just to make sure, however, he telephoned Theo Papadakis and asked if there were any more services he could render him.

"Nothing at the moment. However, I can tell you that your Kokoschka-Böcklin copy has been sold. I was about to contact you about coming to pick up your payment this morning."

"Wonderful! I'll come round immediately."

Karl was tempted to ask Papadakis what he knew about his fellow Greek who lived in Graz, but knew he shouldn't raise any flags as to his plan to visit the lion in his lair. He would tell no one about his plan and could leave for Graz the minute he received a reply from Andriopoulos. Why hadn't he thought about resuscitating Kokoschka's still lifes years ago? Now he would no longer have to marry that wealthy but unattractive widow in Geneva. Things were picking up. And the quality of crystal meth in Austria was better than in Switzerland.

Megan's last day in Vienna before leaving for Greece with Desdemona—and she had finally warmed to the idea—was going to be spent at the University of Applied Art's Oskar Kokoschka Center, which contained not only transcripts of letters and speeches but also the private library of Oskar and Olda. In order to effect this without running into that pest Felix Fichte-Mahler, she skipped her morning exercises, doing only the Pilates plank, and left her hotel at six-thirty in the morning.

She walked over to the Stubenring and a Tutti Frutti shop she knew of opposite the Kokoschka Center. Already salivating, she gave her order: banana, blueberries, strawberries, almond milk, yogurt, coffee, and chocolate. The result was absolutely sensational and Megan sipped the breakfast in ecstasy while gazing across at the Oskar Kokoschka Platz, wondering why Klimt and Schiele had not merited the same honor.

After a final sip of her delicious shake, Megan crossed over to the square and, before entering the building, walked up to admire the Easter-Island-like giant gray head of Kokoschka installed outside it. The carved head was a larger version by a modern artist of the self-portrait bronze head on exhibit that recently had fallen and killed a museum visitor in Berlin. The newspapers and television had delighted in featuring the unsolved mystery of why a woman in a wheelchair was visiting a Kokoschka exhibition with two loaded syringes.

To Megan it was no mystery at all. If only the police could get a handle on who it was who wanted to obliterate the face of Alma Mahler, even if only the doll image of her, as in the two paintings featured at the Berlin show.

She entered the University and in another few minutes had been assigned a chair and monitor in the Kokoschka reading room. She hoped to find something, anything that might aid her and the police in figuring out why such hatred had been ignited toward one of Vienna's most important painters.

Although he detested rising so early, Felix was on duty in the lounge of the Römischer Kaiser at seven-thirty sharp. Evidently Crespi was sleeping late, because at nine-thirty she still had not made an appearance. By ten o'clock the breakfast buffet bar was being taken down and yet the woman still had not shown up. What the hell? And now *he* was starving. He went off to get a quick bite at the end of the Annagasse, keeping an eye on the hotel entrance. Two hours later he was still standing there. The woman simply had not exited the hotel. Bummer. Felix got up his courage, entered the hotel and approached the desk clerk.

"Is Doktor Crespi in?"

"No, she left quite early this morning." Felix was stunned.

"For good? Or just for the day, do you know?"

"Oh, just for the day. It's tomorrow that she leaves us. Off to Greece she told me."

Felix uttered a prolonged fuck to himself, turned, and left the hotel. Oh, hell, can't follow her today and tomorrow she's leaving the country. For Greece of all places! It seemed there was just no way he was going to be able to dispatch her. Maybe his dad would change his mind about her. She was eighty, after all. What harm could she do?

He decided to call his father, even though he would be disappointed by the news. He did and he was. Not so much disappointed as enraged.

"Can't you get anything right? You should have been watching her hotel from six o'clock in the morning on. Did it not occur to you that after your meeting yesterday she might not want to talk to you again?"

"Yeah. But who'd have thought she'd be up and gone by seven o'clock," Felix exaggerated the time of his arrival by thirty minutes.

"You should have been there at six, that's all there is to it."

"So whadaya want me to do now? Fly home?"

"Not yet. You say she's leaving for Greece tomorrow. Haunt her hotel for the rest of today and into this evening. Maybe there will be an opportunity to follow her elevator to the floor her room is on. That's the best spot for you to attack her—when she's alone in the corridor to her room. If that doesn't work, you'll have one more chance tomorrow morning. But get with it, boy, get with it!"

18

Kallias Andriopoulos was a pathetic figure. Eighty-five, grossly overweight, with heavy white eyebrows and long thick sideburns, he had been cursed with a terrible temper. That irascible temper had been the cause of the alienation of all the members of his family. His wife, their two sons, and three grandchildren had returned to Greece five years ago. They had always hated Austria and the "provincial" city of Graz in particular, whereas he had loved it. As a boy he attended the university there and when his multi-million dollar winery business brought him back to Styria's steep, corrugated vineyards he could not have been more pleased. He brought his entire family with him and set up an international headquarters in Graz.

It was there, at the Joanneum Museum that he had, as a student, encountered his first Kokoschka: a large and riveting view of Delphi. Of Delphi! The city of his birth! From that moment on he was committed to collecting the master, a commitment that was strengthened when he learned how much the Austrian artist loved Greece. And how many cities he had visited and depicted there. It was in Greece, in 1961, that Kokoschka created lithographs for his series, *Homage to Hellas*, of which Andriopoulos had several editions.

On business in Switzerland a few years later, Andriopoulos managed to secure an invitation from Kokoschka to visit him at his home in Villeneuve. The artist had been impressed by the fact that the Greek collector had bought his 1925 painting of a ferocious tigon, the hybrid cross between a lioness and a male tiger he had come across and depicted at the London Zoo.

From then on Kokoschka had given Andriopoulos advance notice whenever his Swiss dealer had a new painting by him for sale. Through the years the ardent collector bought some eleven more major late works by Kokoschka, all of them dazzling cityscapes. With one exception. He had placed the winning bid at Sotheby's auction of Kokoschka's large double portrait *Woman and Slave*, also known as *Mania*. Painted during the artist's short stay in Vienna in the spring of 1920, it summed up the enslaved state he then felt had been his relationship with Alma and his mania for her. This confession in paint was a treasure Andriopoulos had to have. It hung in his Graz living room where from the opposite wall the tigon bared its fangs at it.

Without his family, Andriopoulos lived alone in his great yellow manor house out on Erdbergweg overlooking the city of Graz. His needs were few. Once a week a maid came in to clean and bring in food supplies. Otherwise he was alone. He rarely had friends in. His treasured companion was the Internet, which he had mastered with alacrity when he realized he could obtain instant news of the world, and of the Kokoschka market. Because he was not finished acquiring works by the unusual man whose written works—their commentary on the complexity of humankind—he considered as valuable as the artist's paintings. Andriopoulos conducted an active e-mail correspondence with various art dealers around the world.

At noontime a most interesting e-mail had come in from a certain Karl Palkovska of Geneva, presently in Vienna. He introduced himself as Olda Kokoschka's nephew, wrote that he had helped her settle the artist's estate and create the Kokoschka Foundation at Vevey. He declared that he was now ready to sell some of the Kokoschka still lifes with city scenes he had come by, and if Herr Andriopoulos were interested he could bring two of them with him on an imminent business trip that called him to Graz. One of the city scenes was of Delphi, very close to the large view of Delphi in Graz's Joanneum.

Andriopoulos hastened to answer the intriguing e-mail saying he would be happy to receive him at his home when he arrived in Graz. Could it be as early as the next afternoon by any chance? This was all Karl Palkovska needed. He would pack up his freshly minted still lifes that very night and take the noon railjet to Graz the next day. He informed his cyber correspondent that he would appear at his door around 3:30 in the afternoon with the two paintings in hand.

It was hard to tell who was the more excited: Karl Palkovska, the industrious forger, or Kallias Andriopoulos, the fanatical collector.

19

Once again Felix was dogging Megan's footsteps. That evening she was walking from her hotel over to the Parkring and the palais Dumba. He was mystified. The stores were closing, why would she want to go there? But she did not enter any of the shops. Instead, she went to the side of the building facing the Schwarzenbergplatz and disappeared into a small entrance. Felix was mystified. Still, the outdoor tables of the Café Schwarzenberg on the corner offered a perfect view of the side door Crespi had taken. Felix selected a table, sat down, and ordered a Berliner Weisse. Two hours went by. What was the busybody up to now?

Megan had just finished the sumptuous meal Desdemona's cook had provided and they were now taking their coffee in the cozy music room, facing Klimt's Schubert.

"Have you ever been to Greece before, Megan, dear?"

"Yes, twice. Once when I was twenty with my mother to see Athens and climb up to the Acropolis, and once just a few years ago when I was in pursuit of Giorgio de Chirico's Greek roots. His parents were Italian and his father was involved with constructing the railroad system for Greece, as you may know."

"No, I did not know. You mean to say that de Chirico was *Greek*?"

"Yes, he was born in Volos, so I flew up to the port city just to see if I could perceive any pictorial influences there for his empty squares, the ones usually called 'Italian piazzas.'"

"So you mean all those mysterious pictures showing a train engine encroaching upon an empty square go back to Greece for inspiration?"

"Oh, yes. Well, at least the train references could. His father was an engineer of physical space; his son of metaphysical space. By the way, Giorgio also had a brother who became a composer. Did you know that?"

"No, I didn't."

"He took the pseudonym Alberto Savino. Both brothers were sent to Munich for their further studies, and that is where Giorgio encountered the work of Arnold Böcklin. So in a sense we have a direct line from the Swiss artist's mysterious islands through de Chirico's enigmatic city squares—and there are some fifteen major ones in Volvos—to Kokoschka's vibrant vistas of ancient cities."

"Oh, but it all connects!" said Desdemona happily, thinking of her new acquisition, Kokoschka's copy of Böcklin. She could hardly wait to show it to Megan.

"Yes, and add to that de Chirico's interest in Schopenhauer and Nietzsche, and you've got a writer every bit as active as Kokoschka was a painter. Both addressed the mystery of life and art."

"So they were both not only painters but creative writers as well."

"Right. There is a charming self-portrait by de Chirico done when he was only twenty-three. It shows him at bust level, in profile, one hand supporting his chin as he meditates. On the frame below are written words I used to ask my students in Dallas to memorize—perhaps the only Latin to which some of them were ever exposed."

"Latin with a Texas accent?"

Desdemona saw a frown cross Megan's face. "I am joking. Tell me please, what were the words?"

"*Et quid amabo nisi quod aenigma est?*"

"'And what shall I love if not that which is enigma?' Very nice, very nice."

"As I said, de Chirico, like Kokoschka, was a philosopher as well as an artist."

"I wonder if they knew each other?"

"I don't know. Certainly they knew *of* one another. And their dates are remarkably parallel: Kokoschka was born in eighteen-eighty-six and lived until nineteen-eighty; de Chirico was born two years after Kokoschka and died just two years before Kokoschka—very easy to remember."

"Play something for me, Megan, before you go back to the hotel," Desdemona requested, changing the subject and looking at her cast-wrapped wrists ruefully.

"All right. Here's something evocative, since we've been talking about de Chirico. I call it *Manhattan Nocturne*. I composed it when I was living and teaching in New York."

Megan sat down at the magnificent Bösendorfer and played her *nocturne* very slowly and with feeling.

"Oh, that is so lovely!"

"Thank you. It's the only piece of mine that was ever transcribed for orchestra. If you tap the two quarter notes on the menu bar of my website, you can hear it."

"I shall indeed do so, Megan. After all *et quid amabo nisi quod musica est?*"

"Me too," Megan laughed. The two friends talked further about Greece and tomorrow's plans, then finally called it a night around ten o'clock. "I'll pick you up in the limo precisely at seven tomorrow morning," Desdemona said in farewell.

As Megan emerged from the palais Dumba side door a man sitting at one of the Café Schwarzenberg tables shrank into himself, hoping he would not be recognized. Megan passed by without noticing him. The Schwarzenbergplatz was too filled with pedestrians, but the narrower Schwarzenbergstrasse Megan would be taking back into the inner city to reach the Annagasse would be more deserted this time of night. This could be Felix's chance.

As Megan started to turn off the Schwarzenbergplatz she heard her name being yelled. She turned around to see two people running after her: Karin Schwind and Paul Cernak, her friends from Hungarian Revolution days.

"Megan! We dropped in to see you at your hotel," panted Karin, "but they said you'd gone out. We thought we should have one more dinner together at our Wienerwald restaurant. So when you weren't in, we ate at the Café Schwarzenberg instead and just couldn't believe our eyes when we saw you walk by!"

"Well, at least you can walk me back to the Römischer, if you're game."

"Why not? We'll see you right up to your room," laughed Paul.

The trio linked arms and cheerfully set off, singing at the top of their voices.

Shadowing them was a morose Felix Fichte-Mahler.

80

Paul and Karin had indeed seen Megan up to her hotel room where they devoured three tiny Baileys Irish Creams she had collected on various plane flights. They did not break up until just before midnight.

Felix was in the lobby of the Römischer Kaiser at six the next morning. The man at reception had not seen him come in and from his post in the lounge he had a clear view of the hotel elevator and stairs. Crespi would not elude him this time. When she went back upstairs from breakfast to get her suitcase he would follow, wait outside the door to her room and catch her in the corridor when she reemerged. In his left shirt pocket was a handkerchief and a vial of chloroform. He would apply it smack in her face, then twist and break her neck. Shouldn't be hard with such an old lady and couldn't take more than three minutes.

He waited an hour. A few other guests were now in the breakfast room but Crespi had not yet made an appearance. He heard the receptionist's phone ring.

"Yes, we'll send him right up," he heard him say. A few minutes later the elevator door opened and there was Crespi. At the same time, bounding down the stairs that wrapped around the elevator, was the hotel porter. He was carrying the woman's two small but obviously heavy bags. Nodding farewell to the receptionist, Crespi headed straight out the back door to the street where a black limousine was waiting.

Felix stood frozen to the spot where he had witnessed this sudden exit. *The god damned woman had skipped breakfast!*

81

Desdemona beamed at Megan as she climbed into the limo. "I hope this appeals to you," she said, gesturing to the breakfast laid out on the small fold-down table in front of them. It was set with cereal, fruit and a pot of green tea, just as Megan had specified the evening before when she was asked by her hostess if she wouldn't like to have breakfast in the limo on their way to the airport. That had appealed to Megan, as it meant she could sleep a little longer in the morning. Considering that she had not gotten to bed until after midnight, this had proven to be a wise decision.

Unbeknownst to the two women, a tall man with black hair now stood in the street cursing out loud at their disappearing vehicle.

Felix did not have the courage to call his father. His last chance to get Megan Crespi had been nixed by her damned unpredictability. Now what should he do? Fly home to face his father's fury? If only he could do something to make up for his failure with Crespi. He thought about his successful caper in Berlin—how he had managed to slice out Alma's face from Margareta Nussbaum's Kokoschka frieze. He would be bringing that back to his dad. If only there were something else he could bring back. Another Alma trophy.

What about other private collections? Museums were definitely out, considering all the publicity given to recent attacks on Kokoschka's Alma images in their collections. Security must be real tight by now. Yes, it would have to be some image from a private collection. But what image? What collection?

Then he remembered. There was a large painting by Kokoschka titled *Mania* or *Woman and Slave*. It showed a woman with Alma's features dominating the center of the canvas. On the far right side, hanging back, was a man with the features of the artist. Felix knew that the picture was in the collection of a Greek industrialist who lived in Graz. If only he could remember the name of the man! Those Greek names all sounded alike to him—"appalado dappalapados."

Try as he might to pull up the name, Felix was getting nowhere. And he had to act fast. Then he had the inspired thought of contacting Dr. Klug at Nebehay's Antiquariat. He would know who the Graz collector was. And certainly his father had been a good enough customer in the past that he could ask such a question without appearing to pry. He called Klug on his cell phone.

"Hey, there, Doktor Klug. It's Felix Fichte. I was just wondering again if there has been any break in all the Kokoschka happenings. Are the police on to anything?"

"Nothing, I'm afraid. And I presume you've heard about the dreadful attack on Frau Margareta Nussbaum's Kokoschka? Odd, isn't it, you were just telling me you'd like to meet her."

"Oh, yeah, I did, but you advised me not to. You said I didn't have the 'class' to make a visit to her appealing."

"Hope I did not hurt your feelings."

"Hell no. My Dad tells me the same thing. 'No class.'"

"Well, someone broke into the Nussbaum home while she was away and sliced out a portion of her Kokoschka mural. They got away with it and the police have no idea who did it."

"Oh, no! That's awful. Bummer. I guess other private collectors of Kokoschka are feeling pretty scared right about now."

"Yes. I've had a number of calls from worried clients. In fact your father was one of the callers."

"Yeah. And I know he's worried about his fellow collector in Graz. You know, the Greek with all those Kokoschka cityscapes. Um, what's his name…"

"Oh, you mean Kallias Andriopoulos?"

"Yeah. It was on the tip of my tongue. He must be real scared."

"I haven't heard from him, but I imagine he has taken all measures that might be needed to secure his great collection."

"I won't keep you, Dr. Klug. Just wanted to check in with you."

"How much longer will you be in Wien, Felix?"

"Oh, I'm leaving today as a matter of fact."

"Well then I wish you safe travels and say hello to your father for me."

"Will do."

Felix had not lied about leaving Vienna today. Once he hung up from talking to Dr. Klug he looked up Andriopoulos on line and found his exact address on Erdbergweg. Then he checked the railjet train schedule and figured he could be in Graz by four-thirty if he left at one o'clock that afternoon.

82

Desdemona and Megan had gone straight from the Corfu airport to the marina facing her Xenia island, some half a mile out to sea. She had advised her handyman in advance and he had brought fifteen crates, in all, over to Xenia by pontoon. He had installed them in the small study at one end of the long villa that overlooked the vista at the back of the island. Desdemona had respected the tombs carved into the front of the island—Böcklin's view—and she had had her spacious villa carved into the rock cliffs running along the far side of the island.

Down below was a flat beach with a pier for her pontoon. The handyman and his wife, who served as cook when Desdemona was in residence, lived on the island in another small house that had been carved into the back side of the island. It was an idyllic spot and both Alessandro and Harmonia loved their job and their employer. The pontoon was their lifeline to the mainland and they only needed to get supplies once a week. And now all had been prepared for their mistress who was being ferried over by Alessandro. He marveled at the unusual fact that Madam Dumba was accompanied by someone. This was the first time she had ever brought a visitor to Xenia. And she seemed more animated than usual. Yes, in fact, even cheerful as she chatted with her guest.

Alessandro helped the older woman out of the pontoon and onto the pier. They walked slowly up to the house. Megan was vastly impressed. The front part of the villa that stood out from the cliff was made entirely of pure white marble. The façade was punctured with oversize windows for the most part and on the second floor were a series of French doors and a marble balcony running the length of the house. There was a vista from every room straight out to the sapphire sea. The weather was perfect: a warm June day with blue sky and gentle breeze.

Desdemona led her guest to the upstairs spare room that had been prepared for her. Every piece of furniture and every drape was in white. The impression of cleanliness and space was extraordinary. Megan almost felt guilty as she took off her red cap and set her beige Prima Classe bag on the luggage rack at the foot of her queen-size bed.

"Lunch will be ready in twenty minutes downstairs," Desdemona sang out from the hall leading to her bedroom.

After unpacking, Megan checked to see if she could get online and was delighted to discover she had cyber connectivity. Quick calls to Dallas brought her sister and Claire up to date with her whereabouts, and the news that Button had fallen in love. A new Maltese—Pipa—had been introduced into the neighborhood and they met on a walk yesterday. It was a case of love at first sight for both dogs. Megan did not realize how much she missed her Button until she hung up.

At lunch Megan met Harmonia, who had made them a delicious cold soup of chicken broth, eggs, lemon juice, and dill, with grains of rice stirred in. It was new to Megan and she asked its name. Avgolemono, was the answer. This was followed by stuffed grape leaves with yogurt on the side in honor of Megan. Dessert was lemon sherbet with strong Greek coffee. It was too strong for Megan and she discreetly spooned two extra helpings of sugar into it.

"And now a tour of the house and the island, if you like," proposed Desdemona.

"You know, Desdemona, I wouldn't mind having a very short lie-down before we do the tour."

"Oh, but of course, Megan! How very thoughtless of me. And to tell you the truth, I wouldn't mind lying down for a bit myself."

As Megan lay on her bed which obviously must have had a generous topper it was so comfy, she heard the sounds of classical music coming down the hall. Her thoughtful hostess had put on the *Thaïs Méditation* and it was to that lovely soaring melody that Megan dozed off. Half an hour later, feeling wonderfully rested, Megan wandered downstairs into the living room where Desdemona sat on a white leather couch caressing a large yellow and white Aegean cat with light green eyes.

"Oh! Megan, meet Gaia. Gaia, meet Megan."

"You didn't tell me you have a cat, Desdemona!"

"I don't, really. She lives here with Alessandro and Harmonia. They found her down at the port, patted her, and that was it. She jumped into the pontoon and has never expressed any desire to return to the mainland."
Megan gave the friendly cat a massage on its chest and was rewarded with a very loud and steady purr.

"Now shall we see the house, Megan?"

"I would love to."

Desdemona led the way past the living room into a music room festooned with five different wooden lyres on the wall, ranging from child size to contrabass dimension. On the other wall hung a collection of panpipes and panflutes. And, facing the window, was, surprisingly, an electric piano of blond wood.

"What? No Bösendorfer here?" Megan joshed her hostess, knowing full well that the island humidity would play havoc with the tuning.

"I did try one," Desdemona confessed, "but it went out of tune almost immediately and then the strings began popping. It was foolish of me."

The flutist in Megan came out. "May I try one of these panpipes?"

"But of course!"

Megan took one of the larger ones off the wall and blew hard across the open ends of the pipes, applying at the same time a hand vibrato. The result was disappointing and she soon gave up. This would take practice and she was eager to see the rest of the house.

"Let's go into the den," her hostess urged.

They entered the second to the last room of this wing of the house— above it was Desdemona's bedroom, presumably twice as long as Megan's. And beyond the den was what seemed to be Desdemona's private study. Although the music room was large, the den was twice as large—a long rectangle facing the sea. Surprisingly there was only one pane of glass in the room facing out and it was up high, running the length of the room in one continuous band.

Megan understood why immediately. On the opposite wall were fourteen oil paintings. They glimmered in the soft light. The subject matter was immediately recognizable. They were exact painted versions of the fourteen remaining metopes from the north wall of the Parthenon. The Sack of Troy was depicted.

Megan could not help the thought that immediately crossed her mind. Could these fourteen paintings have been in the fourteen crates stolen from Moser's art storage? Could they have been removed at Desdemona's behest?

But the style had nothing at all to do with Kokoschka. They were clearly mimetic, devoid of any style, simply excellent copies of the marble reliefs. Why would the artist have wanted them? Yes, he loved Greece, but he made his own paintings of what sparked his admiration. Well, I guess I'm just too susceptible to the number fourteen right now, Megan explained to herself.

"Shall we go outside now?" asked Desdemona.

They walked back down the corridor, the inner wall of which was faced by the actual limestone of the island's great cliff. The limestone had been chiseled into a smooth flat wall and was carefully polished. The French doors of the living room opened onto a marble-floored expanse with iron porch furniture painted white to match the white cushions upon them. From the porch they had an unencumbered view of the pier and the sea beyond. Two rows of cypress trees framed the vista.

"As you can see there is nothing to disturb us here. We do not even see the mainland from where we are," said Desdemona with what sounded like a degree of sadness.

"Do you miss not seeing Corfu from here?"

"No, not at all. I am happy that I live on the back side of the island. I could not desecrate those rock-cut tombs."

They walked to the bank of cypress on the kitchen end of the house. In front of them was a carefully tended fruit tree grove and a vegetable garden. That explained the crispness of the dill and the freshness of the lemon in the soup at lunch.

"This is Harmonia's pride and joy. And Alessandro provides us with the sea catches. We will be having fish for dinner."

Megan could not help but note that ever since they had met again after lunch, Desdemona seemed preoccupied. The first flush of excitement at arriving at Xenia seemed to have expired.

Suddenly Desdemona spoke and with an earnestness Megan had not heard from her before.

"Megan, I have something I want to show you. Something that may astonish you but I hope not disappoint you. If it does disappoint you, I must beg you not to let me know. Can you keep such a bargain?"

Mystified, Megan agreed and Desdemona led her silently back into the house. They walked down to the room beyond the great den and into Desdemona's private study at the end of the villa. There on a narrow table against the wall opposite the window was a canvas in a narrow frame. Its front was turned to the wall. Desdemona beckoned Megan to a chair across the room under the window. On either side of the chair were stacked some crates, the tops of which had been removed.

"Here is what I have been longing to show you," she said, quickly turning the canvas around.

Megan was astonished. She was looking at what appeared to be Kokoschka in style but Böcklin in subject matter. Impossible! Could Kokoschka have done such a thing? Of course copying the masters was common in art schools, but this was Kokoschka's mature style of wildly lapping, thick brushstrokes. Interestingly, although it was a copy of what looked like the Geneva version of Böcklin's *Isle*, there was one detail that was different. No longer was a woman standing with a coffin in the rowboat. They were gone and only the rower was left. And he was rowing the boat away from, not to, the island. What an enigma. And how did Desdemona come by it? How long had she had it? Why hadn't she told her about it before now? Questions raced through Megan's mind. She started to stand up so she could take a closer look.

Desdemona stopped her. "No! Do not come any closer! I do not want you to study the painting; just to enjoy it. From a distance. I will not have a Janette Killar type destruction of my joy in owning this wonderful painting. Please, Megan, please. Just enjoy it from where you are."

Megan acquiesced to her friend's unusual demand but now felt almost an electrical current course through her. The thrill of beholding something that could either be original or an excellent copy. And yet Desdemona did not want to know. She wanted to believe in this extraordinary picture of her Xenia. All right. Megan would stop being an art historian just for awhile. Just as long as she was visiting her friend. But it went against every fiber of her nature. Could she keep her promise?

As they left the room, Megan turned for a last glance at the work and as her eyes swept the room she noticed the stacked crates again. *Was she mistaken, or were there fourteen of them?*

83

Karl Palkovska's railjet to Graz arrived at three in the afternoon, right on time. With the two "Kokoschka" still lifes in his roller bag, he made his way to a bank of taxis outside the station and gave the driver an address on Erdbergweg. In the taxi he took a discreet sniff of meth. Clouds were beginning to turn the sky gray and it looked as though it might rain. Kallias Andriopoulos's house stood alone on a low hill with a sweeping view of the vineyards below. When Karl knocked at the front door it was the old man himself who answered, after a considerable pause.

"Come in, come in, Herr Palkovska! Ah, it's begun to rain. Let us go into my living room." Slowly Andriopoulos led the way, wheezing as he shuffled ahead of Karl.

What Karl beheld in the living room made his jaw drop. Eleven large cityscapes were on the walls, grouped in clusters of three and two. And, opposite each other on the two short walls were Kokoschka's *Woman and Slave*, which Karl knew as *Mania*, and the famous *Tigon*. A fitting juxtaposition, he thought. Alma Mahler was indeed a hybrid of femme fatale and self-promotion. The paintings were of the highest quality.

"Ah, you like what you see?" Karl's host asked him after a minute of silence had passed.

"*Like* is hardly the word for it. This is a superb collection of Kokoschka."

"Yes. I fell in love with him as a boy visiting Graz's Joanneum Museum where I saw his magnificent view of Delphi. That is why I was so interested in seeing your still life with a view of the city in the background. And also the one with Jerusalem. But first we must have some ouzo together to celebrate your bringing these pictures to me. You do like the taste of anise, do you not?"

"Oh, yes, very much," Karl lied.

Andriopoulos had prepared for his guest. On the table was a bottle of *Sans Rival* ouzo and two shot glasses. He began to pour out a small quantity of the clear liquid, his hand trembling uncontrolledly.

"You know that ouzo is absinthe without the wormwood," he declared, trying to distract his guest's attention from his shaking hand."

"No, but I did know that when absinthe went out of favor, ouzo took over," said Karl, slightly surprised that he knew one fact about the licorice drink.

"I must tell you, Herr Palkovska, that recently I received a young woman who had a gouache sketch by Kokoschka, purportedly a study for his famous poster *Murderer, Hope of Women.* I bought it from her then and there. But as time went by I began to feel there was something wrong with it. I consulted the Killar oeuvre catalogue and it was not listed or reproduced. After some more research and a great deal of just looking at the work, I decided I did not want it in my collection. So I placed it with the Amadeus Auktionshaus in Vienna. Are you familiar with that auction house?"

"Indeed I am." Karl did not volunteer that he had placed one of his faux Kokoschka still lifes with the shady establishment. "Shall we look at the paintings I brought with me now?"

"Yes, let us see them."

Karl removed the wrapping from his Delphi picture and dramatically held it up for the elderly Greek to see. Would it pass?

Andriopoulos regarded the painting in silence. The seconds ticked by. A frown crossed his face. This was followed by a wide smile.

"I cannot tell you how thrilling it is for me to see this second Kokoschka depiction of my beloved Delphi."

Karl could feel the tension in him slip away.

"You know, I was born in Delphi," Andriopoulos said. "But let me get my glasses."

Tension flooded through Karl again.

"We need to take it outdoors when it stops raining and the sun is out again. But I see quite enough here. It is a wonderful work. The agreement between the grapes in front and the view of Delphi in the back is so complete. Ah! Marvelous, simply marvelous."

Karl relaxed again.

"Would you like to see the other one, Herr Andriopoulos?"

"Indeed, indeed."

It only took a minute to unwrap the Jerusalem still life and again Karl flourished it with a dramatic upsweep.

"Ah. It is quite as remarkable as the Delphi one. Yes, yes. I think I would want to add them both as a pair to my collection."

Karl tried hard to keep from cheering. He put on his most serious expression and said simply, "That can be arranged. I am willing to sell."

Just then the front door clapper sounded. Andriopoulos looked at his watch. It was already four o'clock.

"I am not expecting anyone. Let me just see who is outside." He walked slowly to the front door and opened it.

Felix Fichte stood on the threshold, a duffle bag in his hand.

"Herr Andriopolos?"

"Yes?"

"I have a message for your servant."

"Servant? I have no servant."

Upon hearing this, Felix repeated his Berlin maneuver. He simply smashed his way inside the doorway, knocking Andriopoulos to the floor with a body slam. Then he kicked the old man violently in the groin, chest, and head. Andriopoulos moaned, then fell back unconscious.

Alarmed by the noise, Karl came cautiously out of the living room. He gaped at Felix who was now kneeling beside Andriopoulos, choking him with his bare hands. His victim gave one last jerk. Then was motionless.

Karl was frozen to the spot. He eyed the strong young man and thought, oh my god, I'm next!

Felix was furious that there was a witness to his putting Andriopoulos out of the way. He sprang to his feet. Karl suddenly found *his* feet and started to flee back into the living room. But the younger man overtook him and pummeled him to the ground. He twisted his head until he heard Karl's bones crack. Then he pinched his nose closed and held his hand tightly over his mouth. Karl turned red and tried to throw Felix off him, but he was too weak. After a few more minutes he resisted no longer. Like Kallias Andriopoulos, he was dead.

Felix stood up and glanced around the room. This was it! A dozen or so Kokoschkas on the walls and just across from him the *Mania* painting with Alma's gloating face. He whipped out his jackknife and cut the face from out the canvas. Then he rolled it up and placed it in his duffle bag. Another minute and he was walking out the front door. He set the lock on the door and closed it firmly behind him.

The double murder and art destruction was not discovered for three days.

84

"Lord Elgin was a *criminal*, as far as I am concerned."

Desdemona was holding forth over lunch at Xenia the next day. They had spent the evening before playing and listening to music. They agreed on so many things musically, from J. S. Bach to Astor Piazzolla. And now they were discussing the removal of Parthenon marbles from 1801 to 1812 by agents of Thomas Bruce, the seventh Earl of Elgin. He had been given "permission" to do so by the reigning sultan, as the Acropolis was at that time still an Ottoman military fort and had been so since 1460. Turkish soldiers had amused themselves by shooting at the precious statues, friezes, and sculpted metopes. When they arrived in England Lord Byron called them "misshapen monuments" and pronounced Elgin a "vandal."

The greatly respected Italian sculptor Antonio Canova had refused to restore them for fear he might further damage the precious artifacts.

Although Lord Elgin eventually sold the dismantled art to the British Museum, tremendous controversy had accompanied the transaction and just last year UNESCO had agreed to mediate the dispute between Greece and the United Kingdom as to whether or not the marbles should be returned to their home country.

All this Desdemona told Megan with great passion and animation, and Megan could not help admiring her commitment. This explained why her hostess had fourteen oil paintings of the Sack of Troy metopes in her house. She thought again of the fourteen crates she had noticed and subconsciously counted in Desdemona's private study and wondered if she dared bring up the subject.

After lunch, as they sat outdoors on the front patio lazily enjoying the expanse of sea and sky, Megan became emboldened and decided to speak aloud what was on her mind.

"Desdemona, might I ask what all those crates are doing in the house? In your study?"

Her hostess looked long and steadily at her.

"They contain something else I have been longing to show you, but I do not know whether or not I have the courage to do so."

"What do you mean?" asked Megan, now fully alert.

"I must confess to you that although the crates have been opened for me by Alessandro, I have not had the chance myself to give them more than a passing glance. I should love us to unpack them together."

"And I would be happy to help you."

"But first, Megan, I must swear you to absolute secrecy. No one knows about this shipment to Xenia. No one except Alessandro and Harmonia who ferried them over from my warehouse."

"Oh? You've had them for some time then?"

"No, actually not. I shipped them to Greece from another country." Desdemona was beginning to have second thoughts.

"Well, you certainly have my undivided attention."

"Will you swear, Megan, not to reveal the contents to anyone?"

Megan hated being pressed. She felt she was in a trap. But she was touched by her friend's enthusiasm.

"All right. I swear."

"Then let's go and unpack them right now." Desdemona jumped up from her lounge chair and Megan followed suit.

They entered Desdemona's private study and opened the topmost crate to the right of the chair Megan had sat in the day before during the unveiling of the Kokoschka copy of Böcklin's *Isle of the Dead*. That canvas had now been installed in Desdemona's bedroom by Alessandro, Megan learned.

The lid was off the crate and Desdemona drew forth a small horizontal painting that was three feet long and two feet tall. It showed a scene that was vaguely familiar to Megan from her knowledge of the eight fans Kokoschka had painted for Alma. Fans, seven of which had recently been stolen from the Hamburg museum. She could clearly see, against a rocky landscape with mountains and ravines, the figures of Oskar and Alma facing each other. The painting was without doubt by Kokoschka. The style was that jerky, spiked style of his 1912-1915 period.

Rather than examine the picture more closely for the moment, Megan agreed with Desdemona that they should unpack all fourteen crates and line the pictures up along a wall to see what they had. Each picture slid easily out from its close-fitting crate and soon the two women had a small exhibition leaning against the far wall of the room.

"This is amazing," breathed Megan, almost involuntarily.

All fourteen pictures featured Oskar and Alma but in varying circumstances, none of them repeated.

What did not change about the pictures was a pronounced horizontal ribbing that the artist had painted across the width of each work. Before examining the paintings individually Megan wanted to figure out what the ribbing was. It was meticulously painted in and often the pronounced ribs interfered with the continuity of the scene, sometimes even cutting off part of the figures.

Then it hit Megan. *Kokoschka was turning his fans into pictures!*

And there were *fourteen* of them, not just eight. This must be what the artist meant when he said to her about the crates that they were "juvenilia." No wonder he did not want pictures relating to his stormy affair with Alma in the Villenueve home he shared with Olda. Or perhaps it was she who asked him to get rid of them and he could not bear to, so he sent them for storage in Vienna—the locale of his stormy love—for storage "in perpetuity."

"Why the number fourteen, do you think, Megan?"

"This may be a wild guess from my high school days at an Ursuline academy, but might they refer to the fourteen stations of the cross, I wonder?"

"I thought there were just seven stations of the cross."

"There are both sets. Let's look up the fourteen stations on line, Desdemona. May I use your laptop?" Megan asked, not waiting for an answer and walking over to her hostess's desk.

Desdemona joined her. Up flashed exactly what they wanted to see. A terse description of each station of the cross.
They were listed:

1. Christ condemned to death;
2. The cross is laid upon him;
3. His first fall;
4. He meets His Blessed Mother;
5. Simon of Cyrene is made to bear the cross;
6. Christ's face is wiped by Veronica;
7. His second fall;
8. He meets the women of Jerusalem;
9. His third fall;
10. He is stripped of His garments;
11. His crucifixion;
12. His death on the cross;
13. His body is taken down from the cross; and
14. He is laid in the tomb.

Now Megan and Desdemona turned to the paintings leaning against the wall and began to arrange them according to the fourteen stations. Oskar and Alma were in each of the splayed out "fans."

In the first one, Christ condemned to death, Oskar took the place of Christ before Pontius Pilate while Alma was depicted with her hands up in shock, a veil hiding her long hair. She was on her knees next to Oskar as the cross was laid upon him in the next station. At the first fall she was shown scorning the men in the crowd who raised him. In the fourth station when

Christ-Oskar met his mother, Alma was the distraught mother and in the fifth, she stood aside as Simon of Cyrene was made to bear the crucifix. It was not Veronica but Alma who wiped Christ-Oskar's face with her veil in the sixth station. When Christ-Oskar fell for the second time, Alma stood in front of the grieving group of women and mocked him.

What startling contradictions! Alma as grieved lover, Alma as contemptuous hater.

In the eighth station, when Christ-Oskar met the women of Jerusalem, she had a welcoming expression on her face, but in the very next station, as the third fall took place, she was pointing to his collapsed figure with glee. In the tenth station, as Christ-Oskar was stripped of his garments, she stooped to mourn.

The eleventh station depicted the crucifixion and Alma was now shown to be one of the persons nailing Christ-Oskar to the cross. But as he died on the cross, Alma stood below him wailing with grief, and she was shown helping to take his body down from the cross in the penultimate fan. The final picture showed Christ-Oskar being laid in the tomb as Alma climbed athletically into the tomb as well. The couple can only be united permanently in death was Kokoschka's final harrowing message.

Desdemona and Megan looked at each other wordlessly. Such a powerful message. Such raging emotions. Yes. Here it was revealed. Kokoschka's passionate juvenilia, hidden from the world all these decades.

Perhaps Desdemona had done the right thing after all, saving these exceptional works from oblivion. Megan shook her head to clear her thinking. But the *means* by which these works were revealed. Pure, unadulterated theft. And where was the audience for these masterpieces? Not counting herself, it was and obviously would remain, an audience of one. Here in Xenia, remote from the outside world.

No, this could not be. Well, she would deal with that later. Right now she wanted to join Desdemona in relishing these unknown works attesting to an affair the likes of which, in Kokoschka's words, had "not been seen since the Middle Ages, for no couple has ever breathed into each other so passionately."

85

"I didn't get to Crespi, Dad, but I did get something special and you're gonna love it, believe me." Felix was talking to Bruno while waiting for his flight back to the States to be called. In his duffel bag he had not one, but two images of Alma to present to his father: the one from Berlin and now one from Graz.

"All right, Felix. When you get in this evening come straight home. We have a lot to talk about."

"Sure, Dad." Over the phone line he could hear the doorbell ring.

"There's someone at the door so I'll say goodbye," Bruno said. "Just remember, come straight home, don't stop at any bars."

"Will do." Felix was becoming irritated. His father was treating him like a child. A headline on the television screen above him in the waiting room caught his attention. "Murder and Mayhem in Graz!" The camera focused in on the Andriopoulos house and a reporter was talking about two bodies found there. They were identified as Kallias Andriopoulos, owner of the house, and one Karl Palkovska of Geneva. The motive for the double killing was unclear. It seemed nothing had been stolen or disturbed in the house except for a painting in the living room. Two figures were shown in the picture, a man and a woman, and the face of the woman had been carefully sliced out of the canvas and was missing.

Felix was riveted. Then he thought, oh hell, I hope Dad doesn't hear about this before I get back to New York. Otherwise he'll guess what I have to show him. I want him to be surprised. I want him to be pleased with me that although I didn't get Crespi, I did get something far more worthwhile.

Just then his flight was called. Eight hours later, when his plane landed in New York, two policemen met him as he was exiting the plane. His father had already been arrested. The charge: possession of valuable stolen property. Megan's urging of Detective Versteckt to check with the New York police about Nyack had paid off.

86

Megan had left her iPhone upstairs in her bedroom at Desdemona's villa. She and her hostess had spent the afternoon and evening looking at the Kokoschka trove revealed in the fourteen crates. This time Megan was not looking at forgeries. These were the real thing. And they were superb. Iconographically and artistically. A treasure undreamt of by the scholarly world.

How could she keep her oath to Desdemona not to reveal the existence of these fascinating works? She would end up being a partner in crime if she did not speak out, did not inform the Vienna police of the whereabouts of the fourteen stolen crates. Desdemona simply must be persuaded to go to the police.

After they had said an early goodnight to each other and Megan was in the privacy of her bedroom she automatically picked up her iPhone. She had missed one call. It was from Hans Tietze in Basel. She called back immediately.

"Megan! I have marvelous news! Kokoschka's *Tempest* has been found!"

"Found? How wonderful. Where?"

"In Vienna. It is really a strange story and the police do not have all the details yet. But yesterday the neighbor of a man named Leo Lang, puzzled that he had seen no traffic in or out of the house for several days, went over to check on things. He knew the man lived alone. When he got to the front door he found several days' worth of mail on the ground in front of it, so he called the police. They entered and found the man dead in his bedroom under circumstances they have not yet revealed. A search of the house resulted in the discovery of our Basel painting! Because of the publicity over its theft, the Vienna police knew exactly what they had uncovered and I was contacted just a few hours ago."

"Oh, Hans, this is terrific news. I'm so happy for you. And for Kokoschka. What will you do with the other painting?"

"I've already thought of that. Since both paintings are by Kokoschka, we will hang them side by side. And once again we will have overflow crowds."

"And a didactic explaining the substitution of Lilith for Alma?"

"Most certainly. The connection between the murdered man, Leo Lang, and Lilith Lang is clear. He was her and Kokoschka's grandson. Rather thrilling, is it not?"

"Immensely. Do the police have any idea who murdered Leo Lang?"

"No leads at all, apparently. It obviously wasn't to get at the painting. They are still trying to determine whether or not anything was stolen. The news reporters have all sorts of theories, including a revenge killing. But by whom, and for what? Lang was known as a solitary man. His wife had long since passed away and he had no children. So it's an enigma."

"Well then our theory that Leo was the unacknowledged grandson of Kokoschka seems to be right on the mark. His grandmother was Lilith Lang. And it is she who the artist depicted in the ersatz *Tempest*."

They talked a few minutes longer. Megan told Hans where she was, but did not disclose why or what she had come across.

"When are you flying home, Megan?"

"Pretty soon now, Hans. I just have one more situation to attend to and then I can leave for home."

"Well I wish you a safe flight and I do hope you will come back to Basel soon and see what will be our magnificent new double display."

"Do send me a photo in the meantime, promise?"

"That's a promise."

Megan's uncomfortable feelings about the Kokoschkas at Xenia had been pushed to the side. She was thrilled on her friend's behalf that the Alma *Tempest* had been found. She fell asleep with a smile on her lips.

87

Desdemona also had a call waiting for her when she retired to her bedroom for the evening. It was from Theo Papadakis, who urged her to call him back, "whatever the hour." She did so and found her agent to be unusually excited.

"You will never guess what has happened, Frau Dumba!"

"What? What?"

" Monsieur Victor Léman of Geneva has just approached me in regard to putting his Böcklin *Isle of the Dead* up for sale. I wanted *you* to be the first potential client."

Desdemona was dumbfounded. A chance actually to own one of the six Böcklin *Isles*? Without thinking, her immediate response was yes. She wondered what the price might be, not that it really mattered.

"You know, of course, Herr Papadakis, that I am more than interested. Just tell me what the asking price is."

"I have a special price just for you dear Frau Dumba. One hundred and fifty million Euros."

Desdemona did not feel like haggling.

"Tell Monsieur Léman that I accept the price and that I shall fly to Geneva immediately."

"Excellent! I shall do so first thing in the morning."

"And do you know what condition the painting is in?"

"Monsieur Léman assures me that it is in prime condition."

"Wonderful. I shall see him and you tomorrow in Geneva."

Desdemona could hardly wait to tell Megan the fantastic news. But she would have to wait until tomorrow morning. She had trouble falling asleep. Also she was beginning to wonder if perhaps her fourteen new Kokoschka acquisitions should be shared with the world. But how to do so without revealing the genesis of their being in her possession? If she could persuade Megan to accompany her to Geneva she would have a chance to listen to her counsel.

88

On the plane flight back from Corfu to Athens and then on to Geneva, Megan and Desdemona were engaged in a very intense conversation. That morning, because of the phone calls each had received, both women had agreed to cut their Xenia stay short. Megan had the good news about the Basel *Tempest's* having been found, and Desdemona had the equally good news that the Geneva Böcklin was up for sale.

It had been surprisingly easy for Desdemona to persuade her friend to make the trip to Geneva with her. As for Megan, she was truly interested in seeing a Böcklin *Isle of the Dead* that had been out of the public eye for decades. And more importantly, she believed she might have a chance to convince Desdemona that the Kokoschka fans belonged in a museum. Perhaps she would not have to be slapped with robbery charges. After all, it was her agent Theo Papadakis who had engineered the actual theft. How much had Desdemona known about that in advance? Perhaps a good lawyer could argue in her defense that she only knew about the robbery after the fact. But even so, certainly later she knew about the theft—it had occupied television and press coverage for days. Desdemona broke into her thoughts.

"Do you know, Megan, I feel as though some divine plan were steering me, steering me to Böcklin with his beautiful image of my Xenia."

Megan wondered if this might not be a good time to initiate an assault on her friend's conscience.

"I too feel there might be a question of destiny, or the intervention of fate. Of fate's giving you an opportunity to act nobly. Not to make just another acquisition, fitting as it may seem to you, but to right a wrong."

"What do you mean, 'right a wrong', Megan?"

"I am talking about the fourteen Kokoschkas we had the privilege of living with all day yesterday."

"Yes?" Strangely, Desdemona did not sound defensive.

"You say that you have 'rescued' the pictures from oblivion. And in a sense this is quite true. But rescued for whom? For you alone? There in isolated Xenia?"

"It is very complicated, Megan. The content of the fan paintings shows an Oskar who is Christ-like but an Alma who is by turns loving and hateful, caring and contemptuous, soothing and hurtful. Think what this would do for her already questionable legacy."

"But, Desdemona, there are so many scholars now who question the veracity of her autobiographies, who wonder what she suppressed in Mahler's letters to her. You know that she possessed more than three-hundred-and-fifty of them, but she published only about half that number. And her own letters to him have mysteriously disappeared, have not been kept."

"Yes, Megan, I appreciate that all this is now well known, and also the fact that Alma made alterations to some of those published letters. But that is why I don't think these fan paintings should be made public. They would further damage her reputation."

Megan realized she had pushed too far. Had chosen the wrong moment. Desdemona was still under the spell of the magic of having experienced what the contents of those fourteen crates were.

The two women fell silent for a while, then talked of other subjects.

"Megan, I have reserved rooms for us at the Hotel Beau-Rivage *on the same floor as Sisi's room!*"

Six hours later, after a change of flights at Athens, the two women arrived in Geneva and after dining in the hotel restaurant they parted company. Their appointment with Monsieur Léman was for eleven in the morning.

Breakfast at the Hotel Beau-Rivage involved one of the largest buffets Megan had ever experienced. While Desdemona had just scrambled eggs, Megan filled her cereal bowl with her favorite fruits and yogurt. Both had ordered green tea.

"Megan. We have time before our appointment to take a look at Sisi's room. I know you did it once, and so have I, but wouldn't it be marvelous to see it together?" Desdemona's old enthusiasm had returned, here, so close to her idol Sisi.

After breakfast then, instead of returning to their rooms they walked further down the corridor to the famous bed chamber. A plaque commemorating the Austrian empress's stay was on the door. Nearby a chambermaid was at work in one of the bedrooms. A badge on her uniform showed her name to be Luisa Luceni. Desdemona approached her, discreetly holding out to her a banknote of twenty Euros and pointing to the Sisi door. The maid looked around hurriedly, took the bill, then opened the door.

"Only for a moment, if you please," she whispered looking up and down the hotel corridor apprehensively.

Megan quickly took an iPhone photo while Desdemona simply stood in silent reverence. Then they left and returned to their rooms. It had begun to rain and they wanted to pick up the umbrella provided in each room.

Just as the chambermaid was locking the door to Sisi's room, after taking a look in it herself, the hotel housekeeper appeared. She took one look at the girl and exploded.

"Have you been letting tourists inside Sisi's room?"

"Only for a moment."

"You are fired! Leave the premises at once!"

Luisa was filled with hatred. Hatred for the rich lady who had tempted her with money to do something for which she had just lost her job. She went to the hotel kitchen and slipped a long steak knife into her blouse. Then she exited the hotel through the front doors and stood in the rain on the Lake Geneva promenade, waiting.

She did not have long to wait. Within minutes she saw two ladies, one of them tall, the other rather short, exit the hotel. Both were holding open umbrellas. Luisa ran up to them, appeared to stumble in front of the tall lady, and made a movement with her right hand as though she wanted to catch her balance. The hand contained a steak knife and Luisa managed to stab her victim three times in the chest before either lady realized what was happening.

Desdemona fell silently to the ground. Megan shouted for help and kicked out at Luisa who had started to run away. A man who had witnessed the stabbing gave chase. Some passing tourists crowded around the woman who had been assaulted. She was bleeding profusely. Excited voices shouted in French, German, and English.

One of the onlookers kept repeating incredulously: "It's just like Sisi! It's just like Sisi! She was murdered right here! In the same way! It's just like Sisi"! Another one called for an ambulance, something Megan had been too numbed to do.

Two policemen arrived and one of them ran to meet the man who had captured a writhing, screaming Luisa.

Horrified, Megan had knelt down next to her mortally wounded friend and held her head in her lap. Desperately she stroked her forehead.

"Hold on, Desdemona, hold on. Help is coming."

Despite her increasing weakness, Desdemona was desperately trying to tell Megan something. She pressed her ear close to Desdemona's lips.

"Megan! Return the Kokoschkas!"

* * *

After giving her account to the police at Geneva's main police station Megan—still in a shocked state—picked up her bags from the hotel and took a taxi to the airport. She was able to catch a late afternoon flight to Vienna.

Before she boarded she got though to Detective Versteckt and tearfully summarized what had happened. He promised, since Desdemona had no family, that he would make the arrangements to have her buried at Xenia. He also agreed that the Dumba palais apartment should be closed off and a team sent to Corfu to work with the local police in getting to Xenia and retrieving the stolen Kokoschka paintings. Theo Papadakis would be arrested and questioned concerning the break-in at Moser's art storage. The question of which museum would be the beneficiary of the Kokoschka fan paintings would have to be settled by the courts, but the most obvious institutions were either the Wien Museum or the Leopold Museum.

For once in her life Megan did not feel like revisiting Vienna. She would stay overnight at the NH Wien airport hotel, just opposite the arrivals hall, and in the morning would catch a seven-thirty Lufthansa flight that, via Frankfurt, would take her back to Dallas. She would need the time to adjust to the reality of Desdemona's death. What had begun as a strange switch of paintings at the Basel Museum, the caper had taken her from Switzerland to Austria to Germany to Greece. She was ready to go home.

And little Button was waiting.

Readers Guide

1. Retired professor of art history Megan Crespi is reflecting on an interview she had with the Viennese Expressionist artist Oskar Kokoschka (1886–1980) in Switzerland shortly before his death at the age of 93. What is she an expert on? Why is she thinking about Kokoschka? What did Kokoschka tell Megan about some "juvenilia" stored in fourteen crates in a Vienna art storage vault? What has happened to the crates?

2. Megan receives a phone call from the director of the Basel Museum, Hans Tietze. A major double portrait by Kokoschka showing himself with his lover Alma Mahler has been stolen. Left in its place is an exact duplicate, except that Alma has been replaced by an unknown woman. What is Hans Tietze's connection with the artist?

3. Megan goes over the drama concerning the doll Kokoschka had made in the likeness of Alma; she then remembers Oscar and Alma's descriptions of their affair via long quotes from their memoirs. Megan arrives in Basel and meets Tietze at the museum. On the way to his office she stops to admire the riveting painting by Swiss artist Arnold Böcklin, *The Isle of the Dead*. What are the reminisces of Oskar and Alma about their three-year affair? Do they remember it in similar fashion? Do we know yet the significance of *The Isle of the Dead*? Megan meets with the museum's two restorers. All agree that the substitute *Tempest* showing a blonde woman instead of the brunette Alma is also by Kokoschka; not a copy. What leads them to this conclusion? Are there any thoughts on who the blonde might be? What is the significance of a phone call Tietze receives?

4. We meet retired Hunter College professor of art history Bruno Fichte, unacknowledged great-grandson of Alma Mahler. Why does he not use Mahler in his surname? What was his son Felix doing in Vevey, Switzerland? Was he successful?

5. Megan decides to stay another day in Basel. She muses over the two early posters Kokoschka made in 1908 and 1909. How are they so different from each other?

6. We meet Leo Lang, grandson of Lilith Lang, whose love child with Kokoschka in 1914 was Oskar Lang, Leo's father. What did Leo find hidden under his mother's bed when she died? How does Leo intend to make the whole art world know Alma took Lilith away from Kokoschka? Why does Leo employ the shady agent Agnes Sauer? What does she do to forward his plans?

7. We meet Helmut Haesslich, owner of one of Berlin's most prestigious galleries. He has two passions: Böcklin and Kokoschka. What happens when a young restorer shows him his very good copy of the Swiss painter's Isle of the Dead?

8. Now we meet the gorgeous long-nosed, long-limbed, exotic Greek Desdemona Dumba, great-granddaughter of Vienna's patron of the arts, Nikolaus Dumba. She is a throwback to the 19th century in her absolute worship of Sisi, Austria's beautiful but tragic Empress. What else does she have in common with Sisi? What is Xenia?

9. Bruno Fichte is disappointed by what Felix has brought back from Switzerland. What is it and why is Bruno disappointed? What emboldens him to consider a theft on a larger scale? And where?

10. Megan arrives in Vienna, eager to visit the art storage company where the fourteen crates were stolen. What does she want to ask the owner and why would that be important?

11. Now we meet Desdemona's agent, the Greek Theo Papadakis. He is an expert in ferreting out supposedly lost works of art. What has he restituted to Desdemona? Who is second only in fascination to Sisi for Desdemona? What is the unique link between Sisi and Alma Mahler? Who is Constantine Christomanos?

12. Leo Lang has picked up Agnes Sauer and her special baggage from the airport. Back at his villa they open the cardboard container tube and remove the canvas roll that is the Basel Museum's *The Tempest* by Kokoschka. Why is Agnes surprised at Leo's reaction to the painting? What is Leo's grand plan in which she will play a vital part?

13. Megan visits Moser's art storage with her museum director friend Hannes Ohm. What does she manage to find out? How does that help figure out what might be in the fourteen stolen Kokoschka crates?

14. The Albright-Knox Art Gallery plans to hold a "Famous Artists and Their Lovers" exhibition. Why does this fit in with Bruno Fichte's bold new plan? How does he go about realizing the plan?

15. Leo Lang gives Agnes Sauer a new assignment in his crusade to rid the world of images of Alma Mahler. What is it, and where will it take her?

16. Megan visits the Galerie Hummel and is shocked by what she sees on exhibition there. What does she find? When she exits what is the sudden event that causes Desdemona Dumba to say "Oh! You have saved my life!"?

17. In New York Bruno Fichte browses the Internet and comes upon the logo "Remove Nudity in Museums." What does he do next and why? Is he prepared to go the limit?

18. In Tokyo now how does Agnes Sauer plan to deface the "Mona Lisa" portrait of Alma. What steps does she take to execute her plan?

19. Megan accompanies Desdemona to the hospital. How bad are Desdemona's injuries?

20. After visiting the venerable Christian M. Nebehay Antiquariat, Megan goes to the Amadeus Auktionshaus where she is shown a preparatory drawing for Kokoschka's 1909 poster, *Murderer, Hope of Women*. What does she think about it and what seal does she see on the back? Who is Kallias Andriopoulos?

21. Agnes Sauer manages to deface Kokoschka's Alma Mahler portrait at Tokyo's MOMAT museum. What are the tools she uses and how does she gain unencumbered access to the painting?

22. Why does Helmut Haesslich roll up the forged Kokoschka *Portrait of Constantine Christomanos* after paying for it?

23. When and how does Megan reveal to Desdemona that her islet of Xenia is the same island painted by Böcklin in six versions? What do they decide to do next?

24. What is the layout of Jutta Feinstein's "Degenerate Art Revisited?" Which artists are in the bold exhibition at Essen's Folkwang Museum? Why does the layout ultimately cause Agnes Sauer to deface the wrong painting?

25. Where is the painting Bruno has had kidnapped and delivered and how was the art heist accomplished?

26. We meet Karl Palkovska, nephew of Kokoschka's wife Olda. What is his special talent and where has his work taken him? What does he do about the fourteen missing Kokoschka crates, and on what does he depend?

27. Megan and Desdemona fly to Berlin to see what Theo Papadakis has informed them has come to light, the long lost Kokoschka *Portrait of Constantine Christomanos*. What is their reaction when they see the painting?

28. Karl Palkovska successfully creates fourteen small "Kokoschka" still lifes. What does he do then? Why does he decide to go to Vienna?

29. Bruno Fichte(-Mahler) sends his son to Vienna to hunt down Megan Crespi. Why? He learns about 103-year-old Margareta Nussbaum's decision to give the Wien Museum her collection of Kokoschka. What chain of events will this set off?

30. Why does Leo Lang have a life-size cloth doll which, like the original "Alma" doll commissioned by Kokoschka, includes "all orifices"? What does Agnes Sauer think of her employer?

31. Bruno Fichte sends his son Felix to Berlin. Why?

32. Agnes Teuer arrives in Hamburg and checks out the museum where the seven Kokoschka fans of him and Alma are on display. What are the means she will use to steal them? Why does Leo want her not to destroy these particular artworks? Is Agnes successful in her plan?

33. Megan and Desdemona visit Margareta Nussbaum in Berlin and are shown the Alma mural. What happens when the 103-year-old toasts the two women? How does this make it possible for Felix, who has been watching the villa's comings and goings from across the street, to enter the house? What does he do once inside?

34. On assignment from Leo, Agnes is in Klosterneuburg. What is she after in the sleepy old abbey town and what does she do to achieve her mission?

35. Janette Killar, author of the oeuvre catalogue on Kokoschka, arrives in Berlin. She goes with Megan and Desdemona to see the putative Kokoschka Portrait of Constantine Christomanos. What is her reaction?

36. Agnes Sauer is in Berlin to stake out the Neue Nationalgalerie's show of "Kokoschka's Women." What does she see in the third room of the exhibit and why is this so lucky?

37. Karl Palkovska shows photos of his fourteen "Kokoschka" still lifes to Theo Papadakis and a fifteenth one in the flesh, a still life with Venice in the background. What does this move Papadakis to do?

38. Agnes Sauer has cased the Berlin museum and assembles the equipment she will need to get at the two Kokoschka doll paintings. This includes a wheelchair. Also she needs a partner this time and calls her sister Rita Sauer-Luge to come to Berlin. Why the special equipment and do we know what Agnes's plan is yet? What happens when she tries to execute it?

39. Felix Fichte catches Megan at breakfast and importunes her with questions and the assertion that his dad is "real scared" about his own Kokoschka collection with all the "Neo-Nazi" goings-on. She fishes out from him that he and his father are related to Alma Mahler and he inadvertently mentions his father's second home in Nyack. Later Megan conveys this information to Detective Versteckt of the Vienna police. Why is Felix following Megan?

40. Rita Sauer-Luge flies from Berlin to Vienna and cases out Leo Lang's villa. Why? Through a window she observes him at dinner. His companion is the

gynoid-Alma doll. Rita enters the house unknown to Leo and hides behind the drapes in his bedroom. When Leo comes up with the doll what happens next?

41. Karl Palkovska has created two more Kokoschka still lifes, one with a view of Delphi, the other with a view of Jerusalem. Although he could put them on auction with Amadeus, he decides to try to interest the fanatic Greek Kokoschka collector Kallias Andriopoulos in his still lifes, and e-mails him. He hears from Andriopoulos that very evening. Yes, come the next afternoon to Graz. Why is this so important to the plot?

42. All Felix Fichte's efforts to do away with Megan have failed. He decides to redeem himself with his father by executing another act. What does he plan to do?

43. Megan agrees to fly to Greece with Desdemona. Felix's momentous plan takes him to Kallias Andriopoulos's villa in Graz. Who is also there?

44. What astonishing works of art does Megan encounter at Xenia? And further, why does Desdemona decide to share the contents of the fourteen crates with her? What amazing objects do they find? And what do they mean?

45. Karl Palkovska shows old Kallias Andriopoulos the two fabricated Kokoschka still lifes. Who impinges upon their conversation? What terrible events happen next?

46. Felix flies back, successful, to New York. What happens when he arrives? And what happens to Bruno Fichte?

47. Desdemona has a missed call waiting for her. It was Theo Papadakis. She returns his call immediately and learns the astonishing news that Monsieur Léman of Geneva is putting his Böcklin *Isle of the Dead* up for sale. What is the asking price and what does Desdemona do next?

48. Both Megan and Desdemona fly to Geneva to see the Böcklin *Isle of the Dead* for sale. What hotel do they stay in and what do they do there that causes a chamber maid to be fired? What happens as they walk on the Lake Geneva promenade? What does Desdemona whisper in Megan's ear?

www.ingramcontent.com/pod-product-compliance
Lightning Source LLC
Chambersburg PA
CBHW031944010726
47493CB00007B/2073